"Six lost souls find true love in the sweet first romance of the Honey Creek series from Thomas . . . It's the inviting setting and quirky, good-hearted characters that will draw readers in."
    —*Publishers Weekly* on *Breakfast at the Honey Creek Café*

"*The Little Teashop on Main* is a beautiful love letter to the power of female friendship, and when you read it, you'll feel like you've come home. Perfect for fans of Debbie Macomber and Nina George."
    —Robyn Carr, #1 *New York Times* bestselling author

"*The Little Teashop on Main* is tender, heartfelt and wonderful. Jodi Thomas's beautiful writing and her compelling, vivid characters will work their way straight into your heart and stay there forever. I loved every word."
    —RaeAnne Thayne, *New York Times* bestselling author

"You can count on Jodi Thomas to give you a satisfying and memorable read."
    —Catherine Anderson, *New York Times* bestselling author

"Thomas hits another winner."
    —*Library Journal* on *Mornings on Main*

"Ms. Thomas has penned yet another beautiful story that celebrates the beauty of love."
    —*The Romance Review* on *Mornings on Main*

"This is a novel that settles in the reader's heart from the beginning to its satisfying end."
    —*RT Book Reviews* on *Mornings on Main*, 4½ Stars, Top Pick!

Picnic in Someday Valley

Jodi Thomas

ZEBRA BOOKS
Kensington Publishing Corp.
www.kensingtonbooks.com

ZEBRA BOOKS are published by

Kensington Publishing Corp.
119 West 40th Street
New York, NY 10018

All Kensington titles, imprints, and distributed lines are available at special quantity discounts for bulk purchases for sales promotion, premiums, fund-raising, educational, or institutional use.

Special book excerpts or customized printings can also be created to fit specific needs. For details, write or phone the office of the Kensington Sales Manager: Attn.: Sales Department. Kensington Publishing Corp., 119 West 40th Street, New York, NY 10018. Phone: 1-800-221-2647.

Zebra and the Z logo Reg. U.S. Pat. & TM Off.

First Zebra Books Trade Paperback Printing: May 2021
First Zebra Books Mass-Market Paperback Printing: April 2022
ISBN-13: 978-1-4201-5132-9

10 9 8 7 6 5 4 3 2 1

Printed in the United States of America

For my big brother,
Philip Clifton Price

My hero

Friday

Chapter 1

Marcie

Marcie Latimer sat on a tall, wobbly stool in the corner of Bandit's Bar. Her right leg, wrapped in a black leather boot, was anchored on the stage. Her left heel hooked on the first rung of the stool so her knee could brace her guitar. With her prairie skirt and low-cut lacy blouse, she was the picture of a country singer. Long midnight hair and sad hazel eyes completed the look.

She played to an almost empty room, but it didn't matter. She sang every word as if it had to pass through her soul first. All her heartbreak drifted over the smoky room, whispering of a sorrow so deep it would never heal.

When she finished her last song, her fingers still strummed out the beat slowly, as if dying.

One couple, over by the pool table, clapped. The bartender, Wayne, brought Marcie a wineglass of ice water and said the same thing he did every night. "Great show, kid."

She wasn't a kid. She was almost thirty, feeling like she was running toward fifty. Six months ago her future was looking up. She had a rich boyfriend. A maybe future with Boone Buchanan, a lawyer, who promised to take her out of this dirt-road town. He'd said they'd travel the world and go to fancy parties at the capital.

Then, the boyfriend tried to burn down the city hall in a town thirty miles away and toast the mayor of Honey Creek, who he claimed was his ex-girlfriend. But that turned out to be a lie too. It seemed her smart, good-looking someday husband was playing Russian roulette and the gun went off, not only on his life but hers as well.

He'd written her twice from prison. She hadn't answered.

She'd tossed the letters away without opening them. Because of him she couldn't find any job but this one, and no man would get near enough to ask her out. She was poison, a small-town curiosity.

Marcie hadn't known anything about Boone Buchanan's plot to make the front page of every paper in the state, but most folks still looked at her as if she should have been locked away with him. She was living with the guy; she must have known what he was planning.

She shook off hopelessness like dust and walked across the empty dance floor. Her set was over, time to go home.

A cowboy sat near the door in the shadows. He wore his hat low. She couldn't see his eyes, but she knew who he was. Long lean legs, wide shoulders, and hands rough and scarred from working hard. At six feet four, he was one of the few people in town she had to look up to.

"Evening, Brand."

"Evening, Marcie," he said, so low it seemed more a thought than a greeting.

She usually didn't talk to him, but tonight she thought she'd be civil. "Did you come to see me play?"

"Nope. I'm here for the beer."

She laughed. One beer wasn't worth the twenty-mile drive to Someday Valley. He'd had to pass two other bars to get to this run-down place.

"You ever think of buying a six-pack and staying home for a month?"

"Nope."

Marcie couldn't decide if she disliked Brandon Rodgers or just found him dead boring. If they spoke, they had pretty much the same conversation every week. He was a Clydesdale of a man, bigger than most, but easy moving. She had no doubt he talked to his horses far more than he ever did people.

It wasn't like she didn't know him. He was about three years older than her, owned a place north of here. Ran a few cattle and bred some kind of horses, she'd heard. Folks always commented that the Rodgers clan kept to themselves, but lately he was the only Rodgers around. His mother died and his sister married and moved off. He'd never dated anyone that she knew about. In his twenties he had gone off to the Marines for six years.

"You want to sit down?" He dipped his worn Stetson toward the chair to his left.

She almost jumped in surprise. He'd never asked her to join him. But Marcie didn't want to make a scene. He never talked to anyone, and no one talked to her, so they could sit at the same table in silence together.

In a strange way they were made for each other, she thought. "Sure."

"You want a drink?" His words were so low they seemed faded by the time they reached her.

"No." Marcie folded her arms and stared at him. They'd run out of conversation, and with his hat on, she couldn't see anything but the bottom half of his face. Strong jaw. A one-inch scar on the left of his chin was almost camouflaged by his week-old beard. He wasn't handsome or homely.

She decided to wait him out. She guessed he wasn't a man to enjoy chatter.

"I'm not trying to pick you up, Marcie," he finally said with the same emotion he'd read a fortune cookie.

"I know. 'You want to sit down?' is the worst pickup line ever." She raised her voice slightly as a half dozen good ol' boys who smelled like they'd been fishing stumbled in. They all lived around Someday Valley, most with their folks, and even though they were near her age, not one had a full-time job.

Joey Hattly, the shortest of the pack, bumped into Marcie's chair. Joey must have heard Marcie say 'pickup line.'

"I got a line that never fails." The stinky guy pushed his chest out as if performing to a crowd.

Marcie smelled cheap liquor on his breath and fish bait on his clothes. She moved an inch closer to Brand. She wasn't afraid of Joey, but she didn't want her sins listed again. Some of the bar regulars liked to remind her that she was a jailbird's girlfriend.

Luckily, Joey was more interested in talking about himself tonight. "I can pick up any gal with just a few words. I walk up to a table of pretty gals and say, 'Evening, ladies. This is your lucky night. I'm single and here to dance. I've got a college education and I know my ABD's.'"

He held up a finger to silence everyone before adding, "Wanna *C* what I can do?"

The fishing buddies laughed. One slapped Joey on the back. "Don't waste your lines on Marcie; she's not interested. She's sworn off all men since she slept with the bottom of the barrel."

She didn't count Brand as a friend, but right now, he was the safest bet in the room. A pack of drunks was never good, and they all appeared to have more than a few bottles of courage in them.

Another fisherman joined in. "Yeah, she was shacking up with a killer. They say a man who thinks about burning folks alive is sick in the head. If you ask me, she knew what he was planning. She don't deserve to just walk away free when that fire Boone set almost killed four people. Least we should do is give her a spanking."

The oldest of the group added as he scratched his bald head, "Maybe we should strip her and paint an A on her chest like they did in that old book Mrs. Warren made us read."

"They stripped a woman in *The Scarlet Letter*?" Joey's squeaky voice chimed in. "Maybe I should have read that."

His buddy added, "There were no pictures, Joey."

The sound of the bartender racking a shotgun silenced the room. "Closing time. One more drink and I'm turning off the lights." Nothing in Wayne's action suggested that he was kidding.

The gang turned their attention to the bar. Marcie had never seen the bartender fire the shotgun, but Wayne had slapped a few drunks senseless with the stock.

The bald guy gave her a wicked look before he joined his buddies.

Brand slid his half-empty beer across the table and stood. "Get your guitar. I'm taking you home."

Marcie managed to force a smile proving she wasn't afraid. "Brandon, that won't be necessary. I live across the street in the trailer park. I can walk home."

"It's not a suggestion, it's a favor, and I told you, I'm not picking you up. That trailer park isn't safe to walk through in daylight, much less after midnight."

She looked up and for once she could see his coffee-brown eyes. He looked worried, almost as if he cared. "I'm not your problem." Marcie laced her fingers without making any move to follow his orders. "I'm no one's problem. I don't think you even liked me, so why act like you care now?"

She'd slept with some truck driver a few months after Boone went to jail. The trucker had bragged that she told him all kinds of things about what Boone did in bed and then she claimed the trucker was better. The trucker must have known she wouldn't say anything when he bragged. If she had, no one would believe her.

She looked up at Brand Rodgers, wondering if he was looking for a story to brag about. No, not quiet Brandon. He seemed to have turned into a six-feet-four tree wearing a Stetson. Silent. Waiting beside the table.

"Oh, all right," she said as if they'd been arguing. "I'll let you drive me home."

A few minutes later as they walked past his pickup, Brand placed her guitar in his truck bed. The black case vanished in the shadows. "I never said I didn't like you, Marcie. I'm older. You were just a kid."

"I'm grown-up now."

"I noticed."

She thought of telling him they could easily walk to her trailer, but somehow after her day, riding home seemed a treat.

Brand was safe. She'd never heard a bad word about him. Marcie swore under her breath. Thinking Brand was better than most men she knew wasn't saying much.

She gave him directions to her place back in the tree line near the end of the trailer park. She'd grown up here. Lived with her folks until her mom left when Marcie was seven. Then her dad ran the bar for a while until he got sick. She took over managing the place before she was out of high school. Ordered supplies. Cleaned the bar after closing time. Hired the help. Wayne had been a drunk who needed a job. She'd hired him to bartend with the understanding he wouldn't drink on the job. He'd kept that rule until he finally bought the place. Now and then Marcie saw the signs he was drinking again, but she doubted the customers noticed.

Once she thought she had a chance of breaking free of Someday Valley. She'd left to make her way with her songs. Three years later she was back. Her dad was dying and her brother had disappeared. The only good news, she guessed, was that Wayne now let her work for him.

Wayne wasn't a bad boss. He paid fair and she did most of the work while he drank away most of the profits, but he did pay her extra for singing. Twenty an hour and tips. Which tonight had been seven dollars and a quarter.

The lone yellow bulb blinked through the trees as Brand drove toward her ten-by-thirty home. The place didn't seem so bad when she walked through the trees in the dark and slipped inside. But now, with the headlights blinking on the rusty sides and the broken window glass covered with cardboard, the small trailer looked like something abandoned to decay.

"This is far enough," she whispered. "You might get stuck in the mud if you go much further."

He stopped and got out.

She did the same. "I can make it from here."

He started walking beside her. "I'll walk you to your door, Marcie."

Brand didn't seem to notice the mud or the slow drizzle of rain. He was a man who worked outside. He was used to the weather.

She had a feeling she'd be wasting her breath if she argued about him coming to the door. She didn't want to tell him that no man had ever walked her to her home. Boone used to call and wait at the park entrance until she came out. He'd said he didn't want to get his car dirty on the bad roads, but Marcie always thought it was more that he didn't want anyone to see him picking her up. She was small-town trash and he was Austin rich.

Marcie stepped on the first concrete block that served as a step. She turned back to Brand. "Thanks. I'm home safe now."

He touched the brim of his hat and stepped away without a word. It was so dark in the trees that she wondered if he'd find his way back to his truck.

Marcie slipped inside and locked the door. Loneliness closed in around her like a heavy fog, making the air so thick she had to work to breathe. All her life she'd felt alone. Even when her mother was around she never had time for her. Or, when her father was ill and never left the trailer. And now, people only talked to her when they had to.

She curled up on her couch and just sat in the dark. There were times she'd had dreams. This place seemed a pod where she could imagine a future, as a singer in Nashville or a rich man's wife. She could mold herself into anyone. All she had to do was break free of this place, and bloom.

She was almost asleep when she heard movement in the brush outside. A stray dog. Maybe a coyote looking for a late-night snack.

Then she heard mumbling loud enough to pass through the cardboard that blocked her view. What good did it do to lock the door if anyone could come through the broken window? Cardboard wouldn't stop a rat.

"You in there, Marcie?" A voice sounding very much like Joey Hattly yelled, then giggled. "Me and the boys thought we'd come by and talk to you. We brought beer."

"Go away," she said too low for them to hear.

Someone knocked on the door. Tried the knob.

Joey's voice came again. "Now come on, Marcie. You don't want us to have to break the lock. We thought we'd pay you a visit. Just to be friendly, you know. Let us in."

Laughter came from the shadows.

"Go away," she said a little louder. Tears slipped down

her face. She was all alone. There was no one to help her. No one.

The knob rattled again, then someone pounded on the door as if she might not know they were there.

The man on the other side of the door cussed. His buddies snorted. Another yelled, "Hurry up, we ain't got all night."

The man at her door added, "You're going to pay, tramp, for making us wait out here in the rain."

Marcie moved to the window slit in the thin door and peeked out. Four, maybe five men, moving around in the moonlight. More creatures than humans, if only in her mind.

"Kick the door in," the bald man in the yellow glow of the light growled, then threw his empty beer can against the trailer. "Let's get this party started. She'll play along after I rough her up a bit. Women like that. Lets them know who's boss."

Joey's voice sounded a bit panicked. "Marcie. Come out. We ain't going to hurt you. We just want to have a little fun."

She heard the roar of an engine before she saw a black truck seem to fly from the trees. Branches broke and mud sprayed as tires hit the dirt.

Brand!

When he was ten feet away he hit the brakes, cut the engine, and jumped out with both boots hitting the ground with a thud.

He just stood there, his fists on his hips like he was a warlord bothered to have to drop to earth.

Among the drunks, Joey found his nerve first. "You better back down, Brand, unless you got a gun. There's five of us. We're just here to party with the lady. If she cooperates there ain't going to be no trouble."

Brand set his hat on the truck. "I don't need a gun. Which one of you men wants to go first?"

The bald guy laughed. "How about we all go at once? We'll beat you so far into the ground, folks will use you as a hitching post."

"Yeah," another yelled. "This ain't none of your damn business."

Brand didn't move as they all started toward him.

Marcie watched from the tiny window. With the truck's lights she saw the first two men rushing Brand. A heartbeat later their bodies were flying in two directions.

One drunk hit the trailer so hard he probably did damage. Another hollered something about his mother as he sailed through the night air. When he wrapped around a pine, he melted silently to the ground, breaking branches all the way down. Brand was out of the light's beam, but every man that went after him came out crying in pain.

When Joey lowered his head and rushed into the fight like a bull, he boomeranged out faster than he went in. On his second try, he rolled out like a soccer ball and hit the concrete steps of her home.

The last man standing, the bald guy too old to still be running with the others, had enough sense to raise his hands and back away. He bumped into Joey and they both tumbled over her trash cans. The tall man picked up a lid and started beating Joey on the head for tripping him. Then both men fell over the concrete steps again.

Marcie couldn't tell if they were helping each other up or fighting.

Brand finally stepped in front of his truck's headlights

and asked almost politely, "Anyone else want to continue this conversation?"

Joey's voice was high when he yelled for everyone to stop. "I think my arm's broke, damn it. It hurts like hell. One of you drunks has got to drive me over to Honey Creek to the clinic."

"It's closed until six in the morning." The man in the dirt cussed between every word. He seemed in no hurry to get up. "To hell with your arm, I'm spitting teeth."

Joey cussed the world for a while, then seemed to give up. "Just take me there. I'll sit on the porch and cry until it opens. I got to see a doc before my arm falls off."

Marcie watched as Brand moved to her door and the men slowly crawled away. No one tried to help Joey. The gang had become every man for himself. They all complained. One limped. One held his gut, another his head. The one who hit the side of the trailer had to be kicked awake.

As soon as they were gone, she ran out to Brand, then stopped a foot away from him. This cowboy had just proved he could be violent. She wasn't sure she wanted to get closer.

"Thank you," was all she could manage. "I . . . I . . ."

"You're welcome," he said as calmly as if he'd just pulled out her chair.

"Why did you come back?" She stared hard at his sad brown eyes, but she saw no anger in the man.

"I forgot to get your guitar out of the back of my truck." He patted her awkwardly on her bare shoulder. "You all right?"

She was shaking at the thought of what could have happened but she couldn't speak. Slowly Marcie looked up at him and shook her head. She wasn't all right. She hadn't been for a very long time.

Brand pulled her gently against him. "It's all right now, honey. No one is going to hurt you."

She couldn't stop crying. She didn't want to think. Five drunk men and a throwaway woman no one cared for. If Brand hadn't come back, she knew what would have happened.

She also knew Brand was lying. There was no "all right" in her world. Everyone hurt her.

He didn't say another word. He just held her. She heard his heart pounding and felt his rough hands on her bare shoulders. The warmth of him finally calmed her as she melted against him.

Brand gently pushed far enough away from her that she could see his face. "Come home with me tonight, Marcie. You'll be safe, I promise. I'm just offering you a place to sleep. I'm not trying to pick you up."

"You keep saying that." She wiped a tear from her cheek with the palm of her hand. "I'm starting to believe you."

Without another word, Brand walked her to his truck, opened her door, and helped her up as if he'd been doing this simple act all his life.

Chapter 2

Honey Creek

Piper

Mayor Piper Jane Mackenzie paced her tiny office on the fourth floor of city hall as if it were a jail cell. The trees were in full fall colors outside, and for once she hardly noticed. All she saw were stripes from raindrops on her windows. To her, the rain had been tapping on her windows for a month, like a hundred tiny clocks ticking away.

It had been five months since part of the building had burned, and the repairs were almost finished. The arsonist, Boone Buchanan, had been tried as soon as he was released from the hospital. He'd be an old man before his family would be able to get him out of prison. Only Piper, the town's mayor, still awoke at night feeling the heat of the fire, the sounds of chaos crackling around her, and smoke filling her lungs.

Her fear of dying in a fire haunted every night, making her wake most mornings with the smell of smoke in her lungs.

Life was calm now, but the recall of that night remained a scar on her memory. In a strange way the fire in Honey Creek had brought the town together. The people seemed to realize what they had, nestled in a valley in the heart of Texas. Before, they'd loved Honey Creek. Now they also protected it with additions to the fire department and the sheriff's office.

She pressed against the window, letting the glass cool her warm cheek. The repairs were almost done. People had stopped talking about that horrible night. So, why wasn't she happy? Why couldn't she relax?

Simple! She hadn't seen Colby McBride in three months and her pride wouldn't let her tell him how much she needed him. She knew Colby had been a state trooper right in the middle of one of the biggest cases in the state. He'd been sent to protect her, and he had. In doing so, he'd almost lost his own life.

The passion they'd shared might still be mixed up with all the drama of the fire and the trial. Maybe all the excitement had fueled their love affair and now he could walk away. But she couldn't. Colby was too deep in her heart.

Boone not only tried to burn the city hall down, he did it because he wanted to kill her. Boone thought her death would bring him notoriety. He'd made up a story that he was engaged to the mayor, and he planned to play the part of a heartbroken almost widower. He'd thought no one would catch him, but Colby and Sam Cassidy had.

Piper was used to the press, but Colby wasn't. The months during Boone's trial must have been hard on Colby. She was used to it. She'd grown up in the light of cameras.

Thanks to Colby watching over her, Boone's plan failed. Boone was in jail and Colby was now a Texas Ranger.

But what was between her and Colby had nothing to do with the fire or a crime. She'd simply fallen for him hard. Too hard. She was a sensible, career-minded mayor. She wasn't supposed to fall in love with the officer assigned to watch over her. But she had, and now that he was transferred to Austin, she missed him terribly.

Maybe she should slow down this time. Take her time with Colby. Get to know him better before she risked their careers. Play it cool. She could say these three months apart had given her time to think, and she wasn't ready to move to the next level. Colby would understand. He might even be relieved. He was as serious about being a Texas Ranger as she was about advancing in government.

Trooper Colby McBride had been assigned to do a job, then leave town. He belonged in Austin. It made sense to take their time. But she couldn't talk her mind out of what her heart wanted. She loved Colby.

Her heels tapped the polished oak floor. He was doing his job, she knew that, but she wanted him here. Phone calls couldn't substitute for having him next to her. Neither did the public encounters they had in court or interviews during the trial. Thanks to her two big brothers who had both been Texas Rangers for years, Colby and she had never found a moment alone when she had to testify at Boone's trial.

She wanted Colby in her arms, in her life, and in her bed. Slowing down would probably be harder than staying on that egg and grapefruit diet she tried in college. She'd gained ten pounds from celebrating every night after staying on the diet all day.

"Piper!" Autumn, her secretary, yelled from one room away. "You're going to wear out the floor."

The mayor peeked out of her office and glanced across Autumn's always spotless desk. "He was supposed to be here an hour ago."

Autumn stood and leaned against her office window. Her pregnant belly shined the glass. "I think I see him turning the corner. He's riding that old Harley. You've got to tell him to stop riding that thing or before we know it, he'll be nothing but bug guts on the windshield of some trucker's rig."

Piper kicked off her high heels and ran. By the time Autumn turned around, Piper was halfway down the new metal staircase.

She darted out the back door of city hall and ran right into Colby's arms.

The Texas Ranger took the blow laughing. He lifted her off the ground and tried to kiss her as he carried her out of the rain. Bold, fast kisses salted by her happy tears.

They were almost inside when Tyrone Tilley walked past. The chubby little man stepped on the grass so Colby could get by. "Evening, Mayor," Tyrone said formally as if he didn't notice them midnight kissing on the rainy afternoon.

Piper looked up. "Colby's back," was all she could think to say.

"I noticed." Tyrone tipped his umbrella. "Glad to see you're home, sir."

Piper waited three seconds, then she went back to kissing Colby. Maybe she'd tell Colby they'd start taking it slow tomorrow.

Once they were in the stairwell, he let her feet touch the floor and kissed her just like she liked to be kissed. Long and slow with their bodies so close they seemed to melt together.

"I missed you, babe," he whispered. "I've got a three-day weekend, but I have to be back and fully functional Tuesday morning."

"Three whole days."

He laughed. "And four nights. Any chance you're still sleeping upstairs at the Honey Creek Café? We could wake up a few ghosts in that place."

"Everyone in town will know we're there." A perfect weekend lost a bit of its shine. Everyone would watch them, talk about them. They already did.

"I don't care. You're my girl. We'll sleep until noon, then go down and eat, then go back to bed."

For a long moment he held her, rocking her gently as if they were slow dancing. She didn't mention that she'd have to do her weekly radio spot at eight o'clock on Saturday, or that he'd probably have to report in to the sheriff and fill LeRoy in on what was happening with Boone's appeal.

For a while she just wanted them to be a man and woman in love.

In love? Another chip fell off Heaven.

Colby McBride, the man who'd run through fire to save her life, who made love to her like she'd never been loved, who'd do anything for her, had never said he loved her.

He kissed her forehead. "We'll figure it out, PJ. Right now it's enough just to be close to you."

Laughing, she whispered, "The widows want you to come spend the night at Widows Park. They promised to have the downstairs bedroom ready for you and breakfast cooking by seven if you ever came back."

"Where would you sleep?"

"My room upstairs, and every step on the stairs creaks."

He shook his head. "Maybe I can get Digger to reserve the back cabin for us. Then the only one watching us will be that raccoon."

"No luck there. Old Digger left for a vacation. Closed up the lodge."

She could feel Colby's arms tighten slightly around her and she laughed. "Don't worry, I've got a plan."

He smiled. "I hope so, because making love in that tiny office of yours will not do for what I have in mind."

He lifted her up and carried her to the elevator. "We'll talk about it when I take you up to get your shoes."

The ride to the fourth floor was one long kiss that made her forget everything but Colby.

Chapter 3

Pecos

Pecos Smith sat at the dispatcher station, studying his books. Kerrie, his new wife, and he both decided to only take two college classes for the fall semester. With her pregnant and due the first of December and him studying to be a deputy sheriff, they thought starting college slowly might be a good idea.

But nothing about Pecos's life was slow. Their drive to classes two mornings a week always seemed a race to make it on time. He studied police procedures online most nights when the calls were light, and worked all day on Saturday at Kerrie's grandfather's farm.

Five nights a week from midnight to eight he was the dispatcher who handled 9-1-1 calls for the county. Everyone asked if he ever slept. Pecos just smiled. He couldn't tell them how grand it was to curl up with his wife and sleep the afternoon away, or lie next to her the two nights he was home. As she cuddled beside him, she'd put his hand on her tummy and let him feel a baby growing.

He was a lucky man. Twenty years old. Most beautiful wife in town. About to have a child.

The 9-1-1 phone sounded and Pecos pulled out of his dreaming.

"Nine-one-one. What is your emergency?"

"Pecos?" Sam Cassidy, the fire chief, yelled in his usual demanding voice.

"It's me," Pecos answered. "You got a fire somewhere, Chief?" Cassidy was new in town. Of course, pretty much anyone not born here was considered new. Sam wouldn't be calling if it wasn't an emergency.

"Not this time. We got a man someone tried to shove into the newborn drop box. All they got in was his head."

Pecos tried to picture the small box at the corner of the station. Most towns had safety boxes installed in case someone abandoned a newborn. The Safe Haven Baby Box. The law made sure the baby would be safe and the person would not be charged with a crime. The minute the box was closed, an alarm went off in the station and the firemen would take care of the child's needs. In all the years it had been there, Pecos never heard of anyone using it.

"Sam, I got to ask, is the head connected to a body?"

"Yeah, and he's cussing. His friends almost scraped his ear off trying to shove him in, then they took off, probably afraid we'd arrest them for abandoning a drunk."

"What do you want me to do?" Pecos had never seen this in any manual.

"I don't know. He needs more medical attention than we can give him. I got the two men in-training practicing on stopping the blood, but he's fighting them off with his one arm that seems to be working. Maybe you could call the sheriff, get him to wake the doc, and talk him into opening the clinic early."

Pecos tapped in the sheriff's number. While it rang, he asked Sam, "Was he attacked?"

"No, I don't think so. He claims Big Foot came out of nowhere and tossed him ten feet. He's been yelling it so loud I'm starting to believe him."

Another ring from the sheriff's home phone. Pecos enlightened Sam. "You tell the guy that Big Foot doesn't live in Texas?"

"I can't tell him anything," Sam added, "he's only got one ear to hear and one eye that's not swollen closed. The man doesn't seem to be interested in debating."

The sheriff's voice came through the speaker. "This better be important!"

Sam boomed back, "We got a problem, LeRoy. I don't know if it's medical, criminal, or if we're dealing with a drug case, but you've got to come get him."

"I'm on my way. Got a name?"

Sam sounded relieved. "Said he's Joey Hattly."

"Hellfire," the sheriff roared on the speakerphone. "Last time I heard from Joey he was claiming he shot his ass off. I drove all the way to Someday Valley to find out that it was just his left butt cheek."

Pecos fought down a laugh. It was nights like this that made him want to be a deputy.

The sheriff ordered Sam to stop as much blood as he could from dripping out of Joey, while he'd pick up the doc and meet them at the clinic.

Both lines went dead and Pecos leaned back in his chair, already thinking how he'd tell Kerrie all about Joey at breakfast.

He thought of all the things he loved about being married. She cooked omelets for him. They talked about everything. He loved holding her. She told him he was her best friend.

Pecos's smile faded.

Her best friend, nothing more. Her kiss each night was a fast peck. Pecos was twenty, he was a man, he wanted more. He had a feeling when the baby, whom he'd claimed as his, was born, Kerrie would still think of him as her friend.

He knew he was lucky to be married to her. She was beautiful and smarter than he'd ever be. Her family was rich. He was going to college because of her. He had bigger dreams than he'd ever imagined because she said she believed in him.

But . . . he was his wife's best friend, nothing more.

Pecos dropped his head so fast his forehead hit the book he'd been reading. He was in hell.

Chapter 4

Marcie

Marcie Latimer curled up on an old leather couch at Brandon Rodgers's small ranch house and cried while he checked on one of his mares about to foal in the barn. He'd turned on the lights and lit a fire before he'd left, but her world still felt cold and dark.

In her mind she kept envisioning what would have happened if Brand had not come back to her trailer. If he hadn't stopped the drunks.

Her body shook with fear. They would have hurt her and then called her names. They would have threatened her if she said anything about what they'd done to her. It was her word against all theirs. One would probably tell her to forget what happened; after all, she wasn't really hurt, just bruised a bit. Another would whisper that he'd be back for seconds.

She couldn't remember when she'd been so tired. *Bone weary all her life* would probably be carved on her headstone. She saw no way out, just day after day of trying to survive. She'd been burned by her last boyfriend so badly, she'd never even wanted to try loving again. She was a grown woman, but tonight she felt like a child huddled in the woods, shivering and afraid.

When she heard Brand's boots stomping across the porch, she pretended to be asleep. She couldn't stand the thought of him asking questions. She'd seen worry in his brown eyes at the bar. She didn't want to see pity now.

He stepped inside, removed his muddy boots, and came straight toward her.

Marcie couldn't breathe. She thought she could trust him. Suddenly she wondered why. Maybe she never heard of him dating because he killed all his girlfriends and buried them out by the barn. Maybe he wanted what Joey and his friends wanted, all to himself.

As he leaned toward her, she balled her hands, then realized what chance did she have in a fight? He'd taken on five men. Running seemed her only answer. But where? In the dark she'd never find the main road, much less her way back home.

His big hand grabbed the quilt on the back of the couch and lifted it.

Suffocation? That's how he'd kill her. He'd never been very friendly, and now he probably thought putting her out of her misery was being kind. She was simply a wounded animal no one seemed to want around.

As he straightened, he floated the quilt over her. Like a cloud it drifted down, adding a layer of warmth.

Marcie took in air and opened her eyes slightly. As usual, her imagination had taken over. Brand was just a man helping out someone in trouble. She thought of him as someone she knew from school years ago. No one special. Barely remembered.

She watched him walk away from her. He turned the dead bolt, lifted a shotgun from a shadowy corner, and checked that it was loaded before putting it back. Then he turned off all the lights except the lamp by the couch.

"Good night, pretty lady," he whispered as he reached the hallway.

"Good night," she answered in a voice he'd never be able to hear.

The fire slowly died and sleep finally came to her. Even a broken heart has to rest.

Chapter 5

Piper

Mayor Piper Mackenzie pulled the key from a nail just above the back door of the Honey Creek Café. The only sound at the closed café, on the edge of town, was the lapping of the river almost spilling over its banks.

"My cousin reminds me regularly where the extra key is so we can use the bedroom upstairs if you ever come home." Piper laughed. "I think she'd like to have you in the family someday."

He stopped nibbling on her ear long enough to ask, "You're not sleeping here? Every night I imagine you here, waiting for me to make it back."

"No, I've been staying at Widows Park since you left. I guess cuddling with all the old dears isn't near as sexy. Lately they seem to need me more."

"I need you," he added, then pulled a few inches away. "Are all the old girls okay?"

"Yes, except for a cold or two. I just get lonely here without you, and they love having me around."

Colby hugged her. "I try to make it back, but I swear one, or both, of your brothers have something they think I have to check out every weekend. If I didn't know better I'd say they were trying to keep us apart. They both protect their little sister like grizzly bears."

"I'm not surprised. They like you, Colby, but they think no man is good enough for me. Between them they'll make you a great Texas Ranger, but they'll have to get used to the idea of you being their little sister's boyfriend."

"I'll try my best to do the job of ranger. I feel like I'm learning in double time." He laughed. "As for being good enough for you, I'll try real hard, Mayor, but you're the only one who can judge my progress. How about we leave your brothers out of what's between you and me? There's not enough room in the bed."

They both laughed as they opened the café door and ran up the back stairs to their lovers' hideaway. The little room she'd once used to spend time alone was waiting for them.

She needed to hold him, touch him, taste him, and it seemed he felt the same way. They hadn't talked of love and commitment, but she knew he'd always feel this way about her. He'd saved her life. He'd made her feel wanted and needed. He made her laugh.

Tomorrow he'd talk about his training as a Texas Ranger, and she'd tell him all that was happening at city hall, but right now all she wanted to do was make love to her man.

Chapter 6

Jesse

Jesse Keaton checked his watch by the dashboard glow. It was 6:23 a.m. The bakery should be open by now. Of course, he was the only customer parked out front in the dark, so he could be a bit early.

Another fact—he was apparently the only one awake in the whole town of Honey Creek. Didn't anyone know that the day started before dawn?

Glancing at the back seat, Jesse smiled at his three children. Sunny Lyn, four years old, asleep in her car seat. Danny, six, curled up with his safety belt holding him upright, and Zak, seven, silently looking out the window.

Jesse could never forget his Beth, his one love, his wife. Her face shone through in all their children.

"Why'd we stop here, Dad?" Zak met his father's

stare. The boy's blue eyes were always looking for answers.

Jesse sometimes thought there were two kinds of people in the world. Seekers and settlers. The seekers never stop wandering, growing, experimenting. The settlers, like him, build their nest and stay in one spot.

He answered his son's latest question. "Thought I'd pick up donuts for Granny May."

"And us." Zak grinned. "Granny May won't eat them. She says she is too fat to eat anything sweet."

"You guys can eat all of them then, but you have to eat half of your breakfast first."

Zak frowned. "Dad, you know Granny May feeds us oatmeal. Grandma George lectures us while we eat at her house on Tuesday and Thursday, but at least we get pancakes with fruit on top. By Friday it's a toss-up which we get, the oats or the lecture."

"I know, but, son, that's the way it has to be. Grandma George was a teacher; she can't just turn off lecturing because she retired, and Granny May can't cook. When I was in school, I was always the skinniest kid in class. Your mother used to say that having a mother-in-law who can't cook was a great blessing."

Zak didn't smile. He was the only one who remembered his mother, and Jesse knew he didn't want to talk about her dying, but Zak liked it when Jesse told the good stories.

"It's not fair we have to drive all the way to town to eat. Why can't you feed us breakfast at home and take us to school?" Zak complained.

"You know why. I lose half the morning's work. This way I can be in the field by sunup. Plus both your grandmothers love doing this. You three are the only grandkids either will ever have. Since your grandpas passed on, they'd be lonely without you guys."

Zak turned back to the window. "I guess the donut holes will help this morning. I'll take one bite of oatmeal then pop a donut in."

Jesse smiled at his oldest child, but he wanted to roar all the way to Heaven that nothing was fair. Nothing in the world. He had to get up an hour early to drive his kids to Honey Creek so one of their grandmothers could feed them and see the boys got to school on time. His daughter would spend the day alone with a grandmother watching over her. At five he'd stop work and drive back into town to pick them up. By the time they sat down to supper it was dark, almost time for bed.

But it was worth it. He was raising his own kids and keeping the farm going. Sunny Lyn had a playroom at both houses, but no one to play with most days. And since his mother and Beth's mother, Grandma George, lived three doors apart, his youngest was often shifted from one house to the other.

6:26 a.m.

The front lights in the bakery finally blinked on. He could almost smell those pumpkin scones baking. Jesse's life seemed mapped out in routine, but now and then a smell or a touch made him remember what it was like to be aware. Last week it was like the scones woke him up and he breathed for a short time.

Nothing usually changed in his routine, except once a week he made the farmers' meeting at the grain co-op. It started at eight, but most of the men came in early to drink coffee and talk. He'd learned more from the old guys than he'd ever learned in Ag classes.

Jesse fought down a string of swear words. He'd turn

forty-one tomorrow and his only social activity was drinking coffee with a bunch of farmers.

One week ago he walked into the bakery to pick up a box of donuts for the guys and smelled pumpkin scones. He changed his mind and ordered the scones.

Jesse had heard the rumor that the baker and her little sister were witches. A cowhand told him the oldest, the baker, put glitter in her hair and had a tattoo.

Jesse knew ninety-year-old women who glittered their hair for fun, and tattoos were common. He didn't believe the witch handle any more than he believed in ghosts. After all, he was an educated man. He had two years at the junior college over in Clifton Bend and a year at Texas A&M before he started working the farm. Though he didn't finish a degree, he'd always thought of himself as smart. He read. Watched the news when he had time. He even took a few classes online before Danny came along.

But last week one bite of the baker's scones led to another, and before he realized it, he'd eaten three on his way to the weekly meeting. The scones were addictive. Maybe that pretty baker had mixed a spell in with the flour and sugar.

That afternoon, on his way home, he'd swung by the bakery for a dozen more. The kids were only interested in the donut holes he brought home. The scones were all his. Jesse rationed himself to two scones a day.

It was a miracle he could remember back a week. He hadn't had one for twenty-four hours and Jesse was sure he was going into withdrawal after eating them every day for a week.

He watched the baker, Adalee, unlock the door. Her long, curly red hair was tied up in a ponytail, but it was on the side of her head, not the back. Maybe she was a bit strange, but those scones had something in them too good to deny. It seemed the only explanation; they were pure magic. Before long he'd be her mule or whatever folks call people hooked beneath a spell.

Jesse let his imagination run. No telling what she'd have him doing now that she'd pulled him in. Maybe he'd have to kill some animal and drain its blood. Or dig up a body in the cemetery. She might want him to be her sex slave.

Jesse shook his head. He was forty, too old to be a sex slave. He had three kids to raise and a farm where he never caught up on all the chores. He didn't even have time to cook breakfast most days.

Besides, everyone in town knew the whole Keaton clan was homely as mud and he was a prime example of that. Well, maybe not homely, maybe just plain.

If he hadn't lived three doors down from Beth, she would have never spoken to him, they never would have married or had three beautiful children. His own mother kidded him that some folks love ugly dogs and Beth must have been a girl who loved ugly men. Lucky for him he was the first one who came along, or she might have married one of the Brigger boys. Some say when the first Brigger was born, he was so homely the midwife tried to push him back in.

Jesse's people were all tall and thin with hair that went every direction. From the time he started school, he thought his arms and legs were too long and his ears too big. His mother used to say the Lord made the Keaton men out of spare parts but they balanced it with strong hearts. She'd teased her one son, but she loved him *almost* as much as she loved her grandchildren.

His kids were blond like his wife had been. Angels with sky-blue eyes.

Jesse watched Adalee moving around in her bakery. She didn't look like a witch, but then he'd never seen one. He'd asked around but the boys at the cattle auction didn't seem to know much.

Adalee and her sister moved here about three years ago and opened a bakery. They didn't mix with the locals except to do business. Willie said he saw the little sister dancing in the rain once but old Willie had been drunk since '97, when his wife left him. One guy mentioned that the older sister was curvy, not the kind of stick figure like most girls in town.

As Jesse watched her, he saw that the man was right. Nice curves.

One of the cowhands said he saw the top button of the older sister's shirt unbuttoned once, and he swore he saw the curled tail of a snake tattoo. He claimed if that snake went down between her cleavage it would have been crushed for sure.

Hell, the only real evidence Jesse had was that she'd bewitched him with her scones. If he ever saw that snake he'd become a believer. If he went to the sheriff with his theory, LeRoy would tell everyone Jesse finally went mad living out there with the grasshoppers.

Just because Jesse's great-grandfather rode into town nude once when he was drunk, didn't mean Jesse would do anything crazy. Jesse figured being homely was enough of a burden to bear.

At 6:31 a.m. Jesse climbed out, opened the back door, and lifted Sunny Lyn from her car seat so she could sleep on his shoulder. Zak woke Danny and they headed toward the bakery.

Jesse told himself if he hadn't had the kids with him, he'd ask Adalee straight out what she put in the scones and then he'd tell her he was never eating another one of her addictive treats.

The baker smiled like she'd been expecting him. He took a deep breath and stepped forward as the heavenly smells slammed into his senses. Baked apples, chocolate pie, blueberry muffins, mixed with the smell of coffee. Jesse swore even his eyeballs were hungry.

"Morning, Mr. Keaton," she said from behind the counter. "That's right, isn't it?"

"Everyone just calls me Jesse. How'd you know my name?" Mind reader, maybe? he almost said aloud.

"I asked someone when you left last week." She smiled and winked. She had the greenest eyes he'd ever seen.

Jesse glanced back to see who she was winking at. There was no one behind him. He decided it hadn't been a wink. Maybe she had a twitch.

He thought about saying "Morning," but before he could, she handed him a scone.

"First customer gets to sample my newest scone, Jesse. Apple cinnamon."

He knew she was trying to trick him somehow, but he couldn't be rude. One bite. Well, two. Darn it, he ordered a dozen while he was still chewing.

As he ate he wondered which she'd make him do first, drain a wild animal of blood, dig up the dead, or be a sex slave, because he had to have another scone.

Then it dawned on him that all he had to do was buy them.

Sunny Lyn raised her head as the baker passed out free clear bags packed with six donut holes. The four-year-old patted the side of his head, indicating she wanted down, then ran to join her brothers at the table by the window.

For a moment he just stared at them as the first light of day shone on his sunshine children. Beth had named Sunny the moment she saw her light, almost white hair. An hour later Beth had been rushed into surgery with complications.

She never came back.

"You all right, mister?" Adalee asked, tipping her head sideways as if her ponytail was pulling her over.

"Jesse," he offered again, liking the way she said his name.

"Are you all right, Jesse?" she corrected, as if those beautiful eyes could see all the way to his soul.

"No." He pushed the past aside and forced himself into the present. "You've got me hooked on your scones."

She laughed, then leaned over the counter closer to him, as if she was letting him in on a secret. He couldn't stop himself from glancing down to see if one of her buttons was undone. No such luck and he felt like an idiot.

"My plan is to bewitch you."

Jesse froze as she turned back to her work. The baker had just admitted it without him even asking. She must have read his thoughts. She knew he'd figured out that she'd put him under her spell.

When she looked up and winked again, a full-out wink this time, she whispered, "See you next week, Jesse."

He was too shocked to talk. No woman had ever

winked at him, and this one did it twice. Like she was doing it on purpose.

His mind was full of crops and chores and raising kids. He swore he didn't have time to worry about one more thing. Now a bewitching baker had walked into his brain. She was probably still listening in on his thoughts. Facts would have to start falling out to make room for this new worry, because he could not hold much more.

"Do you want anything else?" She tilted her head again and the ponytail brushed her shoulder. "Half pumpkin and half apple cinnamon." She passed him a box.

Jesse nodded and paid. She must have read his mind because he hadn't said to mix them.

A gang of high school kids came in. Jesse watched her as she helped them. She didn't wink at any of them. By the time they left, the town seemed to have come alive. People were rushing in, packing the place and filling the air with chatter.

Jesse walked out, holding Sunny while the boys darted around them. He was hooked and there was nothing he could do about it.

Saturday

Chapter 7

Marcie

A slow rain let morning sneak in wearing shades of watery blue and gray fog. Marcie sat up and studied the room as if it were a painting she'd accidentally stepped into. She had no idea how long ago Brand's mother had died or when his sister left, but it must have been years. Nothing of them, or any other family, remained. Not a picture or trophy, nothing personal. The furniture was definitely picked out by a man, probably on Amazon where someone orders an entire room at once.

As she stood she saw books packed into every shelf. No TV or even a radio, but a new computer was in one corner. Brand Rodgers read in this room and maybe watched the fire or the weather, since no window had a shutter, blind, or curtain. There were stacks of paper and forgotten coffee cups around the desk.

It crossed her mind that there was no music in his life and the thought almost made her cry. He was a man who lived in silence.

He lived with nature. The house was so still she thought for sure she would have heard someone else breathe if anyone was there.

Marcie stood and tiptoed down the hallway until she found the bathroom. She took off her wrinkled clothes and stood in the shower until the water turned cold. Then she wrapped up in one of the big towels and tiptoed back to the living room.

Brand now sat in the huge recliner with a cup of what smelled like cocoa beside him. As she neared to ask if he had something she could put on, Marcie noticed he was asleep. While she'd spent the night feeling safe, he'd probably kept guard.

For a long while she just stared at him in the low dawn light. He looked younger now. What he'd done for her was brave. He'd fought five men. No, four. The bald guy had backed away. Strange because he'd been the loudest when they came calling and he probably would have been the first to rape her if they'd made it through the door. Or maybe he'd have waited to be third or fourth when most of the fight had gone out of her.

Marcie shivered at the memory. The night had been rainy, but she'd been sweating when she heard them call her name.

She had no choice. She needed to talk to someone, and Brand was the only one near. She poked the sleeping bear.

Brand opened one eye. "I made you some cocoa," he

whispered as he handed her the tin cup. "I heard you in the shower when I came in."

"I'll share." She sat on the arm of his chair with the big towel going almost to her knees. "Where'd you sleep last night?"

"On the porch. Thought the drunks might want another round." He laughed. "Doubt they could find the place even if they were sober. Joey came out here once asking if he could hunt dove."

Marcie leaned into his shoulder for balance. "What did you tell him?"

"I said no."

Marcie almost laughed. Brand was the worst storyteller she'd ever met. No details.

They took turns drinking the warm cocoa until the cup was empty. She could feel the warmth of it spreading down to her toes.

"You all right now?" he finally asked.

"You saved me last night. They'd come to rape me and I would have fought them to my last breath."

He tightened his grip on the cup handle. "You don't know that was what they came to do, Marcie. All I saw was you not opening the door so you probably didn't want them around. Are you sure they came to hurt you? Maybe they came to rob you."

She was silent for a long while, then answered, "There is nothing to rob in my house. I am sure what they came to do. It's happened before." Silently she began to cry. This man she'd barely noticed all her life cared enough to get involved. This man who'd never been more than a polite stranger to her was about to see all the scars that had built up in her since she was twelve. This man who rarely spoke to her now knew a secret she'd never told anyone.

Back then she'd held it all in. She'd told no one. She'd been too afraid. She thought part of it must have been her fault. She hadn't locked the door like her daddy told her. She hadn't screamed loud enough. She hadn't . . . Marcie let all the hurt and pain and loneliness inside of her pour out while Brand tugged her against his chest and rocked her.

Somehow he had become her one safe place. She let down her guard and stopped trying to be strong. She crumbled against him.

When exhaustion overtook her, she rested to the rhythm of his heart beating, as she tried to not let another tear fall. The rain pounded harder against his windows. As she drifted into sleep, she felt Brand carry her back to the couch. He laid her down as if she were a baby and covered her with the blanket. He'd kept to his word. He'd taken her home with him and made her feel safe.

Then he turned off the lamp and tossed a few more logs on the fire. The stormy morning seemed to be twilight. He walked away, leaving her to sleep without fear.

Hours later, she woke to a weak sun trying to fight through the clouds. For a moment she wasn't sure where she was. The room was spotless, almost as if it had been a show home that was staged in western décor. A pair of men's pajamas was on the table in front of her. She smelled coffee.

Slowly, as if waking up from days of sleep instead of hours, she stretched and lowered her feet to the floor. As fast as she could, she slipped into the pajamas, rolling up the arms and legs. They were red flannel and soft all over. She smiled as she wondered who gave them to Brand for Christmas. Someone who obviously didn't know him, for the set had never been worn.

"Coffee," she murmured, as if echoing the smell's call coming from the kitchen.

She heard low laughter. "Lunch is almost ready. Hope you like chili and cornbread."

Marcie walked into the kitchen knowing that she looked ridiculous. "Thanks for the clothes."

"I'm glad they fit." Brand set two bowls on the table. "Milk or coffee?"

She took a seat. "How about milk in my coffee?"

He nodded and passed her both. They ate in silence. Several times she wiggled and accidentally brushed his leg. He didn't complain, but once she caught his gaze just as she'd bumped against him. They'd both smiled.

When Marcie leaned back after her second bowl of chili, she noticed her guitar by the door.

"You remembered my guitar."

"Figured you'd want it." He picked up the bowls and returned with her guitar. "Any chance you'd play for me?"

This guy was growing on her. "I usually dress for my performances."

He moved his chair back a foot, put his elbows on his knees, and fisted his hands beneath his chin. "You look fine in my pajamas."

"These are not your pajamas."

"Only pair I have."

"You've never slept in them." She waved one of her sleeves. "They've never been worn by anyone but me, so that makes them mine."

"Nope. I was saving them in case I needed to loan them to a lady wearing a towel."

She was reading between the lines. "How long have you been waiting?"

"A while."

There was so much she wanted to know about Brand, but she had a feeling she'd have time to learn. His brown eyes reflected more of his feelings than his words probably ever would.

Her fingers ran over the strings of the guitar. For a while she just played, then with a low voice she began to sing. He never moved and she knew he was taking in the music as if it were a grand gift.

When she finally stopped and looked up at him, he nodded once. "Thanks," was all he said, then he asked if she wanted more coffee. As she stared at him she saw something in his eyes.

He treasured spending time with her. No one, all her life, had ever done that.

"Can I stay another night? Just one more. I don't want to go home after I play at Bandit's tonight."

"You can stay as long as you want. When you're working tonight, I'll go back to your place. I'll fix that window and put good locks on the door."

"You don't have—"

"I do."

Chapter 8

Pecos

The sun was up by the time Pecos Smith got finished with his job as Honey Creek's dispatcher. On Saturdays he didn't have to drive to Clifton Bend, and because it was raining he didn't have to work at the Lane bee farm. Kerrie's grandfather said if the bees were staying inside, so was he.

Kerrie would still be asleep when he got back to the rooms they rented from Mr. Winston. Pecos could crawl in beside his wife and sleep the morning away.

He tiptoed up the stairs to their rooms. After five months of knowing his in-laws, who lived down the street from Winston's place, Pecos knew no matter how bad life got, they'd never move in with them. Renting a place seemed more independent, more grown-up. With the free room they'd offered would come never-ending advice.

He might be twenty, but Kerrie didn't turn nineteen for another month. The baby might come before then. They'd bring it home here.

Slipping into their room, he stood watching Kerrie in the tiny slivers of light from the window. She was so beautiful. For the rest of his life he'd wonder how he got such a wife. He wasn't her baby's father, but no one would ever know that. He'd love her baby as he loved her.

He moved his hand lightly over her hair as if making a promise.

She'd never said she loved him. But he was her best friend and that was enough.

He slipped off his clothes and slid beneath the covers slowly, so he wouldn't wake her. For a few minutes he was still, letting his body warm next to hers.

As she always did, she rolled toward him, cuddling against him like he was her favorite pillow.

Pecos hugged her close and waited for the sigh that always came like she'd been waiting for him all night. When it whispered against his ear, he slid his hand over her round body, saying good morning to his baby.

He kissed her lightly on the lips as his hand moved up to brush over her breasts. He hadn't asked if it was all right to touch her there, but she'd never objected. Her breasts were bigger than they had been that day they'd graduated from high school. They'd gone skinny-dipping in the river and he'd seen her nude. Her beauty stopped his heart for a moment. The rest of the weekend was crazy. She'd told him she'd slept with a guy while staying at her cousin's place in Dallas. A nobody who said he never wanted to see her again.

One day after she'd told Pecos her secret, her parents had found out and thought the baby's father was Pecos. He lied and said it was. Naturally, after that her dad tried to kill him. Pecos didn't blame her dad. After a trip to the emergency room, everyone finally settled down and he and Kerrie married.

It all seemed like something that happens in movies, but it wasn't, and in the end he wouldn't have changed a thing . . . except maybe the part about her dad trying to kill him.

Pecos smiled as his hand brushed lightly over her breast one more time. "Kiss me good morning before you go back to sleep," he whispered.

She rolled to face him, her body touching his. "Morning, husband." She rubbed her chin against his day's growth of beard. "You smell like coffee and rain. Am I dreaming or awake?"

"You're sleeping. Any objection if I touch you while you dream?"

"No. Just don't wake me. The baby kept me awake most of the night."

He wanted to kiss her deep and hard, but he was gentle. Over the past months they'd learned one another, and it seemed neither slept soundly without the other. He'd gotten used to her walking in while he showered, but he'd never get tired of watching her dress.

He was twenty. He was a man, but he'd wait until she was ready for them to be lovers. Only problem was, her first and only venture into sex was all wrong and he didn't know how to make it right for her.

The guy who got her pregnant had walked away. He'd called her names for being drunk. He'd never mentioned his last name, so she couldn't have found him even if she'd wanted to.

Pecos had given her his name. He'd loved Kerrie Lane since they were in grade school. He knew he wouldn't have had a chance with her if she hadn't met the creep that one night in Dallas. He'd walked away, but Pecos was near when she needed someone.

He slid his hand over her hip and down her leg. He was slowly learning every curve of her body. He'd be ready when the time for loving came.

Chapter 9

Colby

Colby McBride woke alone. His lover, the mayor of Honey Creek, was gone. She left him with the ghosts of the Honey Creek Café to keep him company.

The little room, decorated in mismatched furniture and flowery upholstery, hadn't changed since the night he'd climbed the ivy and talked his way into her bedroom. That night still played out in his mind now and then. A first taste of Heaven, even if it did cost him several scrapes.

He didn't care that everyone thought the second floor was haunted. He just wished he could hear activity below in the kitchen. Colby was starving.

When he'd finally finished being dragged all over Austin by Piper's big brothers like they had to solve every crime before dark Friday night, Colby hadn't had time to eat before he took off to spend a long weekend with Piper. Then, when he drove into town and saw her running toward him, food was the last thing on his mind.

By the time he showed her how much he missed her, both were too tired to move. He thought he'd probably fallen asleep in mid-sentence. She'd cuddled closer and he was back in Heaven.

Now, he wasn't surprised she was gone by dawn. First, always, was her duty to her town. He turned over and saw the note on the back of the door. *Gone to do radio interview. Push the button and you'll hear me.*

Grumbling, he pushed the radio button. Rambling Randy, the local DJ, was popping questions at Piper in his double-time voice.

"So how are the plans for a Thanksgiving parade coming along? And, Mayor, what's being done about the reports of trash cans being stolen? Do you think this rain is ever going to stop?"

Colby closed his eyes and daydreamed of slugging Rambling Randy. He'd never met the man but he imagined him as Gollum from the movie *Lord of the Rings*.

Before Piper could answer either question, Randy added, "I heard we had a drop in the safe haven bin at the fire station. Anyone in town want to adopt a thirty-year-old drunk?" Rambling Randy's laugh sounded like a snort.

Colby thought he heard a door close downstairs. Since Piper was on the radio, it couldn't be her. Maybe it was the cook. Piper's cousin, the owner of the Honey Creek Café, always came in early. Jennifer would start making bread even before the cook came in.

He jumped out of the bed, grabbed his T-shirt and jeans, and dressed on his way down to the kitchen. Maybe he could help cook. That way he could eat sooner.

Jennifer turned as he stomped down the back stairs. Her bright blue eyes missed little and the smile she flashed assured him he was welcome.

"Thank goodness it's you, Colby. For a moment I was preparing to finally meet one of my great-grandparents' ghosts."

He smiled. "Disappointed it was just me?" Colby raised his hands in surrender.

"No." The owner of the café laughed. "Maybe you'll cheer up Piper." Jennifer raised an eyebrow. "You look like you've lost weight."

Colby grabbed an apple and sat down on the other side of the prep table. "I have. No time to eat." Jennifer's words finally sank into his brain. "Piper's been feeling down?"

The cook just nodded as she worked.

"I came back as soon as I could get free."

Jennifer laughed as she whacked a cantaloupe in half. "Men!"

Colby stared at the fruit as he wondered what he'd said wrong. He might not be an expert on women, but this one was fairly easy to read. "What?" No need to fill in any more of the question. He had no doubt she'd tell him what she thought. Piper's cousin had hated men since her divorce. If she hadn't found her love in running the café, she'd probably be roaming the country decapitating every lying husband she could find.

Jennifer pointed her knife at him. "Did it ever occur to you that maybe you're not what is bothering Piper?

Maybe you're not the center of her world. She doesn't need you, Colby. She wants you, or at least she did. Who knows? Your expiration date may be up."

Now he was more confused. He felt like he'd given all of him there was to give last night. Maybe it wasn't enough for Piper and she'd asked her cousin to say goodbye.

Should he leave?

"Is there someone else?" That couldn't be true. He talked to her almost every night. A tiny part of him thought that her finding someone else might be a way out. He wasn't ready for a forever kind of relationship, and Piper would want that, he guessed. He wasn't ready to say goodbye to her either. That thought seemed impossible.

But, he hadn't expected the thought of her moving on to hurt so much. He felt like Jennifer had slugged him in the gut with one of her cast-iron skillets.

He glared at Piper's cousin. She'd lifted her knife shoulder high, as if she planned to whack him next. "No, you idiot, she doesn't have someone else, and having you isn't having much. I like you, Trooper, but I swear every man I've ever known is a few bricks short of a load when it comes to understanding women."

Colby was considering that starving to death might be an improvement over talking to Piper's cousin Jennifer in a kitchen full of weapons. "What's the problem with me?"

"I don't know, really, but she's not happy. You're the obvious place to look." Jennifer went back to her work decapitating carrot tops. "I thought it might be one of the widows at the big house, but they all looked healthy a week ago when I dropped in. As far as I know there is no problem at city hall. Maybe it's this cloudy weather. You want breakfast? The grill's hot."

"No. I'll wait until Piper gets back, but thanks. I think I'll go take a shower." If he hung around Jennifer any longer, Colby feared he'd be suicidal.

He was halfway up the steps when she added, "This may have nothing to do with you. It may be something not even a Texas Ranger can solve."

Colby kept walking. When he reached the second floor, he closed his eyes in the stillness of the darkened hallway. He wanted to be Piper's hero. He wanted to protect her. He wanted to be the one she turned to.

Then one last thought slammed into him. He didn't want to lose Piper. She mattered too much. He couldn't walk away.

Chapter 10

Jesse

Jesse thought of the baker as he watched the dawn sun spread over his land. The view of the day's first light on wet earth was almost the color of Adalee's sunshine-red hair. He liked the way her curly hair bounced when she wore it down, and how her body was nicely rounded. She had a sweet smile and a wicked come-closer wink.

He'd daydreamed about telling her just what he wanted when she'd say, "What will you have today, Jesse?" but his thoughts were just flashes from a lonely man, nothing more. Not plans, only silent wishing.

If he was brave he'd say, "Just you." Or, maybe he'd say, "Can I hold you for a while?" Some nights he couldn't sleep for missing a woman to hold. As if it was some kind of core need, buried deep inside him. But just any woman wouldn't do.

He couldn't help but wonder if she knew she was climbing into his thoughts from ten miles away. If she did, she'd probably be blushing about now.

The air was still and heavy, promising a good rain, but for once his mind wasn't on the weather or the chores he had to finish before he quit and headed back into town.

By the time he got the kids home, fixed supper, got them all bathed and in their pajamas, he'd be too tired to do more than watch the news and go to sleep. If Danny didn't get up for more water or Sunny Lyn didn't start crying, Jesse would try to look at the stack of mail he was always behind on opening.

Only last night he'd lain awake and thought of the green-eyed baker with auburn hair. What does a man do when a woman winks at him? Was there some kind of winking etiquette he wasn't aware of? Did it mean anything? He was a fool for even worrying about why she winked at him. Women like Adalee never gave guys like him a second look. She seemed full of life and he was simply hanging on.

The baker was still on his mind when he dropped the kids off with Beth's mother.

He never stayed long. Grandma George, short for Georgina, decorated her house with memories of Beth. Jesse knew it was good for the kids to remember their mother, but the pictures of her at every age made him sad. He'd never forget Beth. He'd known her all her life . . . loved her most of his. But when he saw the pictures, it was like he'd lost a dozen Beths. The one he walked to school with. His best friend. His partner in games. His girlfriend. His first kiss. His only love. His wife.

Every time he walked into her mother's house, he lost them all over again.

But today he was in a hurry. It was already sunup. The grandmothers were taking the kids to a movie, and he could get in one more day of work this week. It was his birthday and he'd taken the time to let the kids give him his presents, watercolors signed by each.

He was halfway down the walk to his pickup when Grandma yelled from the doorway, "Your mom and I plan to take the kids home for you. We'll feed them a good supper and get them to bed."

Jesse turned back. "But I . . ."

"Take off an hour early tonight, clean up, and come back to town. It's your birthday. Have dinner with friends or check out the movie. Surely it won't be the same one we're seeing this afternoon.

"Your mother and I don't want to see you before ten. Have a little fun, Jesse. You're allowed."

Jesse nodded and walked away. There was no use arguing with them. They wanted to help and if he said no, he'd only hurt their feelings. How could he tell them that he had no friends? The guys at the co-op were all twice his age. His friends from high school had moved away or settled down with families of their own.

But he did as the grandmothers told him. He quit at four, took a shower, and passed them on the drive into the town. The kids waved. He smiled, knowing the ladies had promised them a grand time.

Jesse picked up supplies from the hardware store, then stopped in at the local tourist trap to buy jelly and honey. By the time the shops were closing, it was growing dark.

He got gas and checked the tires before buying a beer at the gas station. He parked downtown and walked the square, not hungry enough to eat and not interested in the one movie showing at the theater.

Jesse liked the trees that lined the courthouse square. They made him think he was in a forest, even though the town lights twinkled among the branches. No one would notice him there among the shadows. In an odd way he felt like he was surrounded by people.

The smells and noises were different here than on his farm.

He might be alone, but Jesse didn't feel lonely. He'd settled into being by himself when the kids weren't around. When Beth died he'd been too busy to think about it, but as time passed he realized he preferred living inside himself to talking to people. Most folks didn't say anything important, or interesting, or even worth listening to. Or worse, they tried to climb into his mind by asking things like, "How does it feel to be a widower so young?" Or "You ever thought of remarrying? Those kids need a mama."

Jesse sat down on a bench beneath the trees and opened his beer as he watched the streetlights come on and the store windows go dark. Fall colors still hung to the trees, but the leaves at his feet were dull and muddy.

He was forty-one today. That was young. A few of his friends were still single. He'd heard others were drifting from place to place, from job to job, still looking for where they belonged.

He took a draw on the longneck. He hated beer, but somehow it didn't seem right to celebrate his birthday with Coke, and the gas station didn't have champagne. Forty-one. He should feel young, but he didn't.

A part of him wished he could run away, but most of him just wanted to go home. He needed to finish reading Zak a book tonight and make sure Sunny Lyn had her floppy rabbit to sleep with. What if the grandmothers forgot to give Danny his medicine?

He closed his eyes and leaned his head back. He was old. He no longer knew who he was—only what he was to others. A dad. A farmer. A son.

There was no him inside his body.

When he leaned forward, a dark form stood in front of him. The night seemed clothed in fog the color of her blue cape. The low streetlights were balls of fuzzy fluff, not offering enough light for him to see beneath the hood of the cape.

"You drunk, Jesse Keaton?" The woman's voice didn't sound too friendly.

"It would take more than one bottle of beer. Besides, what do you care?" He wanted the shadow to go away. He had enough shadows following him.

She moved closer and lowered her hood. Long auburn hair danced in curls around her shoulders. "I don't much care, mister. I like to walk in the stillness after dark, and your long legs almost tripped me."

He folded his legs in. "Sorry. Thought I was invisible." He cleared his throat. "I mean, I thought I was alone."

Her voice softened as she asked, "You all right?"

"Sure. Today's my birthday. I'm celebrating."

"Alone? In the dark? In the rain?"

Jesse hadn't noticed the rain. "I think I'm lost. Nowhere and anywhere are the same to me."

The baker sat down beside him as if she'd been invited. She probably thought he was drunk, or maybe crazy. Or maybe someone told her his story and she just felt sorry for him. To his surprise, she didn't ask questions, she simply pulled off her glove and took his hand.

For a while neither moved. Her hand was soft with a strong grip, almost as if she had to hold tight to keep him from fading away.

Finally, he said, "Did you ever feel like you're falling off the earth? Or maybe one moment your thoughts, your feelings, will just wash away in the rain, leaving a shell to keep moving and working?"

She was a stranger. What did it matter if he let his fears fly? Who would she tell? No one would believe he lost his mind. He was solid as a rock and she was the town witch.

She still didn't say a word. He closed his eyes and released his grip. Maybe she'd vanish as quickly as she'd appeared. This wasn't his best hour.

Her hand slid away from his open palm. Jesse tried to pull his mind back into the real world. He began silently listing all he had to do tomorrow. So much for his birthday. He'd tell his mother and Beth's that he'd had a nice relaxing evening, then his world would settle back in place.

Adalee's fingers touched his cheek. She slowly moved down to his jaw, then back up. She brushed his hair off his forehead and moved over his temples, pressing gently. She might be testing to make sure he was real, or petting him like he was a wild animal. He didn't care. It felt good.

He couldn't move as she touched him, brushing over one eyebrow and lightly pressing his closed eyes. Probably some kind of spell, but he didn't pull away. He'd surrender without a fight. She smelled of the bakery and rain.

Reason whispered he should move away, but it felt so good. It had been a long time since anyone had touched him. This wasn't a handshake or a pat on the back; this was something personal.

The question that sometimes came to him in his dreams of her almost passed his lips. *Would you mind if I hold you, feel you, sleep beside you?*

Of course he couldn't say that.

Her warm fingers moved down his neck and pushed his shirt aside so she could glide along his collarbone. When he didn't move, she pressed her lips near his ear and whispered, "I see you, Jesse. In this moment we're both here. No past. No future. Just now."

He opened his eyes and saw her only in shadow. "I don't want to talk." The last thing he wanted to do was tell his sad story, or worse, hear hers. She didn't look much over thirty, so he'd win the "suffering longer" prize.

The baker moved closer and rested her head on his shoulder. Jesse put his arm along the back of the bench, almost holding her next to him. Even through their clothes, he could feel the warmth of her and she smelled of spices. He wondered if for one long moment she wanted to pretend they were a couple, as he did.

He was so tired of only being half of what he'd always been.

She tapped the toe of her shoe against his boot. "Will you walk me home?"

He nodded and stood. When he offered his hand, she took it and didn't let go. They walked in silence to the back of the bakery. Without the streetlights they were barely visible, but he was very aware of her beside him. At the back door she climbed the one step and turned to him. Now they were the same height. She was so close he could feel her breath against his cheek.

She breathed deeply and her ample breasts, ever so lightly, brushed against his chest.

Jesse took the feel of her like a blow, more pain than pleasure, but he didn't step back.

Her hand cupped the side of his face once more. "I understand," she whispered as her lips glided across his cheek until she touched his mouth. Every cell in his body came alive with panic and need and fear all at the same time.

The kiss was soft, light. "Happy birthday, Jesse," she whispered. Then she was gone.

He didn't move.

The lock clicked. A light shone from a window for a moment, then blinked off. He thought he heard someone running upstairs but he couldn't be sure.

Jesse stood in the black night with rain tapping on his shoulders. Finally, he smiled. He wished he'd said "thank you" to her. He wished he'd kissed her back.

The strange baker reminded him he was still alive. She was there. She wasn't a shadow person passing through. She was, if only for a few moments, there. He'd held her hand. He'd felt her breast touch his chest. She'd kissed him.

Neither of them would probably say a word about what happened. They might even convince themselves it was nothing, but he knew that he would hold this memory in his heart.

Jesse walked back to his bench on the square. No doubt about it, he was still alive. Best birthday in a long while.

Chapter 11

Jesse

Jesse Keaton thought about the baker while he worked alone on his small farm, but once he picked up the kids he didn't have time to think of anything but homework, cooking supper, and getting everyone to bed. Then there was always laundry, and the dishes, and the bills to pay.

Zak had started helping with the dishes and Jesse liked the time with his oldest son. Sometimes he could see the man in the boy.

On Friday and Saturday nights, they'd play board games, with him and Sunny Lyn as partners against the boys, then they'd all cuddle under a blanket on the couch and watch a kids' movie. By the time it was over, all were asleep, including Jesse. He'd finally wake up enough to carry each child to bed and think about how lucky he was. He'd lost Beth, but she'd left what she loved most for him to raise.

Jesse guessed there might be time for him to talk to friends, maybe even date when Sunny left for college. By then he'd be well into his fifties. Until then, he might as well change his name to Dad, for there was no time to be anything else. The baker was just a daydream, maybe a wish, nothing more.

When the house was dark and silent, he'd step out on the porch to watch the rain and think of Adalee. She'd said she bewitched him. That was probably why she came into his thoughts. If she'd put a spell on him, Jesse didn't know if he wanted it removed. He liked having her lingering in his thoughts.

She was so real to him in the stillness of night that he could almost sense her beside him. She was pretty enough that any man would remember her, but she wasn't putting thoughts in his head with witchcraft. There were too many of his own there. The way she smiled. The surprise of her wink. The low way she said his name. He wanted to talk to her, watch her move, and touch her softly, if only in his dreams.

"Adalee," he whispered to the moon before he stepped inside and locked up. Just whispering her name made him smile.

As he moved through the silent house, he realized he wouldn't know how to talk to her even if he had the time to stop by the bakery. The morning he went to the co-op was his only time in town on his own. All others were full. Besides, what would he say to someone like her? She was a flower and he was the weed standing next to her. Red hair. Green eyes. Full lips. Full breasts.

There was no room in his life to date, and he didn't

know how anyway. He and Beth had been best friends growing up, and one day when they were both fifteen she told him it was time they started dating. Three years later she said they should get married, and he thought it was a great idea.

He'd inherited a good piece of land from his grandfather, and both thought it would be a great place to live.

Heaven was living where they couldn't see a neighbor's light.

Beth loved kids. She used to say she wanted a dozen. They thought they'd wait a few years, then it would be easy, but it took a long time for her to get pregnant. Dear God, he was happy eight years ago when it finally happened. Beth made everything seem fun, even pregnancy. The only thing that bothered him about their years together was that he didn't realize how happy he was. He had a lifetime of contentment and he hadn't even known how great it was until he lost her.

Folks say the price of loving is loss. Only, how long would he have to wait to find peace again? The rest of his life, he figured. Even if he did have time to look for another wife who wanted to help raise his kids, it wouldn't be the same. It wouldn't be the perfect match. Some folks never find his kind of marriage. Maybe he should count himself lucky for having it at all.

It had been four years since he'd held Beth, but he knew she'd always be in his heart. The idea that he'd ever think of another woman in a loving way shocked him. Was there even room in his heart when he still loved Beth?

Yet, alone, working, he thought of Adalee. She had called him by his name and she'd kissed him. He had no idea what that meant, if anything.

Of course he'd see her again. The guys at the co-op wanted him to pick up scones. So when he saw her, what should he say? He had almost a week to think about it.

He hadn't made much sense before, so there was a good chance she wouldn't expect much conversation.

There would be no telling the truth, either. Jesse couldn't ask for what he wanted. "Would you hold your body against me?" would probably get him arrested.

He wasn't looking for a wife or even a date. He just wanted to be close to her one more time. He'd memorize her touch, her smell, the taste of her lips, then he'd go away and spend his time remembering that one moment that reminded him he was still alive.

Chapter 12

Honey Creek Café

Colby

When Piper didn't return from her radio interview, Colby dressed and walked toward town, hoping to meet her. The morning was so cloudy it felt like twilight, and rain hung in the air like spiderwebs of ice just at the point of melting. He rounded his shoulders as if conserving body heat, and took long strides.

Colby didn't mind the cold; his mind was too full of thoughts of Piper. Last night in her bed above the Honey Creek Café was paradise. They were perfect together, and the way they made love blocked all thought. But when she rolled away from him, she simply said she was tired and needed sleep. No lovers' talk in the night. No promises.

An uneasiness settled across his shoulders like a weight he didn't want to carry. He was comfortable back in Austin. He loved his work. Being a Texas Ranger was more a way of life than a job, and it fit him. But here in Honey Creek he couldn't seem to get his feet planted flat on the ground. He didn't know who he was.

The hero who saved the mayor from a fire five months ago?

The mayor's boyfriend who was just visiting?

Or maybe only a sometime love? Piper was very career minded. He might be just a weekend getaway from a demanding job.

She had claimed him as hers with one great kiss in front of half the town after the courthouse fire five months ago. But he wasn't sure he wanted to be a "boyfriend." They were both in their thirties. To be more, they'd have to take the next step. Something he'd never done.

Colby smiled and kept walking. He wouldn't mind being her full-time lover, but she seemed to want to keep that fact a secret. The hidden room upstairs at the café was proof of that.

He felt like he was playing poker with two cards. He might be sitting at the table, but he wasn't in the game.

No surprise that he was gun-shy of commitment. His parents played ping-pong with their marriage. When he was five they divorced. A year later they started dating, then remarried six weeks later. That marriage lasted until he was ten. Mom moved out. Dad wouldn't sign the divorce papers. They argued about it for a year. Dad won and Mom moved back home, with her demands posted on the refrigerator.

They had separate rooms from then on. The rest of the house was their battleground. In his teens they'd take turns slamming the door and moving out, but they always came back.

Colby finally figured that they simply loved to hate each other. Last time he called home, they were living under the same roof but not speaking to one another.

Colby never wanted that life, loving someone you can't be happy with. Jennifer had said Piper needed cheering up. Was he the problem or the cure?

He had the weekend to figure it out. He wasn't looking for complications this early. They'd known each other for five months, but they hadn't spent a dozen nights together.

He made it all the way to the radio station, only to find it locked up. Rambling Randy didn't waste any time after his one-hour talk show on Saturday morning. Colby walked the main street. The farmers market that had filled one side of the town square five months ago was gone. Now Honey Creek looked abandoned in the fog.

He peered up at her fourth-floor office at city hall across the street. The entire building looked dark inside. He thought of walking around the square and looking for her van, but it made more sense to walk back to the café and wait. Maybe Piper would remember where she left him and come back for him. Maybe she'd call if she noticed he'd texted her twice during her interview. The only answer was she'd turned her cell off and forgot to turn it back on.

He needed a bit of time to think.

As he walked past a new bakery, Sam Cassidy crossed

his path. The fire chief was so deep in thought he almost didn't look up.

Both men smiled. They'd fought a fire together last spring. They'd forever be comrades.

"Morning, Colby." Sam offered his hand. "Glad to see you back."

"Good to be back, if only for a few days."

Sam tilted his head. "You got a minute, Trooper? I mean Ranger McBride. I need to talk a problem out."

Colby pointed at the bakery window. "Buy me donuts and I'll listen."

Without another word they walked into the town's only bakery and took the table by the window. Sam ordered while Colby watched the street, hoping to see Piper drive by. This was a small town; he'd find her in time, but right now he ached just to see her. During the workdays in Austin he was too busy to think of her much, but at night she kept him awake with longing.

How could the sex be so great but the communication so complicated?

When the baker delivered a plate of donuts and two coffees, the men started talking. They worked their way through the "hellos" and "what's ups" before Sam finally got to the point.

"You probably heard about the excitement last night." Sam looked tired. "It was a long shift."

Colby nodded. "Rambling Randy mentioned it on his morning report. Is the drunk all right?"

"He's got a broken arm, several deep scratches, and part of his ear is gone. In Joey's case I would have sworn he couldn't get much uglier, but somehow he managed it."

"All this from being shoved in a slot meant for abandoned babies?"

"No, he was beat up before he reached us." Sam ate half a cherry-glazed donut in one bite, leaving red icing on both corners of his mouth. "Problem is, Joey wouldn't tell us anything about the fight. Which leads me to believe Joey was probably doing something wrong. We've got a crime, trying to break into the fire station, on top of another crime the sheriff knows about. I saw the friends who dropped Joey off. They all had been involved in something. They didn't want to hang around to answer any questions and all were in bad shape. Black eyes, cuts, bruises."

Colby took a drink of the best coffee he'd had in months, then said, "Let me guess. This Joey isn't too bright sober. When drunk, he's an idiot. Maybe they were in a rival gang fight."

"This town is too small to have two dumb, drunk gangs. Joey and his band of half-wit drunks are an embarrassment to humanity. Something happened over in Someday Valley last night. All we saw here was the end of the trouble. Otherwise, why would his friends abandon him? Why wouldn't Joey tell us how he broke his arm?"

Colby finished off his second donut. "Maybe it was just a bar fight. They'll forget about it."

Sam shook his head. "My wife, who is the lawyer representing most of the Joey-types in court, says people over in Someday Valley hold grudges. She promised me there would be payback."

"And you want me to look into it." Colby knew Sam wouldn't be here telling him the story if he didn't need help.

"If you've got time? Next time someone might be killed."

Colby finished his coffee. "I've got time, but you'll have to drive me over to Someday Valley. I rode in on my Harley. Rain and that windy road don't mix."

Both men stood. "I'll be your driver, but I have to be back for a weather emergency meeting in two hours. It won't last long, then I plan to go home and sleep for twenty-four hours."

Colby followed Sam out. Looking into trouble seemed better than wandering the streets of Honey Creek searching for the mayor.

His cell was charged. When she remembered she left a lover in bed, she'd probably call.

Chapter 13

Colby

On a sunny day, the tiny stop in the road called Some-day Valley wasn't much to see. Now, with rain pouring, it looked more like a set for a horror movie.

A gas station with two pumps, both marked OUT OF ORDER, came into view first. Then there was an abandoned store set back from the road with three five-foot X's nailed to the roof. What looked like a garage and body shop was next, with a sign that said, GONE FOR THE WINTER. Farther down was a bait shop with a dozen old boats stacked on the side of the hut.

The last building, a long, windowless bar, seemed in the best shape. The name on the bar was so rusty Colby could barely read BANDIT'S BAR. A dozen homes were scattered behind the worst strip mall he'd ever seen.

Across the road from the bar was an entrance to a trailer park that stretched all the way to the tree line half a mile back. At one time the trailer park might have been nice, a place for fishermen and families to stop over in the summer, but not now. The abandoned office was missing windows and the door gaped open, a crumbling swimming pool collected trash, and the tennis court was spotted with weeds breaking through the asphalt.

Colby studied the place. In all the beauty of the valley, this scar was dug deep into the side of a hill. Except for one spot north of the stucco wall around the trailer park. A picnic table rested halfway to the tree line, with tall grass around and wildflowers still holding their color against the coming winter. This little spot reminded Colby of a fine painting hanging in a truck stop. A peaceful scene next to a neglected trailer park.

"We might want to try the bar first," Sam said as he pulled into the parking lot. "Any trouble might have started there."

Sam and Colby climbed out of Sam's car and found Bandit's door propped open. As they stepped inside they heard hammering coming from the back.

"Hello," Colby called as he shook off the rain. "Anyone here?"

"We're closed," someone yelled back.

Colby moved toward the voice. "We're not here to bother you. I'm a Texas Ranger and this is Honey Creek's fire chief. We just have a few questions."

The man slapped his hands to clean them. "Wayne Allen, owner of this shack. How can I help you?"

Colby didn't waste time. "We were just wondering if you noticed any trouble last night. A guy named Joey showed up at the Honey Creek fire station, bleeding.

From the description of his friends, they all looked like they'd been in a fight."

The tall bar owner, with a beard halfway down his chest, shrugged.

Colby flashed his badge.

Wayne nodded as if he understood that this visit was official.

"That would most likely be Joey Hattly. He gets beat up on a regular basis. I'm usually the one who patches him up. He has a mouth on him that has no brain driving it."

"Got any idea who broke his arm?"

"Didn't know it was broken. I own this place, but outside that door I don't see much. I've thought of beating on Joey a few times myself. He was picking on Marcie last night. She sings in here on the weekends."

"Marcie? That wouldn't be Boone Buchanan's girlfriend?" Colby didn't add more details. Everyone in the state had followed the trial of Buchanan, the man who tried to burn down the Honey Creek City Hall just to hurt the mayor. Colby had sat in the courtroom every day. So had Marcie Latimer. She cried now and then, but she never made eye contact with Boone that Colby saw.

"Yeah, that Marcie. She's a sweet kid. I don't know how she got mixed up with Buchanan, but I know her. She would never be involved in hurting anyone, not even Joey." Wayne rubbed his whiskered chin and dust seemed to waterfall out. "I've known her most of her life. She's got a big heart but sure can't pick a man."

"Know where we could find her?"

"Last trailer in the park. Back by the trees. If she's not there, she'll be back here singing tonight. You can catch her between sets."

Sam thanked the owner, when Colby would have asked more questions. As they climbed into the car, Sam added, "Forget Marcie. If she'd been involved she'd be the one hurt. Joey was more than likely fighting with one of his drinking buddies. Why else would they run away after they dropped him off? We're at a dead end."

Sam was reading a text on his phone as he spoke. "Besides, I'm being called back to the station. We'll have to cut this hunt short. They've moved the weather meeting up. My guess is that's where you'll find Piper. The mayor usually sits in."

Colby agreed. "I'd still like to make sure Marcie is okay. I saw her during Boone's trial. She looked so broken. If I ever find Piper, I'll try to talk her into going over to Bandit's Bar to hear her sing tonight. Piper and Marcie were friends when they were kids."

"You and the mayor have a date tonight?" Sam laughed. "I don't know about your tracking skills, Ranger. You can't keep up with your lady in a small town. What chance do you have of finding Marcie, who probably doesn't want to see you or any lawman?"

"I hope Piper and I have a date." Colby ran his fingers through wet hair. "She seemed real glad to see me, but she's not the clingy kind. In fact, she's not the cuddling kind either, or the kiss-goodbye kind, or the call-me-back kind."

"What kind is she?"

Colby frowned. "The leave-while-you're-asleep kind."

The fire chief shook his head. "Sorry about that."

"Yeah, me too."

Sam drove while Colby tried to reach Piper. No answer. Maybe she'd turned her phone down while she did the interview and forgot to turn it back on. When they passed the Honey Creek Café, he didn't see her van.

"Mind dropping me at Widows Park?"

"No problem." Sam turned left. "Nowhere is out of the way in a town this small." As Colby climbed out, Sam added, "Good luck."

Colby waved goodbye and headed up the long walk to where all the Mackenzie widows lived. It seemed the Mackenzie men were strong, driven men. Colby worked with Piper's two brothers, and they fit the mold. Max and James Mackenzie were two of the best Texas Rangers in the state, but both pushed themselves to the limit.

Mackenzie women all outlived their mates. Piper's grandfather built the house, which looked more like a small dorm, for the widows in his family. When he died, he deeded the place to Piper. One by one her grandmother and aunts and cousins lost their spouses and moved into Widows Park.

Colby knocked on the massive oak door, then turned back to stare at the town blanketed with low clouds. The weather was as gloomy as his mood. This was not the weekend he'd hoped to have.

The door slowly creaked open. Suddenly he was surrounded by gray-headed women who had shrunk to granny size. He was reminded of a fairy tale in reverse. *Snow White and the Seven Dwarfs.* Only he was the one lost and the ladies were the seven. Every one of them started hugging on him.

Two widows, Aunt Linda and Aunt Morgan, pulled him inside as others hurried to have their turn at hugging him. He was patted on, all the way to the kitchen.

"You're family, Colby, since that night we all saw you in your undies. Remember when you were hurt?"

"I remember."

The one behind him announced, "So, since you're here, you'll join us for coffee in the kitchen."

Colby didn't hesitate. He was still starving even after an apple in the café kitchen and two donuts. If they didn't offer him food, he'd take all of them out to lunch.

Only the ladies kept bringing out food to go with his coffee. After twenty minutes of talking, one lady declared it was close enough to lunch to eat, so out came all the fixings for sandwiches. Colby didn't turn down a single side. While he ate, they told him what was happening in town. Most of the people they mentioned he didn't know, but it was nice listening to them talk.

After eating, Colby drifted through the old, peaceful home. All the ladies went up for their naps and Colby stretched out on the office couch. He'd decided he wasn't leaving until Piper either called or dropped by.

The thought occurred to him that she might be mad about something, but that didn't make sense. He'd thought about how to make love to her every night they'd been apart, and he'd done everything right. Twice.

He felt like he'd just dozed off when he heard the huge front door open and close. No mistaking who it was. Piper's high heels tapped on the entry tile like a clock ticking in double time. When the tapping stopped, he opened one eye. "Afternoon, PJ," he said.

She smiled. "You having a nice nap?"

"Yeah, what have you been doing?" He rose to an elbow.

"I've been at a meeting. Sam was there. He told me he dropped you off here." She pushed into his side, making room to sit. Her fingers brushed through his hair.

Colby smiled. All seemed right. If Piper was mad about something, she wouldn't be touching him like this.

He made more room for her and leaned to kiss her lightly.

She pulled away and smiled. "Glad you got some sleep. We may be in for a bad storm later tonight or to-morrow morning. Possible tornadoes and flooding. Yesterday the weathermen said it'd go south of here. Now it looks like it might come straight down into our valley."

He tried to kiss her again, but his lover had turned into the town's mayor. He liked them both, but it was like knowing Superman and Clark Kent. You never knew which one was coming to dinner.

Piper continued, "There's a chance it'll hit all three towns. Someday Valley is on high ground, but Clifton Bend and Honey Creek are low. Too much rain and we've got a real possibility of flooding. Who knows which way a tornado will turn."

He ran his hand down her back and didn't think she even noticed. She simply kept talking.

"The volunteers at the firehouse are notifying every-one living along the creeks and river to move up. I just talked Rambling Randy into interrupting his usual 'just music' evening with weather reports. Lowland farmers will need time to move cattle up. People near the river will need to tie everything down."

"They can't just walk hundreds of head up the roads." Colby's worries were still on the cattle. Most of the farms and ranches were small, with gateless wire stretched be-tween them.

"If it comes to it, they'll cut fences. If the rain doesn't wipe out farmers' fields, the cattle will as they climb. Winter crops will be trampled."

Colby sat up, finally getting into the conversation. "You think it's going to be that bad?"

"We've had almost double our average rain this year. The creeks are all higher than I've ever seen them, and the ground is saturated. I'd call us lucky if we have only lowland flooding."

Colby started putting on his boots. "How can I help?"

She stood. "We've got time right now. We need to pull together what we need. If the roads flood, we may not be able to depend on help from outside the valley. If you don't mind, I'd like you to stay with Sam tonight at the station. If trouble does come, he'll need all the help he can get. I'll be next door with the sheriff. Pecos will have his hands full with calls coming in. Daisy is on vacation and none of the fill-in dispatchers can handle a heavy load of incoming calls."

He reached to touch her but she stood.

"It's going to be a long weekend. Not what I planned."

Finally, he looped his arms around her, holding her gently. "I'm glad I'm here to help if the storm comes."

"We've been put on alert before and nothing happened, but some of the fishing shacks were flooded." Her smile seemed sad. "Maybe I'm worrying over nothing."

Her body finally melted into him. "I'm glad you're here."

"There is nowhere I'd want to be other than with you." He touched his lips to her forehead. "We'll watch over your town, PJ."

She finally kissed him. Not a passionate kiss, but more of a thank-you kiss. He could almost feel Piper slipping away, even while she was still in his arms. Maybe she was simply worried. Doing her job. But Colby feared he'd stayed away too long, or hadn't done or said the right thing. Maybe she'd found someone else and was trying to choose between them?

If she had another man, half the town might know and not one would tell him. It didn't matter that he'd saved her life, or that she'd kissed him in front of the whole town. Colby was still the outsider.

Now wasn't the right time to ask questions. They'd talk later when this crisis was over.

He feared that it might already be too late. This time when he walked away, as he had when other relationships began to get too serious for him, Colby had a feeling he'd look back.

Chapter 14

Marcie

Marcie spent the afternoon at Brand's ranch and loved every minute, but she knew she'd have to go back home soon. She didn't belong here. This place wasn't hers. Brand wasn't hers. Even if she tried to make him love her, she knew she'd only bring him sorrow.

She guessed he'd had enough of that. Something in his past had molded him into the quiet man he was. Maybe everyone has secrets. Demons who haunt the corners of their minds. She seemed to wear them for the world to see, but Brand kept his buried deep inside.

He'd found his peace here on this rocky piece of land. He could fix her window and add locks to her doors, but he couldn't fix her. If she stayed around too long she'd only end up hurting him.

He wasn't going anywhere, and she was going nowhere. Two very different places.

She figured the man was probably ready for anything except her in his life. Wood was split and stacked by the side of the house almost to the roof. The pantry was packed. He even had enough light bulbs in the bathroom cabinet to last ten years.

The tall evergreens his father had planted fifty years ago blocked the north wind. To the east was a rolling pasture that had never been cut by a plow. Generations had lived here, planning their lives by the seasons. Marcie's kin seemed to live their lives by the day, never planning, never preparing.

Brand was a private man who obviously liked his solitude. They talked of the weather and what was happening on the ranch, but he asked no questions of her. The only time he smiled was when she played for him.

His ranch seemed a million miles away from her world. He stood in silence and watched the sun rise and set as if it were a miracle each day. There was an order to his life and she was a whirling thunderstorm.

But in this place, reality finally crept in. She had to go to work. Wayne had threatened to fire her if she missed one more night. It was time for Brand to drop her off at the bar. He'd insisted on replacing her locks while she sang at the bar.

They didn't talk much on the drive. He carried her guitar to the door of the bar, touched the brim of his hat, and said simply, "See you later."

Marcie nodded. She wanted to thank him, maybe kiss him on the cheek, but somehow it didn't seem right.

Two hours later, when he walked in and ordered his one beer, she knew he'd finished his chore. Her trailer window would be fixed and both doors would have dead bolts.

Brand seemed to think that would be enough to keep her safe, but she knew there would be no safe place.

When he walked to his table in the bar, his gaze never left her.

She smiled. He was her one friend, and one is a long way from none.

The night was cold and the weekend crowd at the bar was smaller than usual because of the rain, but she played for Brand. He hadn't made one advance toward her all day, but he'd held her when she cried and he'd covered her when it grew cold. In her book he ranked high.

She played for him tonight.

When she finished her set, he stood, leaving a full bottle on the table, and walked out on the steps with her. "You all right with me taking you home and showing you the locks?"

"Sure." Her car hadn't started in two weeks and the thought of walking home frightened her tonight more than she wanted to admit. But she didn't want to tell Brand that. "My car has been sitting beside the bar long enough to collect a layer of dirt." She pointed to the back of the lot. "It won't start and I can't afford to fix it. The good news is, I don't live far from work." She couldn't manage a smile.

"You mind if I carry you to the truck? I might lose you in a pothole in this rain." He grinned.

She hugged his neck as he lifted her. "And you said you didn't want to pick me up." Her cheek brushed his. An inch closer and she could have kissed him.

"Hold on tight."

"I will."

Brand didn't say another word until he pulled up to her place. He cut the engine but didn't open his door.

"Did you change your mind about coming in?"

He didn't look at her. He just stared at the trailer. "I thought I left a light on inside." He slowly opened his truck door. "Stay here."

His low, hard tone chilled her worse than any wind. It hadn't been a suggestion, but an order. She watched him walk toward her front door.

Something moved inside the trailer, like a light breeze that crumbled the thin curtains. Marcie opened her mouth to warn him just as he opened the door.

Something black flew out at his face as fast as a cannonball.

Marcie's scream echoed in the cab as she watched Brand fall like a huge oak into the mud. She jumped out of the truck and ran toward his body, spread, arms out, and looking dead in the low light slicing out from inside the trailer.

"Brand!" she cried as she reached him, expecting to see blood everywhere.

But all she saw were two cut lines on his cheek, just deep enough to bleed. He opened one eye. "I'm going to kill that cat."

Reality hit Marcie. What had shot out of the house was one of a half a dozen wild cats that lived around the park.

Laughter splashed away fear. Brand had been attacked by a wild cat.

Brand sat up. "It's not funny," he grumbled. "That cat ate my hamburger when I set it on the step, knocked over my coffee, and almost tripped me twice, getting under my feet while I was working. He's a killer cat."

She offered him a hand. "Come on inside, you poor man. Let me clean you up and treat that wound after your terrible fight with a kitten."

He was grumbling something as he stood and shook off as much mud as he could, then followed her in.

"My brave hero fights off five men and gets taken down by a kitty."

"I'm no hero. That cat is probably a baby mountain lion."

Marcie tugged him to a stool and reached for the first aid kit. When she turned back, his knees were apart, so she moved in close to wipe the blood from his cheek.

Once the Band-Aids were on, she put her hands on his shoulders and pushed, rolling him a few feet to the small kitchen sink.

His dark coffee-colored eyes watched her as she covered his chest with a kitchen towel and began washing the mud out of his hair. "You'll have to wait till you get home to shower. I don't think you'll fit in mine. My brother is six inches shorter than you and he barely fits. In the summer he showers out behind the trailer using rainwater stored in a fifty-five gallon tank."

Brand closed his eyes as she plowed her fingers through his hair. "I could get used to this," he said near her ear.

"Nope. This is a one-time thing. I've sworn off men for good, and much as I like you, Brand, you're a man."

"So can we be friends?"

"Friends. I can deal with that. You know, I don't think I've ever had a boy or a man for a friend. I thought I did once, in the sixth grade, but then he grabbed my developing breasts on a dare."

Brand straightened and she backed away. "I'll make

you a promise, Marcie. I'll never make a pass or grab any part of you. If you ever want more than friendship, you'll have to come to me. If you do, there'll be no flirting or pretending. I don't play games."

"Thanks for making it plain." She shivered at his honesty. "But, Brand, I'll never come to you. My heart, hell, my whole life, has been shattered one too many times."

"Friends," he said. "You'll call me if you're in trouble and you'll always have a place to crash on my couch."

"Thanks. Will you still come to hear me sing?"

"I will."

She thought of hugging him, but he might think she was flirting. She'd never been offered friendship without strings. She wanted to treasure it awhile.

He showed her the huge locks, and she thanked him.

As he walked out and headed to his truck, she smiled. He veered toward the trees to pick up the half-grown cat.

"Come along, Killer," he said. "I've got some barn mice who want to meet you."

Marcie watched until his truck lights disappeared, then locked both her dead bolts. For the first time in years she slept without waking up at every sound she heard in the trailer park.

Sunday

Chapter 15

Jesse

The rain woke Jesse deep in the night. He tossed for a while, then got up and checked on the kids. The storm didn't seem to be bothering them. They all looked so peaceful in their beds.

Sometimes, on nights like this, he would wake and for a moment think that Beth was still in the house. He could almost hear her bare feet walking the hallway. She'd be watching over the kids or tiptoeing into the kitchen to start breakfast before she woke him. He loved waking up to the smell of coffee and rolls baking. He'd smile, then act like he was asleep so Beth could wake him up with a kiss.

But now those memories were like dreams, half-forgotten in the plans of today.

Reality pulled him full awake and he knew she would never walk the hallway again. It was like she'd slipped away when he wasn't paying attention for just one second. From the center of his world to a memory, in a blink.

When her absence slammed into his heart, it hurt just as hard as it had the first night when he'd come home from the hospital with a baby but no wife. No best friend. No partner in life. No Beth.

He grabbed a quilt and went out on the porch. He'd heard thunder earlier, but now the night was silent, as if waiting for the rain. The air had an eerie glow about it. Beautiful and a bit frightening at the same time. The night seemed to be silently weeping a moment before the storm came in, riding a north wind.

Jesse was a part of this land. He understood the weather better than most guys predicting it on TV. Right now his land was taking a beating. There was nothing to do except watch. The hammering of the rain on the tin roof and the swishing sound of water running off and making plopping sounds in puddles was almost like music.

He closed his eyes and drifted to sleep.

In his dream he was dancing with a tall woman to the beat of the storm. He could feel her soft body against him as they moved, almost making love as they glided across the dance floor. His hands were at her waist and her fingers rested over his heart. The touch of her seemed to be healing what was broken inside him.

She had long curly hair the color of the Red River in spring, and green eyes.

In his dreams he looked down at her ample breasts. In the V of her dress he could see the two mounds pushing together. As he watched, thinking he'd like to touch her skin, a snake twisted up out of her dress. A deadly coral. Red, black, and yellow.

Jesse jumped awake so violently he almost fell off the porch. He tossed the quilt and stuck his head out into the rain. The dream left him shaking. The rain left him freezing. But nothing could wash the dream away.

Was it a warning or simply a nightmare?

When the phone rang, he couldn't wrap his thoughts around what the sound was. The dream had been so real.

He was still shaking when he stepped inside and answered the phone. *Hell*, he thought, *am I awake or still in the dream?* No one called this late. "Hello."

"Sorry to wake you, Jesse, but this is Sheriff LeRoy Hayes. We've got a problem on our hands."

Jesse shook his head like a dog, sending water flying in every direction. "How can I help?" Even half-asleep, Jesse knew the sheriff wouldn't be calling unless it was an emergency.

Last year there'd been a wreck a mile from his place, and the sheriff needed his tractor to pull one of the cars out of a ditch. Another time he'd had to house a carload of teenagers who'd run out of gas a quarter mile from his place. Since it wasn't an emergency, and the roads were freezing over, the sheriff thought they could sleep in his barn. He'd said, "I would have them sleep in the car, but there's no telling what would happen with six high school kids in one dark car. We'd probably have ourselves a mini-Woodstock on our hands. One of the mothers said if her daughter got any wilder, they'd have to lock her up in a zoo."

Jesse had smiled while he walked down to the car that night. Then he laughed all the way back. The kids were all blaming each other for the gas problem and by the time he settled them on the hay in the barn, none of them were speaking.

LeRoy broke into his memories. "We got hard rain, and more coming, over here in Honey Creek."

Jesse already knew that.

"The creeks are bursting their banks and the Brazos might overflow. The three hotels in town are full." LeRoy paused. "We can't use the lodge. It's too close to the river. If the creek floods, the Brazos might be next and that'll flood all the way to the edge of town. The river side of Honey Creek could be under water."

Jesse waited as he tried to think how he could help. Both grandmothers were on high ground.

LeRoy kept yelling into the phone as if Jesse suddenly went deaf. "I'll fill all the homes that can take people who are stranded out on the low side of the county road. The church said they could offer fifty beds. Only problem is some of these folks want to bring their animals. You know how it is around here, every person who has three acres thinks they need a horse. We can handle dogs and cats, but we're not prepared for horses. How many can you take at your place? No one will blink at a charge of thirty dollars a night. Your land is so high up, I'll start building an ark if it floods."

"I'll give them the first night free to help out." Jesse reasoned aloud. "By then they'll know if their land will flood."

LeRoy laughed. "I remember that big barn of yours. Thanks for helping me out."

"I can take a dozen in the stalls and I'll rig up another six with the panels if we need to."

"Great. Be ready by tomorrow and pray nothing happens. We may just get rain, but we're going to be ready if trouble comes."

When Jesse hung up, he was wide-awake. He glanced at the kitchen clock. Four thirty. Might as well get up. After that nightmare he wasn't sure he ever wanted to go to sleep again.

If Adalee put that dream in his head to warn him to stay away, it worked.

Chapter 16

Marcie

Sunday was usually Marcie's day to do laundry and clean the trailer. For the first time in months, she'd had a great night's sleep after Brand put dead-bolt locks on both doors and fixed the window. Even the rain didn't keep her awake.

She hadn't heard anything from Joey or the other men who'd tried to pay her a visit two nights ago. They might be laying low thinking Brand, if not Marcie, might have turned them in. No one in the trailer park would be surprised at what they'd tried to do to her. None of her neighbors would get involved, either. With half the trailers abandoned, left to decay, she no longer had a neighbor within yelling distance.

As far as she knew, she was the only woman in the

park without a man living with her, except Momma B. Everyone called the three-time widow Momma B and no one messed with her. She'd raised six kids and was stronger and meaner than most men. Word was she killed her last no-good husband. Apparently, he hit her with a bat and she hit him with a bullet. Her kids helped bury him in the woods and no one called the sheriff over in Honey Creek.

No one would protect her from the wolves, Marcie thought, and she couldn't run to Brand for help every time she was afraid. She barely knew him, even though she'd felt the warmth of his arms as she dreamed last night.

Maybe it was time to leave the trailer park. The bad memories weren't worth keeping. Maybe she could sell the trailer for a few dollars. All that was keeping her here was her job at the bar, and that wasn't much.

Wayne, who owned Bandit's Bar, told her she could borrow his car all day Sunday if she'd promise to clean up next Friday night for free. It seemed a fair trade. Half the time on weekends he was too drunk to remember to lock the bar up, much less clean it up. On those nights she'd stay and pick up until she walked him to his car. Since he lived a half mile down the dirt road behind the bar, he wasn't likely to run into anyone at two in the morning.

As she tied her dark hair into a ponytail, she sang softly. It was time to get on with life. Everyone would forget about her past in twenty or thirty years, but right now she needed to start taking better care of herself.

Step one: Get enough money to fix her car.

Step two: Find a safe place to live.

Step three: Start living.

A rainy day was as good a time as any to start. She'd been saving all she could, but it still wasn't enough for repairs on the car, so her next place would have to be within walking distance.

There were three possible choices she might be able to move into. One was a garage apartment at an old lodge a few miles down by the river. It would be quiet in the winter and in the summer the owner said she could earn her rent by cleaning rooms.

The second spot was renting a room in a two-story house a few hundred feet behind the bar. The street wasn't paved, but the house was big. It was built about fifty years ago when folks thought Someday Valley would become a real town like Honey Creek or Clifton Bend. Someone had built a line of homes that faced the river. Folks said they were beautiful, and to her they still were. A promise of what Someday Valley could have become, a reminder of better days.

The old woman who owned the fourth house from the river already rented to three other women. Marcie would have a bedroom, a bath down the hall, and use of the kitchen if she cleaned up after herself. It was cheap and close to her weekend job.

The third place she might stay was a last-chance possibility, a chicken farm halfway to Honey Creek. A cluster of what would be called tiny houses nowadays had been built years ago for workers at the farm.

Now, young couples had taken them over. They'd painted them bright colors and built a front yard for all in the center of the circle. It was noisy and smelled of too many chickens, but the rent was reasonable. Problem was, the farm was too far for her to walk to the bar, so she'd have to have her car fixed. The mini-town looked peaceful. Sheets flapping on clotheslines and toddlers playing on grass in the center of the compound.

If she fixed the car, she wouldn't have money for the security deposit on a little house. If she put money down for a six-month lease, she couldn't pay for repairs unless she sold the trailer fast.

The *ifs* in her plan outnumbered the *possibilities*.

Her brother hadn't answered his phone the last three times she'd called, so no telling when he'd wander by again. When he did come home, he was usually down on his luck, so she couldn't plan on any help from him.

By full dawn Marcie walked through mud in the sleeping trailer park. It looked almost peaceful so early in the day, but she knew it was time to move on. She'd stayed too long. The few good memories she'd had here had been washed away by the bad. She had to get a day job, keep her night job, then she'd pack up, leave here, and never look back.

She'd start over again. She raised her chin. Brand had looked at her like he thought that she was something special when she sang for him. Maybe she was.

When she darted across the road and onto Bandit's Bar's almost flooded parking lot, she noticed two things.

One, Wayne's car was there waiting for her, the keys under the mat. The bartender had kept his promise.

And two, her rusty Pontiac, which had been sitting in the back of the lot for two weeks, was missing. Someone had stolen her no-good, gas-guzzling, broken-down junker of a car. She hadn't even locked it or taken the keys out, thinking it couldn't go anywhere.

One double-edged thought hit her like the taste of ice cream and brain freeze. She was happy someone got the old car started and it was stolen.

Chapter 17

Pecos

The best day of the week was by far rainy-day Sunday, Pecos Smith decided. He didn't have to work all night or go to school. Even Kerrie's grandfather didn't need help with his bee farm in stormy conditions. All he had to do from the time he finished his Friday shift until Monday morning was sleep and eat and spend time with Kerrie.

He loved dreaming the morning away in bed. He'd wake up to a grand lunch that Mr. Winston served after church. Winston's old friends usually dropped by and they'd talk about things Pecos had never heard people discuss, like planning out their lives by the stars and having adventures that never turned out as planned. They'd talk about loving others and helping people as if it was something everyone on earth did. And best of all, the meal was always surrounded with laughter.

Kerrie said most of the lunch guests were leftover hippies, but Pecos thought they were sages. Alice, who sold old clothes and called them vintage, claimed she had visions, only they came to her like cartoons. Some were warnings but most were funny. Like the vision about naked fishermen dancing that she'd had Saturday night when it rained so hard.

Tall Tim, who was an artist with a buzz saw, talked little, but just seeing him smile made everyone happy.

One old couple, who often came, had once traveled with a circus. She'd told fortunes and he'd been her barker. He never stopped talking and his wife rarely said a word, but she brought the best peach cobbler Pecos had ever eaten.

Pecos noticed the Sunday lunch at Mr. Winston's house grew bigger after Kerrie and he started paying rent. The party expanded from the kitchen table to the grand dining room that hadn't been used in years.

Mr. Winston was sharing the extra money he'd gained by cooking for his friends. They usually had enough for leftovers to last a few nights, and Pecos would always spring for pizza midweek. The rest of the nights might be soup or sandwiches, but Mr. Winston always made it seem like a fine meal.

He had given Kerrie and Pecos a place to live when they got married. Pecos's parents disowned him for leaving the farm, and Kerrie's family was mad about her marrying Pecos.

Their place at Mr. Winston's might just be two rooms upstairs in an old house, but Kerrie loved it and Pecos loved her, so it was perfect. There was a bed in each room, but they slept in one and she used the other for stacks of clothes, and shoes, and endless tiny little boxes.

One night five months ago, Pecos had been sleeping in the bed of his pickup in front of Mr. Winston's house because he'd left home, and then the next night he was married. Now and then he'd mentally tell himself the details in his mind so he could remember to tell his children someday. He'd say, "On our first date we went skinny dipping. On our second we danced together in the moonlight. On our third date, we got married." He'd leave out the part that she was already pregnant.

Kerrie's father blamed Pecos for ruining his only child's life, but Kerrie said Pecos had saved her. Pecos might not be the father by genes, but he planned to be the kid's father for life.

His bride of five months and counting rolled over and bumped her big belly into his side.

Pecos put his hand over her middle and waited for the baby inside her to move. Sometimes the baby seemed to thump at his hand as if saying, "I'm here, waiting, Papa. Should be out in a few weeks."

There was no doubt, Pecos already loved the kid.

"Morning," Kerrie murmured. Sunshine hair covered half her face.

"Morning," he said, letting his hand slide gently up to her breasts.

"They're huge." She rolled on her back, not seeming to notice that his hand followed.

"They are beautiful," he corrected. "You're beautiful." He spread his hand out over her, loving that she didn't mind him touching her. He always caught himself holding his breath when he felt her softness. It was like she was giving him a gift. "You feel so good. So soft. So perfect."

She smiled. "You're delusional, but you're my best friend so I'll accept the compliment."

He brushed her hair out of her face and kissed her lightly. "I'm more than just your friend." *Wishful thinking*, he almost said aloud.

"I know. I like you being my husband. You're so gentle and kind, Pecos. I love that about you. You may be a year older than me, but it's more than that. Sometimes I feel like you're an old soul watching over me. I belong with you, Pecos."

"Always."

"Always," she echoed.

He moved his hand over the thin T-shirt she wore lately. It was several sizes too big and the neck hung off one shoulder, but it was all she liked to sleep in. "There's more of you lately to watch over. You mind if I investigate for myself? The way your body is changing fascinates me."

"No, I don't mind you touching me. We're into this parenting thing together." She laughed. "How about next time you carry and birth the baby?"

He brushed her chin with two fingers, turning her toward him. "Kiss me, wife."

She giggled and said as her lips lightly touched his. "Of course, husband."

When she pulled away, he said again, "No, really kiss me."

Her blue eyes held a question as she hesitated. He threaded his fingers into her hair and tugged her toward him again. This time she gave him what he wanted, one long deep kiss.

When he finally broke the kiss, he asked, "Do you like this?"

"Sure. But you're not going to like what I've got to tell you."

Pecos felt his heart stop beating. Every day of their short marriage he'd feared she'd leave him, or worse, that she'd say she made a mistake marrying him. Maybe he'd gone too far with the deep kiss, but he'd done it before. He'd touched her a hundred times, when she was awake and now and then when she was asleep. He liked helping when she needed lotion on her back or cream on her tummy so she wouldn't get stretch marks.

What if she suddenly hated his hands moving over her?

Kerrie pulled the sheet over her. "Mom called yesterday and said she and Dad want to have a talk with me this morning. I have no idea what is on their minds, but I feel sure it will be something about them running my life."

"Do they want me in on this talk?"

"No. Not this time, but they said I should talk it over with you. I wish my dad would call you something besides 'that guy you're with.'"

Pecos flopped onto his back and stared at the crack in the ceiling. The Lanes would never see him as part of their family. To Mr. Lane, Pecos was just the boy who knocked up his only child. Pecos had thought about telling Mr. Lane the truth, but he'd promised Kerrie he never would. The guy she'd had sex with hadn't wanted to ever see her again, and Pecos stepped up when she needed him. No one would ever know the secret they shared. It bonded them even more than the marriage.

He shrugged and winked at her. "I don't care what

your dad calls me, you're my wife"—he brushed her tummy—"and this is my baby, no matter what your parents want to talk about today."

Kerrie's words came soft, almost apologetic. "How about you walk me over to the house, then go have coffee at the bakery. I'll text you when I'm finished. Then we could come home and help Mr. Winston cook. He's invited some of the crowd from the flea market, as always."

"Fleas or vendors?"

He laughed at his own joke as she thumped him on the forehead.

Pecos slowed his breathing. She'd called this place home, not the big house down the street where her parents lived.

"I could pick up a pie for the fleas while you talk to your parents. I can hang out there until you text, if it's still raining. If it's not, I like to walk around the square. Honey Creek is feeling more and more like my town."

She tossed the covers. "I'll race you getting dressed."

He didn't pick up the challenge. He always lost anyway, because he'd end up stopping to watch her. Lately she needed help getting on her clothes and tying her shoes.

Half an hour later, as they walked toward her parents' home in the rain, neither said a word. He made it to the porch steps, then turned back.

"Later," she said as she disappeared.

Pecos picked up his speed as he headed to the town square and the one bakery in town. Since Pecos had helped save the people in the city hall fire and married Kerrie Lane, everyone now knew who he was, and seemed to care about him more than his own parents ever had. To tell the truth, he liked being around Kerrie's folks more than his own parents, even though the Lanes still held a grudge against him.

Pecos stepped inside the bakery and took a deep breath of the warm cinnamon air. He bought a cup of coffee and a couple of kolaches. He had to wait for a few minutes, holding his bag and coffee, before he snatched a tiny table in the corner.

Finally, he sat on the three-legged chair and began to watch people. Now that he was part of law enforcement, he knew secrets about some of them. Unpaid parking tickets, records of shoplifters and peeping Toms. He'd read so many reports, he was starting to see people and wonder what their file had in it.

Marcie Latimer walked in, fighting with a broken umbrella.

He thought she looked uncomfortable, out of her element. Pecos knew who she was from her singing, but he'd never talked to her before Boone Buchanan's trial. He'd noticed her sitting alone during the trial. No one talked to her; after all, she was the bad guy's girlfriend. Boone never looked in her direction. But Pecos had watched her cry when the mayor, Piper Mackenzie, testified that she feared she was going to die in the fire that Boone had set.

Today the town treated Marcie like she was bad news blowing around in an old weekly newspaper. Most acted like she was invisible.

Pecos knew how it felt to be invisible. He'd spent most of his days at school standing in the center of a crowd with no one to talk to. So, he started nodding hello and waving goodbye the last few weeks of the trial. Once he sat across from Marcie in a crowded hamburger joint and they talked about the weather. She was shy, but she thanked him when he said he loved her music.

When the trial was over and he saw her standing in the stairwell crying, he stopped long enough to say he was sorry for her loss. Pecos considered that to be proper, since Boone would be over a hundred before he was eligible for parole.

When Pecos looked up again, Marcie was standing on the other side of his little table. She had the littlest cup of coffee the bakery offered. It didn't cost anything. It was meant for people to sample different blends.

"Mind if I take this chair?" Her words were polite but the sorrow in her eyes touched him. She reminded him of those ads about dogs at the pound. They seemed to look up with no hope left.

"Of course." He half stood as she sat down.

He watched her as she pulled off her coat and set her purse by the wall. She was thinner than she had been a few months ago. Sadder.

Pecos looked down at his two rolls. "You wouldn't want one of these, would you? My eyes are bigger than my appetite. I'd hate it to go to waste."

"I'll try one," she answered.

"How are you doing?" he asked as he passed her the roll. She was almost ten years older than he was. Too old to hang out with anyone he knew, so he had no idea how life was treating her.

"I'm doing fine. Surviving."

"I'm glad." He'd decided months ago that she hadn't deserved all the gossip. "You hear I got married?"

"No. News rarely makes it to Someday Valley unless it's bad," she answered. "Will your wife be mad that you're eating breakfast with another woman?"

"Nope. She knows I've been nuts about her since we were in grade school." He shrugged. "She also knows I like to talk to folks."

Marcie almost smiled. "Does she feel the same about you? You know, nuts about you?"

Pecos shook his head. "No, but I'm growing on her. Even my mother said I'm not much to look at. Too skinny."

"You're a good man, Pecos Smith. That matters more than looks. I think kind men are always handsome. You were the only one who talked to me that day when Boone's trial ended. I have a feeling that as the years pass you'll grow more handsome and that wife of yours will love you dearly."

"Thanks. Mind if I ask why you're in town so early? Nothing is open but this bakery and the gas stations. Most folks are sleeping in or getting ready for church."

Her eyes turned cloudy again, and for a moment he thought she might start crying. Then she straightened, as if deciding to be honest. "I'm looking for a place to live, but I can't find something I can afford. I'm singing and working a few nights at a bar in Someday Valley, but I have to get a day job. I hoped I'd see a sign in a window of one of the shops or on the *Help Wanted* board down at the grocery." She was silent for a minute, then added, "I'll take anything—housecleaning, waitress, any honest work. I don't know how to do much, but I'm a fast learner."

Pecos knew he should probably stay out of her business, but she had those puppy dog eyes and he knew how it felt to be low.

"I don't know of any work, but I know where you'd be invited to lunch. Lots of us eat at Mr. Winston's on Sundays. Someone might know of a job."

"Would I be welcome?"

"You bet." He wrote Mr. Winston's address on a napkin just as his phone binged. "I got to go. That is my wife telling me it's time to pick her up. Don't forget to show up at twelve thirty. These folks are mostly old, but I swear they're the brain-trust of this town."

Marcie stared at the napkin. "Thanks. I might just come. I haven't been invited to lunch in a long time."

Pecos stood. "I haven't done anything yet, but all of us will help if we can. Marcie, you'll be among friends if you come."

"Thank you for the invitation." She looked up at him with clear eyes. "And yes, you have done something. You gave me breakfast and hope. If I'm still in town, I'll take you up on that lunch."

Pecos waved at her as he ran to pick up Kerrie. The meeting with her parents hadn't lasted long. He didn't know if that was good or bad.

Chapter 18

Jesse

Sundays Jesse dressed the kids in their best and headed off to church. He didn't consider himself a particularly religious man, but since his sweet wife went to Heaven, he'd try his best to get up there someday. She'd need him to drive her around the streets paved with gold, because she always turned the wrong way if she got in a place that had a population bigger than four thousand.

Jesse usually sat near the back of the church, nearest the bathroom. With three kids it paid to be prepared.

When the children's sermon was over, his children left with their friends for the gym. Both their grandmothers were part of the gang of seniors who watched over them.

Grandma George claimed she had heard all the preaching she needed for this lifetime and was too old to do much sinning, so she'd watch the kids.

Jesse would have forty minutes to sit alone before he picked them up. Forty minutes of acting like he was listening to the preacher.

About the time the kids disappeared, someone sat down next to him. No one but Jesse seemed to notice; after all, the preacher had started.

For a few minutes all Jesse saw was a blue cape beside him. Midnight blue, he thought, made for rainy nights. Three more inches closer and she would have been touching him. Slowly, he turned his head. Curly auburn hair overflowed on the sides of her hood.

Adalee, he almost said aloud. He'd never seen her in church before, but then until lately he hardly noticed anyone. He gripped the seat bench space between them. This couldn't have been an accident. He was the only one on the long bench near the back. There were spots she could have claimed anywhere along ten feet of his pew. Plus the bench in front of him was completely empty.

What if she'd had the same crazy dream he'd had? The one where they were dancing, then he looked at the mounds of her breasts and a poisonous snake came out. If she did have the same dream, she probably came to church to slap him.

To his shock, she lowered her hand over his just before her coat covered their fingers.

He could have pulled away. He could have scooted down to give her room. He could have left. No one would notice.

But Jesse sat still, enjoying the touch of her hand. Warm. Soft.

When he turned his hand over, their fingers laced together. The feel of her hand in his made her real. He could actually feel his heart beating. This was no dream.

She never looked his direction. They just sat there holding hands like two junior high kids.

When everyone stood for the closing prayer, she let go of his hand but the feel of her skin against his lingered. The moment the amen came he raised his head to look at her.

Adalee was gone, as if she'd never been there.

He had wanted just one more moment to look in her green eyes or touch her beautiful hair. But it wasn't the right place. There had been no time. She'd always be just a woman he thought of now and then. A might-have-been, nothing more.

Jesse collected Zak's backpack, Danny's coat, and the picture Sunny Lyn had colored in Sunday school. Some of the congregation moved to the parlor to visit over coffee and sweets. Others left, but Jesse just stood in the aisle, wondering if the baker had really been there at all.

When the room was empty, he took the stairs built behind the pulpit. Up one flight, across the back of the choir loft, and down another stairway. The shortcut to the recreational hall, which everyone simply called the gym. The passage never seemed to have enough lighting, and on this cloudy day the passageway was even darker.

His kids would be tired from playing and be pumped full of juice and cookies. He'd be surprised if they weren't all three asleep before he could drive home.

He paused at the square landing. He'd always thought of it as purgatory when he was growing up in this church. A left turn would lead to stairs to the gym, and a right turn went to a door leading to the back parking lot.

Jesse noticed Adalee standing in the shadows near the crossway. She looked a bit disoriented until she saw him, then she smiled.

He started to pass, but slowed. "I didn't know you came . . ."

Her fingers touched his lips. "Don't talk. There is no time."

"All right," Jesse answered as he closed the space between them and kissed her. It was the one thing he'd wished he'd done that night he walked her home. Pure reaction. No thought. Just need. He wanted to feel the woman who'd been haunting his dreams.

One bold, hungry kiss. His hands held her at the waist and pulled her against him. When she opened her mouth slightly, he took the invitation and the kiss washed all other thoughts from his brain.

A door opened down below. He stepped away and was surprised she looked as shocked as he felt. The laughter of children came from the left hallway. She turned to the right.

He wanted to tell her he hadn't planned the kiss. He didn't have time for any woman, much less one like her. He was a simple man. A boring man. She was full of life.

She was gone before he could form words.

"Adalee" was all he had time to whisper before the outside door opened, then closed. She was gone.

On the drive home Jesse thought about what had occurred. Nothing like this ever happened to him. A wild hunger was meant for movies and novels, not simple farmers. He wasn't handsome, or rich. Women didn't even notice him, much less kiss him.

With the exception of guys with rap sheets, he was probably the worst pick in the county. Little farm that would never make him rich. Three kids. One beer on his birthday. How boring is that? He didn't even know how to talk to a woman like Adalee.

A north wind was blowing hard when they made it home. He woke the boys and carried Sunny Lyn into the house. With the windows rattling, he closed the drapes, got out lanterns in case it got worse and the electricity went out. This was definitely going to be an inside day.

"Grilled cheese or ham sandwiches?" Jesse asked as he tried not to think of the baker. She'd be rolling her eyes at his Sunday menu, if he'd had time to invite her to lunch.

All three kids said grilled cheese, so he turned on the TV and went into the kitchen to cook lunch. His hands might be working, but his thoughts were on the woman who'd waited for him in the hallway. Why had she come to church? Surely not just to hold his hand. Why had she waited? What had she wanted of him?

Maybe she'd just delivered the snacks for the Sunday reception and accidentally saw him sitting at the back of the church. She could have been looking for the back parking lot door when he started to pass her.

Then again . . . she'd kissed him back. That seemed a bit over-the-top in the "being polite" category.

One question kept circling in his mind. Had she started this, whatever this was, or had he?

As he served up lunch, he told the kids that they might be having company if it kept raining. People would be bringing horses to their barn so the horses could all have a sleepover.

Zak said he'd help, and Danny said he'd watch over Sunny because she didn't need to get wet. Sunny Lyn said she'd count the horses and write the number down. Since the only numbers she could write were 1 and 4, Jesse doubted an accurate count.

Zak looked thoughtful. "So, Dad, we're running a horse hotel."

"Looks like it, son. If more rain floods the river, the horses will be safe with us."

Chapter 19

Piper

The mayor of Honey Creek stood in Mr. Winston's kitchen in shock. *How did I end up here?* Piper had skipped lunch with the widows to be alone with Colby. She'd thought they'd have a quiet lunch and talk things over. Nothing about this weekend had gone as she'd hoped.

Yet, when the old man invited them, Colby thought it would be fun and said yes for *them both*. Like he could speak for her. Another problem they needed to get straight.

He'd claimed that the old guy's home would be somewhat quieter than a crowded café. Winston collects interesting people. They could talk later. But, later, when no one else was around, talking was never high on Colby's list of what to do.

Piper stood in the kitchen of Mr. Winston's home and just glared at her not-so-secret lover. They were together for the first weekend in three months and Colby didn't seem to want to be alone with her.

Piper put on her public face. Calm, polite, welcoming. It was too late to back out and she didn't want to start an argument. Part of her wanted to curl up in his arms and wish away the rain and all the problems that might be coming their way.

Mr. Winston hugged her and told her what a great honor it was to have the mayor in his home. He placed her hand on his forearm and led her into the grand dining room.

Several guests were standing around talking. Everyone was greeting the crowd, so it was easy to play the smiling mayor. The oak-lined room was warm and inviting.

The lady who owned a booth at the flea market, Alice, was there, obviously wearing one of her vintage dresses and gloves. She looked like she'd just stepped out of the 1950s. Digger, who owned Fisherman's Lodge, had just gotten back home. He hugged Colby like he was a long lost son and not just a trooper who'd rented a cabin at his lodge.

Piper nodded to Pecos and his round little wife. Two kids about to have a kid, she thought. They looked so happy she almost envied them. Young love seemed to come so easy. At thirty-four she'd realized that loving still came easy, but commitment didn't. Maybe that was why Colby didn't make time to talk to her. Maybe he wasn't ready to talk about commitment. Of course, she'd been the one to slip out Saturday morning.

Colby stood close to her, but didn't touch her. Piper almost felt like they were drifting at sea . . . in different boats.

Colby talked of his future with the Rangers. She told him of her plans, but neither mentioned their future together. Nothing beyond things like, "We should go to New York and see a few plays," or "How do you feel about getting season tickets to the Cowboys games next year?"

Again and again one of them was pulled away to talk to another guest.

She looked at Colby laughing with Digger. Part of her loved him and another part wondered if he was just passing through her life. A fling destined to become a memory.

As Piper turned to greet the last guest coming through the door, she froze in surprise. "Marcie," she whispered as Marcie Latimer stepped inside the back entrance of Mr. Winston's house. Her head was down, as if she wasn't sure she'd be welcome. Her hesitance broke Piper's heart.

Before Pecos could introduce her, Marcie faced Piper with fear in her huge hazel eyes. "I didn't know you'd be here, Piper. I can leave." She started stepping backward.

"Wait, Marcie. I invited you. Don't leave." Pecos took one step toward them. When he looked at both women, the fire that night at city hall and the trial of Boone Buchanan seemed to fill the entire room.

Piper's heart felt like her chest was about to break open. Marcie was younger than she was, three grades behind in school, but for a short time they'd been best friends years ago. They'd played together at recess and Piper always insisted Marcie share her lunch when Marcie forgot hers. Piper had told her she'd wished they were sisters because neither had a sister.

Nothing that had happened with Boone Buchanan had been Marcie's fault. Not his lies about being engaged to Piper. Not him trying to arrange a fire so he could be Piper's grieving lover. He was a man who wanted the fast track to his dreams, and it didn't matter who got hurt.

He'd never been Piper's lover, but he had been Marcie's. She admitted in court that he called her his secret girlfriend and sometimes he talked about them running away to live together. He'd never told her his plans about faking an engagement with the mayor, but he'd said money and power would be coming his way soon.

Piper cut Pecos off when he tried to reach Marcie. "No," she said. "Marcie has to stay. I've missed her too long and too much." Piper stuck out her hand. "It is time we remember that we were once friends."

Marcie hesitated.

Piper held out both hands and Marcie moved into her hug as if she was once again the little girl who looked up to Piper. Both women started crying. Everyone in the room watched and smiled, except Kerrie. She cried with them.

Pecos circled back to his wife. When people began to worry about the mother-to-be, Pecos assured them that this was nothing. She cried all during *Frozen*.

When everyone settled down around the long formal dining table, stories and laughter flowed as always at Mr. Winston's place. Piper couldn't stop smiling. She'd set something right that had bothered her for months. She'd been in a media storm during the trial, and that had kept her from speaking to Marcie. Piper knew if she had talked to Marcie, the press would have made something about them being friends and added another layer of drama to the court scene.

But all that was over and Piper had fences that needed mending. She'd had the support of the town and all her family. Marcie had no one. Piper knew she should have found a way to talk to her and let her know that what happened shouldn't break their friendship, but there had been no time.

When Pecos mentioned that Marcie was in town looking for a job, Miss Alice announced, "Let's all put our heads together and think of something. What are you good at, dear?"

Marcie shyly said, "I can sing and play a guitar. My teachers always said I was good with numbers."

"She's kind," Mr. Winston added. "I can see it in her eyes. That's a great quality to have in this world."

Everyone agreed.

As they were having dessert, three cells went off at once. Pecos. Colby. Piper. All three stood and moved away from the table to answer. The other guests remained silent, listening for a word or two that might explain the calls.

Pecos stepped back first and announced, "Sorry, folks, I've been called back to work. We've got a severe weather alert. The sheriff wants me to help man the 9-1-1 calls." He looked at Mr. Winston. "This morning Kerrie's folks were worried this might happen and I'd be called in to work. They want you, Mr. Winston, and Kerrie to go to their house if this storm seems to be coming toward us. They've got a safe room where you'll be comfortable."

Kerrie started crying again. "They want you to come too, Pecos. I don't want to go without you."

"I know, but I'll be safe at the sheriff's office, and I'm needed." He took both her hands in his as if silently saying he was sorry. "You'll be safe with your folks, and people might die if I'm not at my post."

Colby, looking very much like the Texas Ranger he was, walked back into the dining room. "I'll keep an eye on your daddy-to-be, Kerrie. Sam and I will be next door at the fire station, and Pecos will be the first to know if trouble comes." He stared at the mayor. "Piper, I'll get you home before I report in."

"You won't have to. I'm going with you. The mayor needs to be on-site. If it gets bad, I'll be the one to call for outside help."

The people from the flea market all started talking at once. All said their homes were on high ground and they'd ride this storm out playing cards. Digger mentioned his cabins were on low ground, so they invited him to shelter with them and join the card game.

The old cabin owner was far more excited about the game than worried about the storm.

Marcie was the only one who wasn't moving.

"Where will you go, dear?" Winston asked.

"The only place I can go is back to my trailer, and everyone knows storms hate trailer parks. The trees behind me might offer some protection, if one of them doesn't fall on me." She must have seen his concern. "I'll be fine."

Kerrie turned to her. "You're welcome to come with me and Mr. Winston. We'll have room at my folks' house."

Marcie shook her head. "I've got plenty of time to

drive home. The flood won't reach Someday Valley. No one needs to worry about me. I just wish there was some way I could help." She glanced from Colby to Pecos. "Is there something I can do?"

Pecos spoke first. "Come with me. I'm in a solid building and I could use another dispatcher. All the other dispatchers will want to be home with their kids. I'll give you the crash course in answering 9-1-1 calls. You can handle the overflow if there is any. The sheriff always says he will, but he gets too excited and starts yelling at the callers."

Piper couldn't tell if Marcie was nodding or simply shaking. "We'll get through this," the mayor whispered to her friend. "I'll be near. It's just a storm. This town's made it through trouble a hundred times. Tonight, we'll stand ready if someone, somewhere needs help."

Marcie smiled. "The sheriff's office is bound to be a safer place for me tonight than home. I truly do want to help."

"If the alert lasts very long, you can help me pass out coffee. That's my main job in times like these." Piper's calming voice seemed to settle the room.

All of Mr. Winston's guests from the market headed out.

Pecos kissed his wife and left with Marcie in a run.

Kerrie waddled upstairs to get a few things and Mr. Winston asked if Colby and Piper could drop them off at Kerrie's parents'. While they waited for Kerrie, he packed up the desserts.

"If this takes all night, we're going to need food." The old man showed no fear. "Take half to the sheriff's office and I'll take the other half to the safe room, whatever that is."

It took all four to get Kerrie's bags and the food to the car. Rain seemed to be spitting at them in short blasts caught in the wind.

Five minutes later, Piper helped Kerrie and Mr. Winston unload at the Lanes' house. She kissed the old man on the cheek and she could have sworn he blushed.

As Colby drove the few blocks to the town square, Piper realized she hadn't said a word to Colby since he'd accepted the lunch invitation from Winston for her. And now, her head was filled with what needed to be done. She had to take care of her town, her people.

She hadn't even sat next to Colby at lunch. Marcie and she had far too much to talk about.

In the silence of the car, they were alone with nothing to say. This was not the time to make up or break up.

Colby must have felt the same way because his jaw was set as he herded everyone to the cars.

Piper glanced at Colby. Wishing they had time. To talk. To make love. To understand why what they had was crumbling.

"I'm sorry," she said, touching his arm as he swung into a parking place and cut the engine. "I guess I was mad at you earlier, and then Marcie came in and I needed to set things right with her."

Colby turned toward her. He looked confused. "Why were you mad?" He reacted like she'd pulled him away from his concentration on the storm with a slap, not an apology. "I don't understand."

She'd finally got his attention. It wasn't the time or place, but she had to say something. It couldn't end like this.

"It bothers me when you speak for me. I'm perfectly able to make decisions and answer questions."

He glared at her as if he had no idea what she was

talking about. "What are you sorry for again? It sounds more like you think I did something wrong." His voice came hard and fast. "I think sometimes we're on different planets and are trying to yell at each other."

"Never mind. It's nothing." She watched the rain and felt trapped in the car.

His words sounded ice-cold. "Maybe I should make a list of all the *nothing*, Mayor. I've spent one day of my weekend looking for you. No sleep for two days to get here, and you didn't even notice. We haven't spent ten minutes alone together all day today." He swore under his breath. "And now with the storm is not the time to talk about what's wrong with us." Colby gulped down his anger. "We've both got a job to do and the job for both of us always comes first. Right?"

"Right." Part of her wanted to be mad at him again for not saying he was sorry, but now wasn't the time. He seemed to think what was wrong between them was her fault.

Piper shoved the door open and ran for the sheriff's office. Raindrops fell on her as tears ran down her face. Colby would have had to look at her to notice.

He caught up with her and managed to hold the door for her as she darted inside.

Both froze as a roar of voices met them. The room was packed with firemen, deputies, volunteers.

She instinctively leaned closer as the noise all but drowned out her question. "What's wrong with us?" she whispered. She could almost hear the bond between them tearing. She told herself when this crisis was over they'd talk, but deep down she knew it might be too late.

He dug his fingers through his wet hair and moved into action. She did the same.

Chapter 20

Pecos

Pecos moved into place like a seasoned fighter pilot going into battle. Everything was ready. The desk was made in the shape of an S. Usually there was just one dispatcher on duty, but if another was needed she'd sit on the other half of the desk. Her computer screen faced the main operator's computer so all Pecos had to do was turn his head to see both. They'd each have their own headset but they'd almost be shoulder to shoulder, making passing information easy. If only one line was active, the other dispatcher could listen in.

Pecos sat down at his cluttered station and Marcie took the other. When she swiveled toward him she could see everything he was doing. If he wasn't on the phone, he was talking or filling her in on the rules, answers, and information she had to collect. Numbers she might need were taped to both desks. She would be taking a crash course in being a dispatcher. If she didn't learn fast, the country singer would be out the door within an hour.

"I can switch over if you get a call that you can't handle."

She nodded, then sat quietly as Pecos answered a few calls, sending one call to the fire department. A fall victim called, needing to be transferred to the clinic. The next call was a woman who couldn't find her cat. Pecos explained that cats hate water, so it was probably up high and dry. He also said if it was not an emergency, she'd have to wait until the storm was over.

The woman was not happy with that answer and wanted to be passed to the sheriff, so Pecos did. Three calls followed, asking about the weather.

The sheriff wandered in to complain about the cat call and gave them both the official statement about the weather. "It bugs me when people call in like we're the weather channel. They'll want to know what to do, like they've never even thought a flood might come along. Hell, they live on a river. Our job is to give them direction and keep them from doing something stupid like trying to float out on their blowup mattress."

Marcie nodded, taking in every word.

Sheriff LeRoy Hayes continued, "Tell them if they're between the river and the highway to evacuate now. Let us know if they need help. That means to evacuate, not move out. Back in '93, a fisherman wanted to take all his trophies with him. Turns out they filled the whole boat. That flood wiped out a dozen fishing shacks, but they came back the following spring like weeds."

"What do I tell the folks on the other side of the highway?" Pecos asked.

"Hell, I don't know."

Pecos could almost see the sheriff's blood pressure rising as he thought.

Finally the answer seemed to slam into his brain and he yelled, "Tell them to move inland if they've got a friend or relative on higher ground. If they live in town, just say 'shelter in place.' Water might reach Digger's cabins or even the Honey Creek Café, but won't flood into town unless it keeps raining for another week."

LeRoy scratched a spot on his chin that he'd forgotten to shave. "If they're sick, tell them to go to the clinic. If they're scared, go to the church. Both are setting up extra beds, and we've got volunteers to help with transport."

The sheriff noticed their guest still sitting beside Pecos. "Dang it, what's she still doing here? Shouldn't she be making coffee or something?"

"She's here to help me, sir," Pecos answered. "She has some experience handling a crisis. She'll keep calm and help."

After staring at her for a moment, the sheriff seemed to accept the idea. "Well, Marcie, you'd better do just that. We may need all the help we can get. Call Rambling Randy over at the radio station and tell him to broadcast every fifteen minutes. Relay every word I say, except for the swearing. One thing that will save lives should this storm hit hard is the folks around here having a plan, and I aim to give them one."

Marcie nodded.

The sheriff added, "Make up the ten most asked questions Pecos gets, and the answers, and send them to

Randy. He can read them out over the air. Maybe it'll cut the calls to nine-one-one." He turned to Pecos. "Don't send me any more damn cat calls."

Pecos smiled and said, "Got it, boss." He'd given up being afraid of LeRoy's yelling months ago.

The sheriff turned and walked out, mumbling something about how he should have retired months ago. "I could be on one of them islands on a beach drinking them fruity drinks called Maytags."

"Mai tai," Marcie whispered.

Pecos laughed. "Don't correct him. He hates being wrong almost as much as he hates his wife not letting him have sweets."

The phone started ringing. Pecos watched Marcie taking notes. Like clockwork she called Rambling Randy to tell him the latest alert. If the sheriff didn't deliver the report, she chased the old guy around the office asking him questions.

The old man treated her like he did everyone in the office. Pecos admired him for that. Hayes didn't hold grudges. He'd told Pecos once that a lawman can't afford to or he'd run out of friends fast.

After a few hours the phone calls came faster. Marcie put on her headset and went to work. The main office beyond the small 9-1-1 room began to fill up. Pecos could hear Sam Cassidy, the fire chief, organizing men. Ranger Colby was by his side. The Texas Ranger carried a portable radio in one hand and his phone in the other. His job seemed to be keeping up with the boats sent out and the huge pickups that could drive through almost a foot of water if they could find the road.

Colby remembered every detail as if he had a whiteboard of notes in his mind.

Volunteers kept coming in, shaking water off like sheepdogs, gulping down the mayor's coffee, and heading out again. All the homes along the river had to be checked before it got dark or the water got too deep.

"What's happening out there?" Pecos asked when Marcie came back from tracking down the sheriff for his report.

Pecos was leaning back, scratching his head with both hands. He might look tired, but he was pumped up on coffee and worry.

"Some of the older fishermen are refusing to leave and the water's already sloshing over its banks." Marcie gave him a quick report. "Someone said that if it was just a few inches, folks might be all right, but it'll come in deep and fast by dark. One man said six inches of running water will knock down a man. A foot can float a car." She took her seat. "That's all anyone is talking about out there."

Pecos played with his pen, waiting for the next call. "I've heard if you toss a stick in a shallow creek and the stick floats off as fast as you walk, then the water will knock you down if you try to cross the stream. Some of those old-timers can't stand solid on dry land. They won't have a chance."

The phone rang. Pecos took the call. Five seconds later the other phone rang and Marcie answered.

Marcie took all the information and read the latest weather report to the caller. When Pecos finished his call, he put her call on speaker. A panicked mother of three was crying. "If the water comes I'm afraid I can't hold on to all three kids. I'm alone. No relatives live close. My husband's deployed to Afghanistan."

The fire chief and the mayor had been standing in the

doorway listening. "You got her address?" Sam yelled at Marcie.

She nodded. "But it's not in where we think the town might be flooded."

"It doesn't matter. Tell her we're on our way." When Marcie hesitated for one heartbeat, the chief repeated, "Tell her we're moving her to the second floor of the firehouse. She'll be safe there."

Marcie relayed the message as Pecos passed the address. Sam was gone before Marcie hung up.

She and Pecos both took a deep breath. "The kids will love a sleepover at the station. Too bad we don't have a great place for the old fishermen, then they might move to safety. Some are so old I doubt they could swim ten feet if they fall in the river."

Piper, who was still standing at the door, interrupted. "Let me make a call. I might know just the residence. There's only one place in town where everyone would go if invited."

Ten minutes later three trucks were headed out to pick up a dozen fishermen. The fishermen were going to Widows Park. Not one man turned down the invitation.

Pecos glanced at Marcie. "A handful of old fishermen who haven't seen a napkin in years and a houseful of tea-drinking ladies. What could possibly go wrong?"

"I'd like to drop by and see."

"Nope." He laughed. "You're needed here."

Chapter 21

Marcie

As the hours passed and the storm raged, Marcie worked beside Pecos Smith like a pro. When she wasn't calling in reports to the radio station and answering questions like, "When is this going to be over?" or "Is it safe to drive now?" she was serving coffee to people who were being transported from their homes to safer ground. All looked worried or frightened and most were dripping water on the floor.

The sheriff ate most of the sweets Mr. Winston sent over, and the firemen on call kept sandwiches and soup for anyone who wanted them.

When she finally took a break, Marcie called Brand, the only person who would worry about her, she figured.

He answered on the first ring. "You all right?" He sounded like he'd been sitting by the phone.

"I'm fine." She laughed. Who would have thought Brand was a mother hen? "I'm helping out with the nine-one-one calls at the sheriff's offices over in Honey Creek. How are you handling the flood?"

"I'm fine, Marcie. I live halfway up in the hills. Dolphins would be swimming by if the water got this high."

"I know, Brand. I was out at your house, remember?"

"I remember. I wish you were here right now. This storm is putting on quite a show."

"And what would we be doing if I was with you?"

"We'd be watching the storm and probably eating the leftover chili. We could share a cup of hot chocolate. I liked doing that." He hesitated, as though he thought he might be asking too much. "You could play for me. I love listening to you sing."

Maybe she needed normal right now, or maybe she just thought she'd tease Brand, but she asked, "Would you let me curl up in your lap and sleep?"

The phone was silent and she almost thought they'd lost the connection. Then, in his low voice he answered, "You can curl up in my lap anytime. I'd keep you safe, I promise."

His words sounded so honest she almost cried. In a whisper she asked, "Brand, when the rain stops will you come get me? Another shift comes on at eight. I drove Wayne's car over here to Honey Creek and I thought I'd better make sure it was safe, so I left it in Mr. Winston's garage. After the rain stops will you help me get it back to Wayne?"

"I will. But I'd like it if you'd come home with me

and rest first. He couldn't get that car down the road behind the bar even if he wanted to."

He was honest. His answers were always simple. She knew she'd never have to ask twice or call him to see if he meant what he'd said.

"Thanks. I think I'd like that." Marcie dropped her phone in her pocket and went back to work. The hours passed with no thought of her own problems. Tonight was about helping others. Near dawn the calls became lighter. Rambling Randy had almost lost his voice, but he kept reporting.

The rain slowed and the sun would rise to weak storm clouds trying to hang on to the sky. Marcie heard Pecos call his wife in the now silent dispatch room.

"It's over, wife," he said. "I'll be coming to pick you up soon."

She sounded sleepy when Marcie heard his pregnant wife's voice. "Mr. Winston said he'd make up a bedroom for Marcie if she wants to crash over at his place."

"Thanks, I'll tell her." Pecos looked at Marcie, a foot away. She shook her head. Pecos went back to his wife. "How'd you make out at your folks'?"

"We just watched old movies and I slept. Dad listened to the radio. Randy said he'd relay any report from the sheriff if a tornado was spotted. That'd be our notice to move to the safe room. Mom packed a week's worth of food in there but we never had to go."

Pecos seemed to have forgotten Marcie could hear every word they both said.

"How's my baby?" Pecos asked.

"Moving around more than usual. I keep trying to get some sleep but can't. I think the kid wants you to pat on him."

Marcie picked up the empty coffee cups and gave him some privacy.

As she walked to the small kitchen, she noticed the deputies nodded a greeting. Even Rip, the youngest deputy, who sat at the middle desk, said "Morning." It was almost as if she was one of them. One of the team.

The sheriff watched her walk to the kitchen. When she headed back, he said, "Marcie, could I have a word?"

She was too tired to care what he planned to say. "Yes, Sheriff."

He grumbled as if the words he was chewing on were rocks. "You were a big help tonight. Pecos could have handled it alone, but you've got a soothing voice. That seemed to help the panicked women. I don't know anyone who can handle Rambling Randy better. He got most of the news right for a change."

Marcie smiled. The old goat was actually complimenting her. Months ago he'd been cold and official when he'd questioned her about Boone, but she never thought the sheriff unkind. He might have hated what her old boyfriend did, but he never took it out on her like several folks did.

"I'm not saying we have an opening or that you'd get it, but you might think about applying to be a dispatcher. When Pecos finishes his studies, he'll be moving up to deputy, and I don't have anyone who could fill in for him."

She was so shocked she couldn't answer. Marcie had applied for every kind of job she heard about in the valley. Now, the sheriff was almost, maybe, offering her one.

"Thank you, Sheriff. I might just do that." Then she outright lied to the man. "It was a pleasure working with you tonight."

A few minutes later she walked out to the first light of dawn. Brand was standing beside his truck as if he was thinking about storming the office. In an odd way, this loner of a man looked out of place in the middle of town.

Marcie ran to him and jumped into his waiting arms. He held her close, then slid his arm down her back, over her hips and lifted her up. He carried her to his truck as if he thought she might be too tired to walk. To tell the truth, she almost was. He drove home with her head resting against his chest and one arm holding her there.

Almost to his ranch, she asked, "You going to say anything, Brand?"

"Yeah," he said as he turned onto his land. "I'm picking you up." She felt the rumble of laughter in his chest. "Thought I'd take you home with me, any objections? I'm guessing you've been up twenty-four hours. You need sleep and food." His voice lowered a bit. "And someone to watch over you."

She raised her head and started to say thank you when she saw her car parked beside the barn. "You stole my car?"

"Nope. I fixed it."

"What was broken?"

"Pretty much everything. Lucky I can fix pretty much everything."

Without another word, he carried her across the yard and into the house. First light seemed so bright after a week of cloudy, rainy days that she leaned her head back over his arm and took in the warmth until they stepped inside.

As she pulled off her high-heeled western boots, she asked if he'd been up all night watching the storm. She wasn't surprised when he said yes.

"You mind if I take a shower?" Hot water might do wonders for her tight muscles.

"No, I don't mind," he said. "You want something to eat?"

"No, thanks. I'm not hungry. I just want to sleep."

"I'll get the red pajamas. I washed them. Turned all my underwear pink."

Just the facts, she thought, but she didn't miss the slight lift of a smile on the left side of his mouth. Brand was warming up to her.

She laughed as she walked to the bathroom. There was something endearing about this quiet man.

A few minutes later she was stripped and standing under hot water. It felt like Heaven. When she dried off in the steamy little room, she noticed the red pajamas on the table by the door.

Sometime during her shower he'd opened the door. Knowing him, he hadn't tried to look at her, even if the steam wouldn't have allowed much of a view.

After dressing in red, rolling up her sleeves and pants, she stepped out into the hallway. He'd made up her bed on the couch. Two pillows this time, and a low fire to hold away the morning chill. One heavy blanket waited for her to curl up in.

When she looked the other way, down the hall, she saw him lying atop his bed. As she tiptoed toward him, she noticed he'd taken off his boots, and his white socks were now pale pink. His shirt was half unbuttoned and he was totally asleep.

Marcie glanced back at the couch, then at the half of the bed he wasn't using. She'd always been a jumper every time she came to a cliff. She tiptoed back to the main room and pulled the blanket off the couch. Then returned to his bedroom.

She spread the blanket over Brand, climbed in beside him, and pulled her half of the covers over her. Marcie rolled against him and used his big arm as her cuddle pillow.

Brand didn't make a move, so she drifted off to sleep. Her last thought was if he could fix anything, maybe he could fix her.

But when she woke, the room was dark and Brand was gone. When she walked into the kitchen, he was pulling two steaks off a small grill.

"You cooked for me?"

He looked up and acted surprised. "Oh, you're still here. I forgot."

She saw the table set for two, baked potatoes already on the plates and a salad in the middle of the table. "You cooked for me."

As he forked the steaks on their plates, she kissed his cheek and took her place. They talked about the storm, and she told him about all the things that happened last night at the station.

He listened, really listened, and asked a few questions.

"I'm going back to Honey Creek in the morning and apply for a job. I think I could handle it." She smiled suddenly. "I have a car again. I can drive back and forth to check on you on my way to work, if the sheriff hires me."

She jumped up and kissed him again. "Thank you, thank you." His kindness had given her a running chance to change.

"You don't have to do that," he said as he brushed her kiss off his cheek.

"What? Kiss you or check on you? We're friends. I have to keep up with you now, Brand. One of those horses could kick you in the head and no one would know for weeks."

"I just wanted you to be safe and not have to walk home at night. You needed a car you could depend on."

"How much do I owe you?"

"Nothing, Marcie. Absolutely nothing."

"But I can pay some of the cost. I can't just depend on you to save me every time I have trouble. I can't drop in on you when I need a place to crash or a great meal."

"Yes, you can. You could pay me back by playing for me now, and then I'd count us even." His low voice sounded more a wish than a bargain.

When they moved into the living room, she picked up her guitar, which she'd left in his truck. She sat on one end of the couch and he sat on the other. As he always did, Brand didn't move as she played but he smiled as if her songs rested his soul.

He thanked her and they settled in to watch the late news. She made one big cup of cocoa and sat next to him as they shared. Then, as if it was routine, she wrapped her arms around his arm, leaned her head against his shoulder, and closed her eyes.

"I feel like I'm a tree branch and you're a koala bear."

"I feel like that too. Do you mind?"

He shifted down so his head rested on the back of the couch. "Nope."

Marcie smiled. The big silent man was growing on her.

Monday

Chapter 22

Piper

Piper leaned against Colby as they walked out of the fire station and into clean morning air.

One of the deputies yelled, "Thanks, Mayor, for spending the night with us."

"You're welcome, Rip," she answered. "Get some sleep. It's over."

"You too."

Colby ended the exchange by closing the station door. He looked tired and in no mood to talk to her or anyone else.

But talking was how Piper calmed, and the ranger would just have to put up with her. "We dodged a bullet last night." The gutters ran, full of leaves floating on fast-running water. The buildings and trees were wet, making the whole town sparkle. "Another few hours of rain and the water would have crossed the highway and flowed into town. Then, we might have had serious problems."

"You're right," he managed to contribute to the conversation as they walked toward the parking lot.

"I feel like everyone worked together, don't you?"

Colby didn't answer and she knew he wasn't in the conversation. They were side-by-side, but they were not together.

Piper continued. "Thanks to a few firemen and several men with boats, the folks in danger were moved to safety. There were more people living out by the river than anyone knew about. That new housing development called Brazos Ranches didn't look close enough at the flood zone to consider where they were building. Homes, not even finished, are standing in two feet of water."

Colby didn't seem interested, so she changed the subject. "I called Jennifer. Water flooded up to the porch of the Honey Creek Café, but it'll retreat fast too."

Colby laughed as if finally waking up from his sleepwalking. "Your cousin Jennifer stayed with the ghosts, didn't she? Glad she didn't call in to be evacuated. Half of the firefighters would head upstairs as they turned into ghost hunters."

Piper finally linked her arm in his. "Another strange fact. Most of the folks who were trapped hadn't been listening to the warnings from Rambling Randy. In truth, I don't think anyone ever listens to him."

Colby pulled her closer. "We were lucky the boats found them. Several people in town took in the folks that flooded out, but if it had rained a little harder for a little longer, we would have had hundreds to move."

Piper jerked away from him and started running toward her van. "Oh no," she yelled. "I forgot. I told the firemen to take the old fishermen, who said they had nowhere to go, to Widows Park. I said the ladies would welcome them in."

"That's nice," Colby replied, jogging along beside her.

"No, it was a bad idea. I just realized that old men, living out there alone with little or no contact with humans, probably live out there for a reason. Wanted criminals. People who don't do well in society. Mass murderers. Men who don't bathe regularly."

"We'd better hurry. They may be having your grandmother and the other widows for breakfast," Colby teased. "To your aunt Linda, not taking a bath probably ranks up there with being a mass murderer."

She slapped his arm for making fun of her. She was pulling away from the curb by the time he jumped into her van.

Colby swore. "Your van smells like cow manure."

Piper fought down her anger. "Of course it does. I garden, remember. I have to do something when my boyfriend doesn't bother to come home for three months." She was tired and frustrated and angry with herself for putting the widows in danger. None of the men in those shacks had wives, and there was probably a reason.

She'd opened that anger at him. Nothing seemed right between them, so any subject was on the table to fight about.

Colby must have felt the same way, but he changed the direction of the argument. "Anyone ever tell you that you are the worst driver in the state? If you were on the highway, I swear I'd pull you over. You've broken three laws and you've only gone three blocks."

She was too exhausted to defend herself. "Then get out, Colby."

"No way." He sounded just as tired and just as angry. "If you kill us both, I want to tell you 'I told you so' when we get to the hereafter."

She slammed on the brakes in front of Widows Park. Colby hit the dashboard.

"You really should wear your seat belt." She stepped out.

"I had to jump into a moving car to get in. I figured you already had your best chance at killing me. When you wreck, I wanted to be able to crawl away."

She didn't wait for him to come around the van. She started toward the house.

As they walked up the drive, Piper noticed the drapes were drawn. They were never closed during the day. It was a house rule. First one up at dawn opens all downstairs drapes.

Something was going on. Piper could feel it. Something was terribly wrong.

She started running and darted for the side door. Colby was five feet behind her when she reached the study.

The sight before her chilled her to the bone. It was worse than she could have imagined.

Aunt Morgan was dealing cards on a hand-carved Lincoln dining table loaded down with empty beer bottles. Aunt Dee sat beside her, counting her chips.

Piper stopped breathing and stared.

Two men lay on the Persian rug her grandparents had brought back from Paris. Both men looked dead. Another was under the coffee table, looking like an improbable version of Sleeping Beauty in a glass coffin, and six more men were sitting in dining chairs wearing only their underwear. No, five had on underwear. One must have forgotten his because he was covered by one of Linda's hand-embroidered tea towels. The last fisherman, tall and bony, was standing in the double doors leading to the kitchen. He was wearing what looked like long johns that might have survived the gold rush.

"Anyone want some more cheese and crackers?" he offered. He was eating off the tray as he served.

Piper started hyperventilating just as Colby looked over her shoulder. His reaction to the scene fresh out of an old *Gunsmoke* episode was to laugh.

She jabbed him in the ribs.

All he did was smile and rub his side. "Morning, kids," he said to the seniors. "You guys having an all-night poker game? Hope you're not betting with money. It's illegal in this state if the house takes a cut."

Half of Colby's relatives played a round of poker now and then, and none used chips.

"We're not illegal." Piper's Bible-thumping aunt Morgan stood up and used her teacher voice. "We're playing strip poker. I'll have you know, no money is involved."

Colby couldn't seem to stop smiling.

If Piper hadn't been about to faint, her aunt's comment might have pushed her over. She crumbled, suddenly boneless. Colby's arm circled her waist a moment before she hit the ground.

The room began to fade.

Vaguely, she was aware of everyone at the table rushing toward her. Well, everyone but the guy with the tea towel. He stood up for a moment, but then just sat back down.

Piper welcomed the blackness. Maybe she'd wake up and all would be normal. This could be some kind of hallucination. No sleep. Nothing to eat. Being panicked with fear most of the night. Twenty cups of coffee.

Slowly, as if coming out of a deep well, she began to hear voices, then a tiny bit of light shone from beyond her closed eyelids.

"Piper, can you hear me?" Colby now sounded worried. "Piper!"

She didn't answer. But she heard her grandmother say, "She used to hold her breath when she was a little thing. First few times we all got upset and tried to keep everything calm around our fragile little Piper. Then the doctor told us she did it just to get her way, so her grandfather told everyone to leave her alone. Let her faint, then she'll start breathing. Of course, unless she breaks her nose. If that happened, blood would be everywhere and we'd never get the poor child married off with a smashed nose. He was just kidding, it was his way, but Piper never held her breath again."

Colby had to ask, "Because she wanted to get married?"

"No. She can't stand the sight of blood."

Piper decided she'd just stay down in the dark well. She didn't want to wake. Colby had just learned her worst two secrets. He'd never look at her as the mayor again. All he'd see was that little girl holding her breath or afraid of blood.

Aunt Linda lifted Piper's head and inched a throw pillow under her chestnut-colored hair while Colby used more pillows to elevate her legs.

"She'll come around." Piper's practical grandmother added, "Men, your clothes are all washed and dried. Why don't you get dressed before she wakes? The sight of those hunky bodies might make her faint again."

They all laughed and shoved their hairy, wrinkled, baggy bodies back into clothes.

Piper heard Colby ask, "How come all you men are naked and all the ladies are fully dressed?"

"They cheat," one chubby man who seemed hairy from his toes to his eyebrows said. "But we didn't mind. Let 'em look."

Piper heard the other men agreeing and the women giggling.

Colby asked the next question. "What about these two on the floor?"

"All they wanted to do was sleep, and the ladies wouldn't let them lie down on the furniture." The chubby man's whole body jiggled as he laughed. "Goat over there stunk, so he went under the glass coffee table, but it didn't help the smell much."

"Goat is his name?" Colby asked.

"I don't know. Probably. I ain't ever heard him go by anything else. We call him Goat because he eats everything. Last Christmas we gave him our expired cans, and he thanked us."

Piper opened one eye and realized she was a foot away from one sleeping man. His snoring was blowing alligator breath her direction. It was time for her to wake up.

Chapter 23

Pecos

When Pecos rushed in the door of Kerrie's parents' house, he could hardly wait to hold her. It seemed like he'd been away for days.

"Kerrie!" he yelled.

"In the kitchen," she answered. A moment later she was waddling toward him and he was running to her.

As he hugged her close, rocking her in his arms, her father's voice came from the kitchen doorway. "Don't hold her so hard, boy. You'll squeeze that baby right out of her."

Pecos didn't turn loose of Kerrie and she held on tighter to him. Pecos stared over her head at Mr. Lane. "I'm not hurting my wife and I'm not a boy."

There was that hate-look Pecos was used to in Mr.

Lane's eyes. Like the *get off my property* look, or that *I plan to kill you as soon as you let your guard down* look.

Pecos wondered if the parents lectured Kerrie all night long. Their range of advice was endless. They wanted their daughter back, but Pecos wasn't sure if they wanted the baby. He knew they didn't want him.

Mr. Winston circled around Mr. Lane like he was one of the columns in the living room that seemed to have no practical purpose. He carried a plate of tiny cinnamon rolls with a pecan half on top of each. "Oh, Pecos, I'm so glad you're here. These are fresh out of the oven. Kerrie made them."

Pecos looked down at her. "You made them?"

"I did."

"Then I'm sure I'll love them." He'd managed to get down her first meatloaf and a dozen first casseroles she got off of Pinterest. He could handle this.

Mr. Lane stormed off to the back of the house and everyone else sat down to breakfast. While Kerrie's mother got the egg dish out of the oven and Mr. Winston poured himself another cup of coffee, Pecos leaned close to Kerrie. "How was it last night?"

"Not as bad as I thought it might be. Mr. Winston helped. Dad makes a point of never yelling in front of strangers. He did try to lecture me to death. I pretended to be asleep most of the time."

He kissed the top of her head. "I missed you, wife."

"I missed you, husband. Can we go home and go back to bed?"

"I'd like that. I'll have to be back at the station by eight tonight." He leaned close and kissed her right in front of her mother and Mr. Winston.

When Pecos looked up, Mrs. Lane had tears running down her cheeks, but she was smiling.

Mr. Winston patted her on her shoulder. "Even an old man like me can see true love."

Mrs. Lane nodded her head so hard, tears flew off her face, but she didn't say a word.

After eating everything on the table, Pecos and Kerrie walked back to their home with Mr. Winston between them. He was doing all the talking. Apparently this had been quite an adventure for the old man.

As soon as they got home they all climbed the stairs and said good night even though it was morning, then headed for their rooms.

Pecos helped Kerrie with her clothes, then he stripped and they both tumbled into bed. The heavy old drapes turned their quarters into twilight.

He loved everything about this room. The heavy old-fashioned furniture, the soothing colors of deep blue and burgundy, the way Kerrie felt beside him. The feel of her against him would warm his heart until his last breath.

"Pecos," she said as she cuddled closer. "I don't want us to be separated if trouble of any kind comes again. Do you think the sheriff would let me stay in the dispatch room? I want to be with you, not with my parents."

"No. The sheriff wouldn't let you hang out and watch me work, but the firemen might let you stay next door. Then I could check on you and you could walk over and wave at me from the front office."

"Could Mr. Winston come too?"

"Sure," Pecos promised as he prayed trouble never came again while he was a dispatcher. If the old man thought the Lanes' safe room was an adventure, he'd have a heart attack in the sheriff's office during a crisis.

Just as he was dozing off with his cheek against her hair, she said, "I asked Mr. Winston what his first name was. He said Abraham."

"That's a nice name," Pecos mumbled as he drifted off. There was no place in the world he'd rather be than right here. He smiled even in his sleep.

There are times, Pecos decided, that life is so perfect you feel like you might explode with happiness. They had next to nothing, but at the same time, they had it all.

He moved his hand over her tummy and the kid tapped against his palm.

Chapter 24

Piper

Piper and Colby spent two hours moving cots into the study of the Widows Park home so the fishermen would have a place to sleep. The water was starting to recede, but not enough for the old men to go home for a day or two.

The widows had figured everything out. The men would all sleep in the study. That way only one room in the manor would need to be thoroughly cleaned and fumigated when the men left.

Surprisingly, none of the men was offended by the announcement.

Colby had laughed when he'd asked if they had enough food for everyone. The widows had shown him their freezer and the pantry. "We're from pioneer stock. We plan for trouble. We keep stuff we don't even need, just in case. If we drive somewhere, even for a day, we pack enough food to last the journey, just in case the stores and Dairy Queens are closed." Aunt Dee laughed. "I fear the habit is cell memory from the covered-wagon days."

Colby didn't argue. "My mother is the same way." He turned to Piper. "I think I'll go back to the station and check things out. You want to come along?"

"No," she said, feeling like she was half-asleep and still standing. "I think I'll eat an early supper and crash here. You're welcome to come back and sleep in the study with the men."

Colby frowned. He seemed to be listening to what she was not saying. This was his last night in Honey Creek and they were *not* sleeping together. Obviously not the way he'd planned, but she'd watched them slowly falling away from each other for two days.

I won't be sleeping with him tonight circled in her mind like drain water. He'd had three nights to be with her. The first was great. Last night was duty. And now she felt she had to step out of the game they'd been playing. Maybe for a night. Maybe for good.

She was too tired and too upset to talk about it. "We'll talk tomorrow morning. Stop by before you take off."

"I'm heading back to Austin by dawn." His words fell like a hammer.

She knew there was so much neither said. They'd argued earlier, but she couldn't remember about what. Her being busy yesterday? Not saying goodbye when she'd left him sleeping? Not calling? Her driving? Him not coming home in three months?

None of that mattered really. How could such little things change anything between them? Their relationship was dying, not by a cannon shot, but by pinpricks.

Then one more little thing walked into her thoughts. He'd never said he loved her. He'd said he loved her body. He loved making love to her. He loved her laugh. But he'd never even whispered that he loved her.

"Good night, Colby," she said as she opened the door. "Call if you have time for breakfast before you go."

"Good night, Mayor." He bowed slightly but his words seemed colder than the night air.

Piper watched him walk away, splashing water as he moved toward town. It was only a few blocks. She could have driven him. But she didn't offer. She had too much pride. She didn't even know what she'd done wrong, and somehow she had a feeling Colby felt the same way.

He was right about one thing. They both were their careers. Maybe that was why he never said the words she wanted so dearly to hear. He thought it would be easier when they had to walk away. He was a Texas Ranger. It wasn't just his job. And she was the mayor.

But tonight, if only for a moment, she wanted to be his. Just his. She wanted him to be all hers with nothing between. One man and one woman who could get lost in each other.

Maybe it was pride or maybe a strong independence that wouldn't allow her to let go and fall into his arms. She wanted to tell him she needed love as much as any woman, maybe more. He'd run through fire to save her but he couldn't seem to talk to her.

No tears fell as she drove home. It was too late. Something inside her had already died.

The next morning when she drove past the fire station, his Harley, which had been parked at the back of the bay, was gone. She didn't have to ask. She knew he was gone too.

Chapter 25

Jesse

As he picked up from the storm and welcomed horse after horse into his barn, Jesse's thoughts were on Adalee. He wondered if she'd been afraid last night during the storm. The bakery was in the heart of town, but winds could have blown out windows, or her roof might have leaked. He could call the business number, but somehow that didn't seem right. She might be with a customer or busy baking.

Besides, they were barely speaking friends. More like kissing friends.

He knew of no other way to check on her other than driving to town and walking into her bakery.

Jesse had spent two days trying to figure out what exactly had happened in the stairwell of the church. He felt like nothing strange had ever occurred in his life before Adalee came along, so he had to assume that she was the catalyst, not him.

He knew the facts of what had happened. He'd kissed her and she'd kissed him back. The kind of kiss that made him believe his ears might let out steam.

The *why* part was a bit more confusing.

Was it the start of something, or some kind of freak thing that just materializes when a man and a woman bump into one another in a stairwell known as purgatory? Like lightning in a snowstorm.

Maybe it was animal attraction. You know, like two rabbits bump into each other in the field and they start mating. But that didn't make sense, he was a human. There is a way these things are done among people. A man and woman meet, they talk, they talk some more, then they meet for coffee or something, then they talk some more. Then, they have a few dates. Talk about where their relationship is going. The guy thinks of feeling her up and the girl thinks of names for their children.

People don't just bump together and start mating.

If he hadn't had his barn full of horses, Jesse might have driven into town and had a talk with the redheaded baker. But the morning before the storm hit, trailers delivered a dozen horses from individuals who kept their pet horse in little more than a backyard. A pony is a grand gift to give your kid, but it takes a hell of a lot more work than a dog.

When the storm ended, every one of the one-horse owners had called to ask if Jesse could board the horses a few more days, maybe a week. Jesse didn't mind. It was work and it meant three hundred sixty a day extra coming in. If they did board for the week, it would add up to over two thousand dollars. He could use the money.

Plus, when he worked in the barn he had time to think about Adalee. He'd never been a spontaneous kind of guy. So why had he kissed her like the world was about to end? He'd kissed her in a church, of all places. Well, it was in the hallway of a church. That didn't sound so bad. After all, she was the one who kissed him first. He had no idea where he got the idea to give her a kiss back.

He had kissed her!

It didn't make sense. He liked women who were petite and blond. Beth had only been five-two, and she wore her hair in a pixie cut. She was so cute. The kind of woman who gets called a *girl* even after her children are grown.

Adalee was nothing like her. She wasn't fat but she wasn't small, either. She was about two inches shorter than he was, making her five-eight or five-nine and just right to kiss. They hadn't talked much, so he had no idea if they had anything in common. Probably not. He'd bet she never lived on a farm. He rationed happiness and fun. She was the type who went full out wild. Glitter in her hair and maybe a tattoo. Fact was, she downright terrified him. The baker was not predictable and apparently it was rubbing off on him.

Jesse burned the first grilled cheese sandwich he was cooking for the kids. He started over and went back to thinking. You'd think cooking the same meal every other day would get easier. He tried cooking other things, but the boys liked order, sameness. Maybe they needed it for a while. So, he went back to thinking of the baker as he tried to make what might be his thousandth grilled sandwich.

He didn't know who, or what, Adalee was. All he knew was that they shared one thing. Touch. No, two things. They both didn't want to talk. That was fine with him. He didn't know what to say anyway. But he wouldn't mind touching her again, if she was willing.

If he ever had time to get to town. There were way too many *ifs* in his life right now.

He'd decided to concentrate on cleaning up after the storm, even though his place didn't flood. The winds had made a mess of the barn roof, and taking care of a dozen horses kept him even busier than usual. The grandmothers agreed to drive out every morning and relay the kids to school, but Jesse had to go into town to pick them up by five. Both ladies said they wouldn't mind keeping them later if he needed to finish work before driving in.

After dragging branches off to burn all the next morning, Jesse decided to clean up and go into town early. He thought he'd check to see how Honey Creek had weathered the storm, pick up some more supplies for the horses, and then buy something sweet before he collected the kids.

When he walked into the bakery an hour before school was due to let out, he still hadn't figured out how he should act around Adalee. Should he be a polite stranger, or should he smile and say "Afternoon, beautiful"?

He wasn't the "Afternoon, beautiful" type. Maybe he should just stick with "Hello" and order a pie or something.

The conflict over what to say was void. Adalee wasn't behind the counter. The lady taking orders was about fifty and didn't look happy.

"Afternoon," Jesse managed without any enthusiasm. "Where is Adalee?"

"Hell if I know." The woman, with a frown that looked tattooed on, answered. "I work in the back from seven to eleven, mostly doing cleanup and prep. She called me over as I'm packing up and asked me to stay until closing."

The woman leaned on the counter like it was a fence gate. "I got varicose veins. I'm not meant to be on my feet for more than four hours. Now, all at once, I'm a saleslady. There better be more pay for having to put up with people. One idiot after another wandered in. Whad-daya want?"

Jesse frowned. No free coffee. No donuts for the kids. No Adalee. "A pie."

The woman's frown turned into a sneer. "I ain't no mind reader, mister. What kind of pie do you want?"

"What kind you got?"

She pointed to a list posted behind the counter.

"Apple." He went with the first on the list.

"We just ran out of apple."

"Peach."

"We've only got two slices left. If you want a whole pie it's chocolate or coconut."

"I'll take a whole coconut pie and two dozen donut holes." He felt like he'd just played *Jeopardy!* and ended up minus any money.

As she boxed up the pie, she said, "We don't sell bags of two dozen holes. They come twelve to a bag or thirty-six."

"Give me two bags of twelve and put them in the same bag."

"Can't do that. No mixing the bags. You want a bag of twelve or thirty-six?"

He gave up. "Two bags of twelve might work."

"About time you made up your mind, mister. I ain't got all day."

Jesse's good mood was ruined. He walked out of the bakery and sat in his pickup. He couldn't keep from wondering where Adalee was. Of course it was none of his business. He hadn't been able to stop in on Monday, so she might think he didn't want to see her again.

What if she'd packed up and moved? She obviously was a drifter. She'd only lived here three years. Maybe that was her limit in any one place.

He got out and walked among the trees near city hall. The chilly wind didn't calm his mood. Winter was coming on, and as the days got shorter so would his workdays. He'd have time to get all the equipment ready for spring. Plan for next year's crops. Fix a dozen things around the house that needed fixing. He even planned to take the kids fishing some cool Saturday.

With the extra money coming in from boarding the horses, he might have a few thousand to put back for hard times.

When he reached the bench where he'd talked to Adalee that night, he stopped for a few minutes. He could remember every moment they were together, but he couldn't see one minute of a future. She'd been little more than a stranger, but she'd held his hand the night of his birthday when he'd felt so alone.

Jesse walked back to his pickup. It was still too early to collect the kids. The grandmothers both had their routines. Granny George usually had a game or art project waiting. Sometimes they cooked or formed a band using kitchen pots. On Grandma May's days it was always snacks, juice, and cartoons. Whoever's day it was didn't matter, if Jesse got there too early he'd have to wait until grandmother time was over.

The little town seemed so peaceful in the stillness. He thought about stopping back by the bakery, but he didn't want to see Adalee's replacement again. So, he drove over to the Dairy Queen and bought a root beer. While he drank he ate one bag of the donut holes, and he hated donut holes.

Finally, it was almost time to pick up the kids.

Jesse had to time it just right. Too early and he'd be part of their grandmother time. Too late and the kids would be tired and whiny. So he decided he'd just drive by the bakery again. Wouldn't do any harm to glance in to see if Adalee was back.

The sign in the window had been flipped to CLOSED and all the blinds were shut. That worried him.

He drove to the side street, parked, and walked into the alley. It looked so plain and ugly in the daylight. At night it seemed mysterious.

Jesse knocked on the back door Adalee had disappeared behind that night he'd walked her home.

No answer. He knocked a bit louder. No answer.

Then he heard the tap of feet. The door opened. For a moment all he saw was Adalee crying. Big tears were drifting down her pretty round cheeks.

Jesse had no idea what to say. As he had before with Adalee, he simply reacted. Stepping inside, he wrapped his arms around her and held her tight. She didn't say a word, but her tears puddled on his shoulder.

When she pushed a few inches away to blow her nose, she made a hiccup laugh and said, "I'm a mess."

He patted the side of her hair, which seemed to have gone wild. "Yes, you are."

That made her laugh more. "Just my luck, I found an honest man."

She had on an old, faded sweatshirt that hung off one shoulder, and baggy pants. He had no idea if she was wearing clothes or pajamas. He didn't care.

"You all right?"

She shook her head. "I don't want to talk about it. The crisis is over, but I can't stop crying."

Jesse just stood there. Was she over whatever problem existed, if she was crying? Did she want him to ask again? Should he leave?

He patted her on the shoulder.

"You want a cup of coffee?" she finally asked.

"Sure."

As she made coffee, she stopped crying. "My little sister tried to run away again."

"How old is she?"

"Fifteen. She's hated this town since the day we moved here."

"How . . ."

She stopped him with one hand up like a traffic cop. "She's all right. I don't want to talk about it. She's upstairs with her door locked now. She claims she's going to run again as soon as she can. She hates the town, the school, having to live in the back of a bakery, and me."

"What does she like?"

"Watching TV. Making my life hell." Adalee frowned. "She loves animals, but I can't have pets in a bakery."

Adalee set the cups on the table. When she took the chair next to him, her leg bumped his knee.

The cloudy day made him think it was almost twilight. With a smile, he bumped her back. They both smiled.

"Maybe my sister and I should both calm down. I'll try to talk to her later," she added. "Why'd you come by, Jesse?"

"I just wanted to see you." It wasn't much of a reason, but it was the truth.

He couldn't think of any advice to offer. He thought about how upset he'd be if he didn't know where one of his kids was. "I'm sorry. I'd probably cry if one of my kids ran off."

She smiled, and he knew she was doing that thing again. She was seeing him, really seeing him. "Her name is Starlett. Star for short. I was almost fifteen when she was born, and I thought Mom had her just for me to play with. My folks ran a bakery in New Orleans, and I spent more time with Star than our parents did put together."

Jesse sat at the little kitchen table and didn't talk. He looked around, surprised how small and plain her kitchen was. Then he realized she probably never cooked in here. She had a bakery out front.

Her tears dried and she said, "Sorry you found me like this. You've visited on the one day I'm falling apart."

"You want to talk about it?"

"No. Not anymore. I'll just cry again."

"You're a hard woman to get to know, Adalee."

"All women are hard to know if they are worth the knowing."

She refilled their coffee and both relaxed in silence. He liked watching her, talking to her. Some men think women are the most beautiful when they're all dolled up with makeup and fancy hair. But he liked them natural. No makeup. Hair wild. Cheeks still wet with tears. She was a beautiful woman and didn't seem to know it.

"Would you mind if I kissed you again sometime?" He thought of adding that it had been a long time since he'd kissed a woman, but he didn't want to hear himself say the words.

"I wouldn't mind, but I'll need a minute."

She was halfway up the stairs before he realized she was leaving him. For her, *sometime* must have meant *right now*.

Jesse drank his coffee and waited. In a few minutes he heard her coming back. Just before she touched the last step, she hesitated.

It looked like she'd washed her face and tried to comb back her hair. She was wearing the same soft comfortable clothes. Touchable clothes, he thought.

Jesse walked up to her and took her hand in his. He tugged her down the last step and stared at her. Everything about her fascinated him. She had light green eyes that seemed to look deep inside him, as if she could see all the way to his soul.

He noticed her full lips. The need to push his mouth against them was strong. He didn't know if what he was doing was right or wrong, but he'd asked if he could kiss her again and she'd said yes.

He gently placed her hand behind her waist, drawing her against him. Her clothes were so soft against him, and what was beneath her clothes felt even softer. She was full breasted, turning him on as she leaned against him.

Digging his free hand into her hair, he brought her

mouth to his and thought that kissing her seemed the most natural thing in the world to do. They matched perfectly when he lowered his head slightly and she lifted hers, as if offering up those full lips for him to taste.

This was no hard-and-fast kiss like they'd had in church. This one was slow tasting. He moved both of his hands to the middle of her back and hugged her closer until he felt the heat of her body warming him. The fullness of her breasts on his chest made him heighten the kiss. She felt so good against him. He'd been flying blind for so long, and suddenly he'd found a safe landing.

As he deepened the kiss, she followed him into passion just as he hoped she would.

When she tugged to free her hands from his, he held tight. "I don't want you to touch me. I'm afraid I'd shatter. Just let me hold you for one more minute."

"Take all the time you want," she whispered against his ear, "but keep kissing me. I like the way you make love with only a kiss. It's like you're starving and I'm your only satisfaction." She melted against him and he sighed.

She smiled, obviously knowing what she was doing to him. "I don't need my hands to touch you, Jesse." Her lips moved across his face to his mouth. Words tickled his lips. "I can touch you every time I breathe."

Then she proved it as he tasted her throat. She pressed against him with each breath. The sensation made him feel half drunk.

As the kiss deepened once more, he let go of her hands and touched her bare shoulder. Slowly, like a man molding clay into perfection, he moved his hands down her body, over the soft shirt, memorizing every curve.

When he lightly brushed over the side of her breast,

she made a little sound and he knew he was doing something right. She was welcoming him.

"You like that?" He smiled as his fingers made the journey along the side of her breast again.

The tiny sound she made was all the answer he needed.

She pulled away a few inches and leaned her back against the wall. He felt for a moment that she was giving him a great gift. His hands grew bolder as she rested her head back so he could kiss his way down her throat.

He slid his hand beneath the soft material of her shirt and lightly moved his knuckles beneath her free breasts. "You want this?" he whispered as he moved an inch higher.

"Yes," she whispered back, then made that little sound of pleasure before she kissed him deeply while his fingers covered one breast as his palm took the weight of perfection.

She didn't hold him except to kiss him as completely as he kissed her. She gave in to his touch. Letting him learn her body. Rewarding him when he slowed long enough to whisper in her ear.

He'd never kissed so deeply or with such a hunger. For this moment in time, she was his. All he didn't know about her didn't matter. All he wanted was her near.

When he finally pulled away to let them both breathe, he didn't stop touching her. Her eyes were closed. Her mouth slightly open as if waiting for his next kiss. And best of all, her body moved slightly with each brush of his fingers.

As his hand tightened around one mound, he whispered against her ear, "I want more of you. I need more."

She let out a sigh of pleasure. Smiling, he pressed against her ear once more. "You feel like you are paradise in my arms."

When he returned to her lips, to his surprise, Jesse felt her deep hunger for more.

"I've never felt this . . . I've never lost control . . ." she whispered.

"Me either. Not like this." Love had always been a gentle summer rain, but this was more a raging storm sweeping both of them into deep water.

For one long minute they just held each other, then she slowly moved away. Sadness brushed her eyes, maybe fear, definitely longing.

She stepped up two stairs. "I know you have to go."

Reason registered, replacing passion with reality. "I do." For the first time he heard the kitchen clock ticking, as if time had stood still for one beautiful moment and now had to catch up. "I have to be somewhere."

"I understand, but when or if you come again, ask for what you want so we won't waste time. Then when I say it's time for you to go, you must leave."

He was halfway across the kitchen when she added, "Agree?"

It seemed a strange thing to say, but he nodded. "You do the same. Ask for what you want."

"I will not have to ask, Jesse. You've already given me what I wanted . . . what I needed." She smiled. "The best kiss ever."

When he started to say more, she turned and disappeared in the bend halfway up the stairs.

Jesse backed away and silently walked to his truck. Part of him wanted to run and never come to her door again. He'd never felt so out of control, and he feared he might not be able to give her everything she wanted.

Another part of him wanted to go back inside and say

that he wanted more, much more. He'd take all she wanted to give.

He'd given up trying to figure out which one of them started this. Now he was wondering which one's daydream they were playing out. His or hers.

He'd never tell anyone what had just happened. No one would believe him. Part of the time, he wasn't sure he believed it himself.

As he drove home after picking up the kids, he tried to figure out what this was between him and the baker. It wasn't an affair. They weren't dating. Most of the time she didn't even want to talk. Were they closer to being lovers than friends?

But she said so much without talking when she moved her body against him. As long as she didn't stop, he wouldn't care if they never talked again.

Maybe they were just two rabbits who bumped together in a field.

Chapter 26

Marcie

After filling out an application for a dispatcher position in Honey Creek, Marcie walked out of the sheriff's office. Deputy Rip Carter, who helped her through the whole process, told her the sheriff said she'd be coming in. She didn't know if that was a good sign or a bad sign.

When she left, the deputy waved and said, "I'll be seeing you."

She drove back to Brand's place with a six-pack of beer to thank him. It wasn't much for all he'd done, but she wanted to give him something.

He smiled one of his rare smiles and said, "Thank you," then helped her get Wayne's car back to the bar in Someday Valley. She'd taken the rancher home in her car, which was running like it was new, then she'd circled back to the trailer park and packed.

She had lived in the trailer park for as long as she could remember, but as she filled one suitcase she realized there was very little she wanted to take. A doll she'd loved at five. A few outfits and a picture of her father. He hadn't been much of a dad, but he'd stayed, and that was more than her mother had done.

Marcie left everything else. If her brother came home, he could have it all.

When she was packing a few blankets in the car, Joey walked by, carefully keeping his distance. His arm was in a cast and one of his eyes was still swollen closed. A bandage covered what was left of his ear, and his lip was busted. He had so many bruised spots he looked like he had blue chickenpox. He was a strange color, with orange-red hair, blue patches, and mud-spotted clothes.

"You moving out, Marcie?" he called.

She acted like she didn't hear him.

He didn't come closer but he yelled louder. "I came over to tell you I'm real sorry about the other night. I'd been drunk all day and my brain wasn't thinking straight."

"Your brain hasn't worked in years, Joey. Go away."

One look told her he probably was sorry, but she didn't care. "Stay away from me from now on."

"I ain't coming any closer. You don't have to worry about that. After I saw what your boyfriend did when we all attacked him, I'd hate to imagine what he'd do to me one-on-one. You tell him I just thought we were coming to party, nothing more."

She thought of telling Joey that Brand wasn't her boyfriend, but she decided to let the lie remain.

"You know me, Marcie. I get drunk and don't know what I'm doing. How about we agree on no hard feelings?" He lifted his arm out from his body. "I got the worst of it. It'll be six weeks or more before I can work, even if I did have a job."

Marcie finally turned and faced him. "You are lucky my boyfriend didn't kill you all. I suggest if you ever see him or me again you walk the other way. Fast."

Joey paled, making his bruises look darker. He turned and limped away, mumbling about how life never gave him a break.

She watched him go and smiled. She'd stood up to Joey. She felt a bit stronger. After climbing into her car, she drove slowly through the trailer park, remembering how people used to have flower gardens in front of their homes and colorful lawn chairs so they could visit with neighbors. The kids couldn't wait for the pool to open the first day of summer break. On hot nights all the children would get together and play kick-the-can, and as it got late you could hear mothers calling their kids in.

Like an apple rotting in the sun, the place had slowly deformed.

When had it changed? What day had it gone from safe to twisted? Where had the grass gone that used to crowd the roads? When had the potholes and trash taken over?

All her childhood hadn't been bad, but it was time to put it aside. She'd sleep somewhere else tonight, even if it was in her car. Marcie no longer wanted to belong to this place.

When she turned out of the park, she noticed the little picnic table someone had put out in the open field beside the park when she was a kid. It didn't seem to belong now. Maybe it had been set up to invite travelers into the park, but as far as she knew she'd been the only one to go there.

Someone had planted grass in a ten foot square around the table. Now the grass had spread all the way back to the tree line.

As a kid she'd come out to the table to play. She and her doll had had tea many afternoons when the shade spread over them from the trees. Sometimes she'd crawl under the table and it would become her own little house. In her teens she'd sit for hours and write her thoughts down. Once she'd planted wildflowers all around the table. They still bloomed every spring.

When she was afraid or broken, she'd come out to this one beautiful place to be alone. She'd watch the cars going by and pretend she was leaving. Leaving and never coming back.

Like today, she thought. Funny, the only thing she'd miss from this place was a spot of grass in a place where the valley looked all beautiful, all peaceful. A place for pretending.

As she drove back to Honey Creek, she passed the road that turned off to Brand's ranch. Part of her wanted to go back there. He'd welcome her, but she had to stand on her own for a while. She was tired of being shattered then broken again before old wounds healed.

As she moved toward Honey Creek, invisible bricks seemed to fall off her shoulders. No matter what happened next in her life, it had to be better. She wouldn't move her past this time. She'd leave it behind.

Her phone rang.

"Hello."

"Marcie Latimer, this is Deputy Rip Carter, who took your application."

"Did I forget something?"

"No, miss. I'm calling to tell you that you need to show up for training as soon as possible. The sheriff wants Pecos to train you. Then you'll take over the midnight-to-eight shift two nights a week, plus cover for the gaps in the schedule. The dispatcher, Wanda, who had the night shift when Pecos wasn't working it, just quit."

"That was fast. Pecos said Wanda only finished her training two months ago. I'm surprised she didn't last longer." Marcie considered this job might be harder than she'd thought.

"I'm not," Rip answered. "Old Jones Whicker calls every week with his newest obscene call. Wanda hadn't had much sleep 'cause of her twins being sick. She cussed him out and walked away. When she was walking through the office, she was yelling she had to put up with enough shit at home."

Marcie didn't know what to say.

The deputy added, "It's my opinion that women who have babies two at a time tend to be a bit sensitive."

"Thanks for calling. I can start training tonight. Is that okay?"

"I'll let the sheriff know. Don't forget to clock in."

"I will." She didn't ask what the pay was. It didn't matter. She had a real job. A job that paid her for eight hours twice a week. With the two nights of helping out at the bar, she might just make it.

Now she had to find a place to live. The chicken farm had been her first choice two days ago, but then she heard that Mr. Winston might let her stay at his big house. She'd sleep in the attic if he had a bed up there.

When she got to Mr. Winston's house, no one answered the front door. She went around to the side.

Again no answer, but there was a note taped to the window. It read, *Gone to talk to the mayor, W.*

Marcie waited awhile, then decided to walk toward city hall. Maybe she'd run into him coming home.

She made it to the first floor of city hall, where everyone pays their traffic tickets and votes on election day. No Mr. Winston. He might be four floors up with the mayor. Maybe she should wait down here in the huge lobby where people crisscrossed from one office to another.

She blinked, letting her eyes adjust to the shadows after the sunlight. For a moment she thought a bald man five feet away looked familiar, then she remembered him. He'd been with Joey that night. The loudest one. The oldest.

She took a step backward, but he saw her before she could disappear behind a column.

"Marcie, isn't it." It was a statement, not a question.

The one man that Brand had not touched had bruises on his face and what looked like a slash on his neck that ran from just below his ear to his collar. It had to be from when he fell over Joey. Both men had hit the cinder-block steps hard that night.

She turned away. Of all the men who came to party, he was the worst. He hadn't seemed drunk, and from his harsh words she knew exactly what he planned to do once they got into her trailer.

Marcie wouldn't turn around now. She wouldn't look at him. Maybe he'd go away. There were too many people around. He wouldn't dare touch her.

She could feel the heat of his breath against the back of her neck.

In a low voice, he said, "Tell that giant who attacked us that me and the boys have been talking. He's going to pay for what he did. All of us have scars and pain from him crashing our party. He won't stand so tall when a chainsaw accidentally cuts him down to size. It'll take a while for him to bleed out, and I plan to make sure my face is the last one he sees. I've been pushed around enough. This time I'm fighting back."

Marcie still didn't look at the man. She never wanted to see him again. Just knowing he was near now would haunt her dreams.

She started shaking as tears dripped unchecked down her face.

In a whisper he added, "When we finish with him we plan to visit you. You won't fight much when you're tied to the ground back in those trees behind your trashy trailer. We'll make sure to go far enough into the trees that no one will hear your screams. And, trust me, you will scream."

His laugh was hard and loud, then his words came low and harsh. "I'll be the last to take a turn with you. You'll be tired of screaming by then and the fight will have been beaten out of you. So, I'll have to cut that soft skin of yours just enough that you'll bleed and beg me to stop. Before I'm ready to have fun, you'll be covered in your own blood. It'll be warm when I smear it all over you. After a while you won't mind it. You might even stop trying to scream, but that won't keep the cuts from slicing deeper." He laughed a hard bark of a laugh then added, "You want me to tell you where I like to cut first?"

There wasn't enough air in the huge foyer. Marcie began to rock back and forth, trying not to faint. Trying to move away. Trying to survive.

He was so excited he almost giggled. "I love the smell of blood."

Someone called her name from the second floor landing, but she couldn't move.

She heard his footsteps moving away, then a side door open and close, but she remained still. Afraid to look. Afraid to hope he was gone.

When a hand touched her shoulder she let out the beginning of a scream. Then gulped it down as Piper Mackenzie moved in front of her.

"Marcie. Are you all right?" Piper asked in a worried voice. "No. You're not all right."

Marcie made a little nod, then kept nodding as if she had no way to stop.

Piper put her arm around her friend and walked her to the elevator. Marcie was still nodding when Piper sat her down on the couch in her office and grabbed a coat from a hook behind the door. "You look like you could be going into shock. Are you hurt? Has something terrible happened?"

"I'm not hurt," Marcie whispered.

Piper opened a door to the next room and said, "Autumn, hold all my calls, and would you please get me two cups of coffee?"

A voice beyond the door yelled, "I get coffee now? Since when?"

Piper looked back at Marcie, then ordered, "Since now. Tap on the door when you're back and I'll take them. And no one enters my office. No one."

Marcie took a long breath and finally uncoiled her hands. "I'm all right. I'm sorry I screamed. I don't mean to be any trouble."

"You're not. I saw you work the worst shift ever as a dispatcher and never even look panicked, which I was, several times during the storm. Whatever has upset you, Marcie, is real, and we're going to deal with it."

Piper pulled her chair around to face Marcie. "I saw that man talking to you. Did he frighten you?"

Marcie bowed her head for a moment, then looked up at her friend. She felt like the little kid alone on the playground again and Piper was waiting to help her.

They drank their coffee in silence, then Piper said, "Tell me what he said to you."

"I can't."

Piper took her hand. "I swear it will never go beyond this room if that's the way you want it. You're not alone. If I can't help, I'll cry with you, but I'm not going away."

Marcie set down her coffee and began. She told her the whole story from the time Joey talked to her at the bar to the bald guy saying what he planned to do to Brandon Rodgers. She said he sounded excited when he told of what he wanted to do to her.

Piper never let go of her hand.

"This is all my fault," Marcie whispered. "Because of me, they are going to hurt Brand."

Piper finally stood and paced. "We can go to the sheriff. He'd talk to them."

"I don't even know their names. Joey, I know, but he'll be too afraid to talk. I think some of them live in Someday Valley, but I'm not sure. I've just seen them around."

"What do you want to do?"

"I want to warn Brand."

Piper agreed. "As bad as what the bald man said was, the guy made a big mistake talking to you. He let us know his plan. We'll be ready if he comes. Promise me you won't go back home."

"I'm already packed. I'm never going back."

"Good," Piper said as she continued to pace. "Where are you staying?"

"I came here to find Mr. Winston and ask if I could rent a room. He mentioned that I could stay there."

"Great. I'm having lunch with him. Let's go. I'm not leaving your side until I know you are safe."

Marcie went to the restroom to wash her face and Piper told her secretary she might be gone the rest of the day.

Thirty minutes later, when they were eating chicken salad at the Honey Creek Café, they made all the plans. Marcie could stay in a downstairs room of Mr. Winston's home. It had a little parlor off the bedroom and a very small bathroom. The water didn't work in the back of the house, but Piper said she knew someone who could fix it before dark.

Mr. Winston didn't ask any questions, but Marcie saw his wise eyes. He knew she was troubled. The kindness in him wouldn't let him turn her away. "Can you cook, Miss Marcie?" he asked when Piper stepped onto the café's porch to call the plumber.

"I can. Simple things."

"That's wonderful, dear. I was thinking of offering a simple dinner each weeknight. If you'd be able to cook for four or five people three nights a week, there would be no extra charge on your rent, for food. Now I'm renting rooms, I find I love inviting people in to eat."

"I'd love to cook."

He stood and insisted on picking up the check. "Will you be moving in today?"

"I'd like to. I'm working tonight." After her first

night of work, she'd love walking back to his place and dropping into bed.

"That will be grand. We'll talk later about the meals." He handed her a key that looked like it might be older than she was.

Mr. Winston left as Piper returned, saying the plumber was on his way.

The two friends decided to order dessert. "You'll be safe there," Piper commented.

Marcie answered, "I hope so." She wanted to believe it, but deep down she knew evil would come. Even if they didn't kill Brand. Even if she moved. Even if the other men didn't go along with his plans.

The evil man would be coming to cut her, just to hear her scream.

Tuesday

Chapter 27

Colby

"Hey, McBride, is there any chance you just heard what I said?" Texas Ranger David Hatcher asked as he kicked Colby's desk.

They'd signed on within a week of each other and had become close friends. When you're sloshing through tons of paperwork and getting every dirty job no one else wants to do, it helps to have a buddy in the mud with you.

"Nope," Colby answered honestly. "Did I tell you about my weekend? Worst one ever, even worse than the ones I barely remember in college."

"Yeah," David said with a groan. "You've told me about five times, and it's not even lunch. With my luck you'll write a book about it and beat me over the head with the hardback."

Colby smiled for the first time since he left Honey Creek. "How about we go have a few drinks after work and I'll tell you again."

"You buying, McBride?"

"I'm buying. Beer and wings."

"Then I'll come, but you've got to keep the drinks coming as long as you're whining."

"I wasn't whining. I just don't understand why she'd stay with her grandmother and a bunch of widows when she could have slept with me. You ever notice women don't think like men do? I've given up even trying to follow their squirrel-trail logic."

"Yeah, if they thought like most men, we'd all be living in caves and hunting food with clubs. I'm telling you, Colby, no man in the history of the world has ever said, 'Let's move, honey, get a bigger place that costs twice as much and needs fixing up and painting and has three times the yard to mow every Saturday.'"

"Since you got married you've become a sage, Dave, my man."

Dave leaned closer, forgetting the paperwork they were supposed to be finishing up. "Then I'll give you some advice. Send that mayor flowers and sign the card, 'I'm sorry.'"

"But I'm not the one who did anything wrong. I had been up all night and all day, but I was still willing to sleep with her."

The seasoned ranger who'd been stuck with the two newbies close to her desk finally interrupted. "I hope you two are not thinking of breeding. I'd hate to think your kind of philosophy might spread."

Ranger Sandy James pointed her pen at Dave. "But

Hatcher, that idea of sending flowers was a good one. Men should always apologize after any argument. Nine times out of ten, it's their fault anyway."

Colby kept his mouth shut, but Dave dove in. "How do you know? You're not married."

She hit back. "That's right, David. I dated too many guys like you two. If my common sense is the reason mankind dies off, so be it."

They all laughed. Sometimes their jobs could be intense, and picking on each other eased the load.

Colby's cell rang. He took a quick look at his phone. "I got to take this," he said as he rushed into the hallway for a bit of privacy.

As the door closed, he heard Dave say, "Bet you five it's the mayor."

Ranger Sandy James shook her head. "No doubt. No bet."

Colby moved into the stairwell. "McBride speaking. I mean hello, Piper." She'd never called him at work, and after their last words a day ago he doubted she'd ever call again.

"I'm calling about a legal question."

He relaxed a bit. Answering a question about the law would be much easier than talking about them as a couple. "At your service, Mayor."

"If you had a friend who said she heard a man talk about a crime he was going to commit, say he said he was going to kill a man, are you legally obligated to inform the police, or in my place, the sheriff?"

Colby needed to break her question down. "Did you hear the man say he was planning a crime?"

"No. He whispered it to my friend."

"Did the person who told you what this man said know the potential victim of the crime?" Colby felt like he was trying to solve a code.

"Yes, but she didn't know the guy who said he was going to kill a local rancher, Brandon Rodgers."

Colby shifted his phone to his other ear. "PJ, just tell me what you know and then I'll know what we're really talking about. If it's a crime I can take action. If it's not, I'll try to help you deal with the problem. Start with who is making threats."

"I can't. This guy was bald, skinny, and looked like a bum. That's all I know. No name. This bald guy told my friend he was going to kill her after he killed Brand, so that's two crimes. What do I do?"

"You saw the bald guy?" Now Colby was full into details.

"Yes, but I don't think he saw me. I didn't know him. I don't think I've ever seen him, but I'd know him if I saw him again. He's one of those creeps who makes a woman hold her purse closer and walk faster. I was on the second-floor balcony looking down. I saw both him and Marcie. He was standing behind her, whispering what he'd do to her. By the time I got to her she was shaking and snow white. He was gone."

"Where are you right now?" Colby's heart was pounding.

"I'm in my office."

"Good. Stay there. I need to get to my desk. I'll call you back in five."

"All right. I swore to my friend I wouldn't tell anyone. So unless I legally have to, I can give you no details." The phone went dead without even a goodbye.

Colby leaned against the cold brick wall and tried to

slow his heartbeat down. Some man had threatened one of her friends and Piper had seen the man doing it. That could mean, if the man was serious, Piper might be in danger. Although Piper said her friend told her what the guy said, she had no firsthand knowledge of any crime. She might be safe.

Loving a woman like Piper Jane Mackenzie was like running live shooter drills in double time.

He pounded the back of his head against the wall. He'd used the L-word. Wrong. Once any man says that word, the woman starts planning the wedding. Colby had been too close to that trap before. He didn't have time for any complication in his life, worst of all falling in love with a small-town mayor. He'd finally gotten to the place he'd always dreamed of being in his life, and nothing was going to slow him down.

When he got back to the office, Dave and Sandy were gone. *Routine follow-up on a case* was written on a note taped to Colby's office phone. *Be back in a few hours. Hold down the fort.*

Colby spent a few minutes checking his facts before he called Piper back. She answered on the first ring. "PJ, you've got to tell me the whole story. Think of me as your priest. I'll never tell anyone unless it's a matter of life or death."

"I can't think of you as my priest. First, I'm Methodist and second, I've seen you naked."

"Mayor, focus here. If I'm going to help you and your friend, I'll need facts." In his mind he could see her pouting. That cute bottom lip sticking out as she paced her tiny office as if her brain didn't work unless her feet were moving. She'd have her shoes off and maybe her jacket. Man, those silk blouses she wore showed off every curve.

Focus! He silently yelled at himself. *Focus.*

When she didn't say anything on the other end of the phone, he began in a very official voice. "As to the question of whether to report what a friend told you. No. You don't have to report it. Your friend, the one who was threatened, could report it, but all that would happen would probably be a restraining order, and she'd have to be the one to file it."

When Piper didn't answer, Colby figured getting information out of her would be like interrogating a carrier pigeon. She was twice as smart as he was and knew the law. So why had she called him?

The answer hit him hard. Mayor Piper Mackenzie needed him. Both her brothers were rangers. Her dad was a lawyer and a state senator.

But she'd called him. When she was scared and worried, she called him.

Her voice finally came through the line, confirming his reasoning.

"Tell me what to do, Colby. I have to help my friend."

"If I were you, I'd make sure your friend is safe. Anger usually blows over, and people who get mad are usually mad at the world. Maybe all the guy wanted to do was frighten her. People like him usually find someone else to harass after a few days or a few drinks."

He hesitated, then asked, "Are you all right? Are you sure he didn't see you? Do you want me to come home?"

Hell! He almost said it aloud. Why did he call Honey Creek home? He'd never lived there. It wasn't his town. He lived in Austin.

"I'm sure he didn't see me. He was out the door by the time I got to Marcie. I'm worried. I want to do something to help and no, you don't have to come home. I want to find a way to help Marcie. I'm worried about them. Brand is a loner, a rancher whose family has lived in the valley as long as mine has. I don't know him well, but I've never heard any bad gossip about him."

"Tell me the facts, PJ."

The line was silent for a moment, then she started. "This guy said he'd kill Brand. Make him bleed out slow, and then he'd torture Marcie with knife cuts where no one would see while he raped her. He said he'd leave her weak from loss of blood, but he'd let her live so he could come back for seconds." Piper took a long breath. "If you could have seen her eyes, Colby, you'd know she was frightened. She believed what the creep said."

"Why Marcie? Why Brand?"

"She told me a few nights ago this guy and a few of his buddies decided to have a little fun with her. But she wouldn't unlock her door. Brand Rodgers came by and broke up their plans."

Colby wanted to hold Piper right now. Her voice was shaking and he knew her whole body was too. She'd used nice words but he knew exactly what the men had planned.

Colby keyed in Brandon Rodgers on his office computer. Simple law-abiding citizen. Fourth generation on the same land. No arrest record, not even a parking ticket.

The ranger flipped photos. Nowadays people had pictures on the internet that they didn't even know were there.

He paused at one, staring.

He recognized Brand Rodgers's face. He'd seen him somewhere before. Colby tried to pull the memory out. Three years ago. He'd been a trooper then, answering a call for backup at the end of a long shift. Two rival drug gangs were fighting it out in a warehouse on the east side of Austin. Colby was just told to secure one back entrance. As he waited by a back gate a few hundred yards from the now quiet building, one lone man walked out of the loading dock entrance. Tall, lean, with wide shoulders.

Colby watched the guy. He came right toward Colby as if he was out for a stroll. As he moved, he tossed off his vest and his shirt. Colby clicked on his headlights, pulled his service weapon, and stood ready behind his open car door.

The man looked as solid as if he'd been chiseled.

When the lights flashed on the stranger's bare chest, the man raised his arms, indicating he was not armed. As he drew nearer, one fact surprised Colby. The stranger showed no fear.

"Stop right where you are," Colby ordered.

"Will do," the man answered as he raised his hands higher. "I'm not armed, Trooper. I don't plan to cause you any trouble."

From nowhere a black Lincoln pulled up, sending dirt flying. Four men in suits hurried out. One flashed a badge and told Colby to stand down. Another walked slowly to the stranger and handed him a black windbreaker. The stranger lowered his hands, gave a quick salute to Colby, and disappeared into the back of the black car.

As three of the suits climbed back into the car, the fourth walked toward Colby. The Lincoln and the stranger disappeared into the night.

The one left behind walked over to Colby. "Any chance you could give me a ride, Trooper?"

"What just happened?" Colby holstered his weapon.

The suit moved toward the passenger door. "You just saw a legend. A ghost. On the way back I'll explain why you didn't see anything at all, if anyone asks."

Colby had looked for the stranger after that night. Tall, built solid, like the guy was all muscle, but he carried his body light. A plain face not many would remember. Someone, if you passed on the street, you wouldn't notice.

Now Colby had a name to go with the stranger's face. The legend. A ghost, and he lived in the same valley as Piper. She'd given him a name. Brandon Rodgers. A rancher who'd never had a parking ticket but somehow worked for the government. A lone ranger, Colby thought.

Piper's voice came through the line a bit panicky. "Colby, you still there?"

Into the phone he said almost calmly, "Keep a close eye on Marcie and don't worry about Brandon Rodgers. Trust me, he can take care of himself."

"But—"

"No buts. If this creep visits Brand, he'll be the one to die." Colby had to think fast. "He's a cowboy, PJ. If he can throw a wild, half-grown calf, surely he can handle a skinny drunk guy who goes around frightening women."

"Thanks, Colby. You've made me feel better."

Colby gripped the phone hard. "I'm sorry you had this happen, but I'm glad you called me. I was going to call you tonight. I don't know what happened between us last weekend. Maybe worrying about the storm and no sleep had something to do with it, but whether we're over or you want to step away for a while, I need to say something. I'm sorry."

The line was silent and he'd have to abide by whatever she said.

"Come home," she whispered. "We'll talk."

"I'll be there by dark, Friday."

She hung up without another word, but he hung on to the phone for a while. Then he smiled and called the Honey Creek florist. A dozen yellow roses would be on her desk in an hour.

Chapter 28

Marcie

Marcie spent twenty minutes moving into the small quarters behind the kitchen in Mr. Winston's house. She guessed the room had been a maid's quarters years ago. There was a little seating area with two beautiful old chairs and a tiny table between them, a bathroom with a big claw-foot tub, and a nice bedroom. Best of all were the high windows, too small for anyone to break and crawl through. She would be safe here.

Mr. Winston had explained that he always locked all the doors at sunset. She'd have her own key if she needed in, and he'd leave the porch light on for her. Plus she had a lock on her door. If for any reason she was afraid, just use the broom to bang on the ceiling and he'd come down.

She hadn't said anything about being afraid, but Marcie guessed the old man could read people about as easy as Charlotte Jordan from the flea market could read palms.

After Marcie was settled in and had paid her first month's rent, she decided to go out to Brand's place and warn him. The idea of him living out there all alone frightened her. Men could sneak up on him, ambush him, and leave him for dead. If they brought weapons, it wouldn't be a fair fight.

Maybe the bald man had simply wanted to frighten her. He'd done a good job of that. He probably figured if she told anyone, it would just be her word against his, and everyone knew she was a con's girlfriend. No one would believe her. He could say he was just joking around like people do.

She couldn't protect Brand, even though it was her fault he was mixed up in this. All she could do was warn him.

The day was growing cold as she drove out to his place, but she kept the window down in case panic visited her again. She parked in front of the house and hurried up the steps, surprised he hadn't met her at the door when he heard her drive up. Her light knock was met with silence.

No worries, she decided, he was working somewhere on his land, of course. She wasn't exactly sure what he did. Raise horses. Breed horses. Train horses. The man never talked.

Fifty yards away from his house was a huge barn surrounded on two sides by corrals. It had been built on an incline, making the front thirty feet tall and the back only fifteen. Marcie thought she heard music coming from the barn. Odd. She'd never heard him play music in his house or in the truck. Maybe he played it when he worked.

She followed a worn path in the grass and stepped through the back doorway of the barn. In front the barn had a thirty-foot ceiling with wide lofts built beneath the overhangs of the roof. By stepping in the back entrance, she found herself in the loft. Brand could easily haul in hay and supplies for the horses below.

She walked along the railing, looking down on the main part of the barn.

There were stalls for two dozen or more horses; most looked empty. Hay stacked above and beside the stalls. Near the front she saw what looked like a blacksmith forge and a tack room without a top, so she could look down and see saddles and all the gear he'd need.

At one time this ranch had been a huge operation, but now it must have hit lean times.

She could hear the music. Country. But she saw no sign of Brand. As she circled so she could see the other side, something strange came into view. First, she saw long racks of weights lined up like she'd seen in gyms. The equipment was orderly and formed a circle on a foot-high platform. This was heavy, expensive workout gear.

Then she saw Brand stripped to his waist and wearing tight shorts that went to almost his knees. His body looked carved in stone. Big, but toned like a runner. All muscle as he moved as fast and liquid as water. He worked hard, pushing himself. The day was cold, but she watched him wipe the sweat away as he moved from one piece of equipment to another.

For a few minutes all she saw was the beauty, the fluidity of his movements. He wasn't building his body up like a weightlifter. He was toning it as if it were a machine and needed to be in perfect working order.

Then, suddenly, as she studied him, she saw the scars. His back. His chest. His legs. All deep and jagged. Wherever he'd been, whatever he'd done, there had been pain involved. She had the feeling that sometime in his life Brand hadn't been the hero, he'd been the prey. She remembered someone saying he'd been in the service. Had he been in a battle?

For a while she stood perfectly still and watched him. When he put on gloves and began attacking a bag hanging in the center of the area, Marcie realized he could take care of himself. Four fools coming at him hadn't been a challenge.

As he moved around the outer circle, running, dropping to do sit-ups, jumping up to do pull-ups, boxing, kickboxing, she couldn't help but wonder why a small-time rancher would need this kind of training.

Suddenly the quiet cowboy didn't seem boring at all. When he darted down steps to a room near where the saddles were stored, he disappeared. She thought she heard a shower come on.

Marcie walked back around the loft and silently opened the door she'd come in. Retracing her path to the porch of his house, she tried to put all the pieces together. He'd said he'd grown up here. Someone had told her he'd been a Marine in his twenties. He kept to himself. But the scars? They spoke of so much more she didn't know about Brand Rodgers.

As Marcie stepped on the porch, she doubted the front door was locked. He wouldn't have minded if she'd gone inside to wait, but she wanted to stand in the fresh air and watch him walk toward her.

Ten minutes later when he came out of the barn dressed in jeans and a white shirt, he was back to being just a rancher. He saw her and waved, then jogged to the porch.

"This is a surprise." He calmly walked up the steps. "You want some supper? I've got a stew slow cooking that will be ready in a few hours."

"I came to take you out, if you're available. We have to eat early because I start training tonight. I got a job today and a new place to live. The rent was half what I thought it might be, so I thought I'd buy you supper." She was rattling. Knowing his secret made her nervous.

A slow smile spread across his face, making him look almost handsome. "You asking me out, Marcie?"

"I am."

He stood so still, she thought he might turn her down, then he took off his hat and said, "I'd be honored to go anywhere with you. You mind if I ask for something first?"

"Name it." She'd guess he wanted to know more about her new job or where she was living or even about how her car was running.

"I wondered, with this being a date and all, if I could have the good night kiss before we start. I might do something or say something wrong and I don't want to miss the last part of the date."

Marcie had slept beside the guy all night and he hadn't touched her, and now all he wanted was a kiss.

She moved in front of him, stood on her tiptoes, and smiled. "You got it."

The moment her lips touched his, Brand reacted. His arms circled her and he raised her off the ground. She felt like pleasure hit her full on. A tender kiss. Her body melting into his hard chest. The fresh smell of shampoo and shaving cream from his shower in the barn. The thrill of knowing how he looked without his clothes. And last, the knowledge that he liked her enough to want to kiss her.

She'd thought she was tough. She'd been around trouble most of her life. Men were hard to understand. They'd say anything to get what they wanted. A one-night stand. Her money. Sometimes her heart. But this man was so different.

Brand wasn't just some man kissing some woman. He was a gentle man who'd gone far beyond being kind to her. She had no doubt he'd been thinking about this one kiss for a long while, and she'd finally made the first move. For the first time she felt herself starting to believe in a fantasy. One good man.

Marcie relaxed and let the kiss carry her away. She wasn't sure what a perfect kiss would be, but this was as close to it as she'd ever had. The gentle way he held her made her feel cherished. The hunger in his kiss made her feel needed.

When he lowered her down to the ground, his hands lingered at her waist. She leaned her cheek against his chest. For a long while she just rested as she moved with his breathing. His hands traveled slowly up and down her back.

He wasn't pushing for more. He seemed to simply enjoy this moment.

Finally she pulled an inch away. "I was wrong to kiss you before the date."

The warmth in his gaze told her he'd loved the kiss as much as she had. "So, what do I do to correct the error?"

"You have to give the kiss back."

A smile spread across his face. "Fair enough."

She wouldn't have believed it, but his second kiss was better than the first. He was learning how she liked to be kissed. Deep and tender. She felt herself melting against him once more. The way he kissed wasn't just foreplay to the main event. This was pure satisfaction. Something full and complete all by itself.

She broke the kiss. "I could do this with you forever, but we have to talk."

He shook his head as if he planned to object.

"Brand, we have to talk."

He pulled her closer.

She smiled as if he were a defiant child. "I'll make you a deal. I haven't had breakfast or lunch. Let's eat dinner in Honey Creek and I'll give you one more kiss before I go to work, but until then we talk."

He nodded and let go of all but one hand. "I'll follow you into town so you don't have to bring me back. That will give us more time. I plan to walk you all the way to the sheriff's office."

As she waited for him to pull his pickup around, she tried to figure out how a quiet man who lived alone learned to kiss. She doubted an online class was available.

One other question lingered. Why would a small-time rancher need to keep in perfect shape? It felt almost as if he was preparing for a battle he knew would come someday.

Chapter 29

Colby

For a change, the office in Austin was quiet and Texas Ranger Colby McBride could comb through the files for answers, but Piper never left his mind. Maybe it was just coincidence that a man like Brand Rodgers lived near Honey Creek. He had to live somewhere, and it made sense that he'd keep a low profile. What better place than his family home. Colby had no idea exactly what Brand did. Maybe some kind of troubleshooter for the FBI, but Colby had seen the respect the suits paid him. Whatever he did, he did it well.

When the story of the warehouse shoot-out came out in the paper, there was no mention of a stranger being among the drug gangs.

Colby made a mental note to look up this Brand

Rodgers when he got back to Honey Creek. And he would be going back to Piper. Not because she needed him but more because she was part of him.

Friday seemed too far away, but Colby wasn't ready to bring in anyone else on the mayor's problem. He'd promised Piper, for one thing, and secondly, no crime had been committed. Even if Marcie went to the sheriff and filed a complaint on the thin guy, not much could be done. A restraining order, maybe a charge of harassment. But then it would be down to who said what. Her word against his, and she didn't even know his name.

As Colby left work for the day he called Piper. He wasn't surprised she was still in her office. The second she picked up he could see her in his mind.

"I'll be home in two more days," he said before she had time to even say hello. "I need to hold you. I'm worried about you."

"I'm fine, Colby. I'm staying at Widows Park. How could I be safer? I'm in the middle of my town." She hesitated and whispered, "But come."

"I'm sorry I didn't hold you before I left last week." Colby considered himself a fairly sensitive guy, but Ranger Sandy James told him a man has to tell a woman three times he's sorry before she believes him.

There was silence on the other end, then she whispered, "Maybe we moved too fast. Maybe we should back off a bit."

Her words hurt more than he expected they would, but now wasn't the time to talk about it. He'd thought the same way when he'd pulled out of Honey Creek Monday.

But not now.

He needed to be able to see her forest-green eyes when she said those words. He wanted to hold her close and know that she was safe, then he'd have time to straighten out what went wrong the night of the storm. It would probably frighten her if he told her now that he wasn't backing away.

"We'll talk about it Friday," he said. "I'm driving into traffic. I've got to go. I'll see you soon, PJ."

"All right," was all she said before the phone went dead.

Colby ordered his phone to call the fire station in Honey Creek.

Sam Cassidy answered, "Chief here. What's up, Colby?"

"Sam, would you mind going across the street and walking Piper home? It's probably nothing, but I'd like to make sure she's safe."

"Sure. Want to tell me what this is about?"

"I can't. I just need a favor."

"You got it, Ranger. I'll take my little redheaded wife along. If anyone bothers your girl, she'll talk them to death."

Sam laughed and Colby had no doubt Sam's bride was standing beside him. When the fire chief said, "Ouch, Anna," Colby knew his little wife was beating on him. They were an odd couple. She was a fireball and he was a fireman. A matched set.

"Thanks, to both of you." Colby smiled at the mention of Anna.

As Colby ended the call, he had a feeling he'd be apologizing later for asking Sam to help. Piper never thought she needed help. Maybe he'd save time if he just had a T-shirt painted *SORRY* and wore it anytime he was around Piper. Everything he said or did lately seemed to be wrong.

He'd known the moment he saw her that she was out of his league. She'd probably be governor one day. She was the whole package. Brains, beauty, and family money. Add a heart afraid to love and he had kryptonite to his career.

But, how could he stop loving her? It would be like forgetting to breathe.

Chapter 30

Jesse

Jesse did all the things he always did, being a dad, a son, a farmer, but Adalee and how she'd kissed was always thick in his thoughts. She'd said for him to tell her what he wanted. He had a feeling she wasn't talking about them going to a movie or him ordering scones from the bakery.

A man doesn't kiss a woman like the world is coming to an end any second, and then calmly ask her to dinner. His answer to her question was simple. He wanted her.

He'd always thought he was a smart man, but there was so much he didn't know about the world. Was the woman who bewitched him asking what he wanted as far as sex was concerned, or was she talking about being friends? If it was sex, he'd have to show her what he wanted. Some of those words he'd never said aloud.

He was an idiot. Women don't just ask what a man wants. She was probably talking about what he wanted to eat. She was a baker after all.

Jesse figured most men never get what they really want anyway. Or maybe women would be surprised what simple things men need. He didn't want to make love by the refrigerator light while they ate olives, like he'd seen a couple do in a movie once. He wanted to be in a warm bed. He wanted to make love and then hold her all night long.

He'd seen a few R-rated movies. The idea of tossing all the dishes and making love on a dining table left him wondering who would clean up the mess. Making love then pulling up the covers and cuddling seemed just right.

In Hollywood, couples might have wild, crazy sex, but marriages between stars have the shelf life of bananas. Here, in the quiet country air, most couples mate for life. Every Sunday he saw old people holding hands, walking through life together.

Did she want that? Probably not.

He'd planned that kind of life with Beth, but it wasn't meant to be. Maybe he should try something different. An affair with a woman he was attracted to, and she made a good cup of coffee. That might just have to be enough right now.

Problem was, how could he work an affair in? Between homework and baths? Not likely. As for work, he was always a week behind.

He decided he couldn't take away from those he loved

to make time for himself. He had no time he could call his own. He didn't even have time for dreaming most days.

Well, there was the meeting at the co-op every week. He might have to give up his one hour of social life to make room for his love life.

He shook his head. He was worrying about hail while the sky was clear. Adalee probably only meant friendship. If she had meant more, Jesse doubted one hour a week would do.

Chapter 31

Marcie

As the sun touched the horizon, Marcie drove back to Honey Creek, with Brand following in his big black pickup. Even though the sky looked the same, she felt the air was clearer. She'd finally quit feeling sorry for herself and changed some things in her life. Somehow she'd found a new start. She planned to make the most of it.

New place. New job. A new man who seemed good to her, but she'd never trust anyone completely again.

She thought about the kiss Brand had asked for before their date. Just thinking about it made her lips tingle. If he kissed like that, how would he make love?

She'd promised after her last boyfriend that she'd never sleep with a man who she didn't know completely. She knew Brand was kind, quiet, and polite. But there was so much more she didn't know. After seeing him work out, she feared he did much more for a living than just breed horses. No man would be in that kind of shape unless his life depended on it.

What if he'd been in prison and got in the habit of working out like that?

Maybe he was a hit man for the mob. Being a rancher could just be his cover. He could be into the drug trade, or he might be a spy. No one in the valley kept up with him. He could disappear and be gone for weeks. No, that wouldn't work. He showed up once almost every week to listen to her play.

Who knows? He could be one of those fighters they lock in cages to fight it out. But how could such a kind man be a fighter?

Another thing. He lived fifteen minutes from a gym. Why would he spend all that money to build his own gym with a shower room? He could have just walked across from the barn to the house to shower. Unless he needed to go into the barn in western clothes and come out the same way.

Brand pulled up behind her when they parked at Mr. Winston's place. Then they walked two blocks over to a popular bar where Marcie had once worked for a few months. This one street in Honey Creek had always been a bit dark, a bit shady. The sidewalks were broken in places and kids had written on the sides of buildings. The locals tended to come here for the food and the beer, but tourists never bothered.

Marcie circled one arm around his upper arm.

He smiled. "My koala bear is back."

When they got to the Pint and Pie Bar, it was noisy and crowded. Marcie didn't recognize the bartender or, thank goodness, anyone else in the bar. The pizzas looked great. Thick crusted, loaded with meat, then covered with cheese so high it ran off the crust when it melted.

The bartender raised his eyebrow when they both ordered iced tea with their large pizza. When he walked away, Marcie leaned close. "You can have a beer. I'm the one who has to go to work tonight."

His lips almost touched her ear as he answered, "I don't like beer."

"You are kidding. You order a beer every week while you listen to me sing."

"I come to see you, honey. I wouldn't order anything, but Wayne might kick me out."

Marcie laughed. "I'm finally learning something about you, Brand. Tell me more."

"There's not much to tell about me. Fill me in about this job you've landed. It sounds exciting. You get to know everything happening in the valley."

She told him details, including about how fun it was to sit beside Pecos when the calls came in. "People will be in trouble when they call, and it'll be my job to get help to them.

"But it's funny sometimes. The cat call made everyone in the office laugh, except the sheriff. While I was working, I felt like I was doing something good, something worthwhile. For the first time since I was in a band at eighteen, I was part of a team. It's boring when I have to study the book, but time flies when the calls start coming in."

"You do something good when you sing. There were weeks when I couldn't wait to see you again. Your music, your voice lets my soul rest."

She started to laugh, but his eyes told her he wasn't kidding.

When the pizza arrived she was telling him every word the sheriff said when he insisted she apply. "When I was in trouble once, he was hard on me, but he was never cruel. I always had something to drink, and he'd tell me to let him know if the questioning got too much for me. During those days, I was mad at the world, but I knew he was just doing his job."

The bar was getting louder. Some football game had started on the dozens of mounted TVs. They ate and talked with their heads close so they could hear. Marcie noticed a few people watching her, but Brand acted as if she was the only one in the room. She wished she could wrap her arms around his arm. She felt safe from any pain in the world with him so close.

When they walked out, the fresh air and silence felt grand. He took her hand and they walked without talking for a half block. She thought that they'd finally grown comfortable with each other. Men had always come and gone in her life. Not one stayed around long. Brand probably wouldn't either, but something about him settled her.

It felt nice when she shivered and he put his arm around her shoulders. When they crossed the street he switched to the outside, silently protecting her.

Almost to the town square, on a piece of sidewalk where no streetlight brushed their path, Brand tugged her toward him and kissed her lightly. When she didn't pull away he kissed her deeper and cocooned her in his arms. She felt warm and cared for, but this time she wouldn't let feelings get all mixed up with love. Her fairy tale never turned out "happily ever after."

She simply enjoyed him so close.

When he finally broke the kiss, he whispered, "I like kissing you."

"I like kissing you." What were they, in third grade? By the third kiss men were usually whispering what they planned to do to her as soon as they were alone with her.

"Don't go to work. Quit." Brand leaned down and whispered in her ear.

She laughed. "I can't quit yet. I haven't even started."

He kissed her throat and murmured, "When is your day off?"

"I don't know. I'm on the schedule for two nights, but I'm also willing to fill in for any of the others."

"All right. I'll call you tomorrow. You should be awake by the time I come in near dusk."

"You have a phone?"

"Sure. Somewhere."

She pulled away and took his hand, then gently tugged him along toward the sheriff's office half a block away. "Promise me you'll be careful." Marcie was afraid what Brand might do if he knew the bald man had frightened her. "Those drunks might decide to come after you."

"I doubt it. Men dumb enough to travel in packs usually aren't brave enough to hunt alone." He took a few steps and said, "Damn, I wish I had time to kiss you again."

"I should have warned you that I'm addictive."

"You are," he answered, as if he believed her.

When they reached the sheriff's office, Brand opened the door for her, and to her surprise he followed her in.

"Evening, Sheriff." Brand nodded a hello to LeRoy.

"Evening, Rodgers. Nice night."

"That it is," Brand said softly as his gaze studied her.

The desk phone rang and Brand winked at her as the sheriff rushed back to his desk.

Brand was leaving, closing the door behind him before the sheriff looked up.

Marcie waited for LeRoy to finish his call. She was not sure what to do. The chubby woman who worked afternoons at the dispatch desk wasn't due to leave until Pecos came in. Marcie thought her name was Daisy, and she had to be seventy at least.

When the sheriff finished his call, he showed her to an empty desk and handed her a manual to read. "Afraid our training program is mostly just reading this and watching Pecos. I don't want you to watch anyone else. You'll pick up bad habits." He looked toward the old woman. "When I started, I hired all young operators."

"What happened?"

"They all got old and cranky."

Before she could start reading, he said, "If you have any questions, just ask me or Pecos."

"Will do," she answered.

When he kept standing in front of her, she looked up. "Is there something else?"

"No, no," LeRoy answered. "I was just thinking, do you know Brand Rodgers? It almost looked like you two came in together."

"I do know him." She tried to start reading again, but he seemed nailed to the front of her desk.

"Anything else?"

"Not really. I was just curious if you're dating Brand?" LeRoy's serious look wrinkled the bottom half of his face.

She smiled. "We had our first date tonight. It was nice." She saw no point in lying, since half the town probably saw them at the bar. "Do you not like the idea of me dating him? Or, is your objection that he's interested in dating me?"

The deputy just beyond the open door yelled, "Before you two girls start talking about the prom, would you mind breaking it up so I can concentrate on my report?"

"Sorry." Marcie lifted the manual.

"Shut up, Rip." The sheriff stomped back to his desk.

Rip turned around to face her and grinned. She could tell he loved bugging the sheriff.

Marcie was beginning to think she was going to like working here. Two hours later when she got herself a cup of coffee, she took the sheriff one also.

"You don't have to do that," he grumbled. "But if you ever do it again, I like a bit of sugar."

"I'll remember that. I like a little cream."

The old guy toasted with his paper cup. "I'll remember that."

When Pecos rushed in thirty seconds before his shift started, he picked up a stack of papers off Rip's desk and darted into the dispatch room. Marcie followed with the manual. The real training was about to begin.

Daisy rambled out, still working on her crossword.

Pecos smiled. "Welcome to the nut house, Marcie. You're going to love the job."

Four hours later she'd read the entire manual. Pecos was studying an online class the sheriff had signed him up for. The 9-1-1 phone hadn't rung for over an hour. Marcie stared at the same page she'd been looking at for thirty minutes while she thought about Brand. There was so much about the man she liked and so much she didn't know.

Pecos glanced up and shrugged. "Sometimes the hardest part of this job is staying awake. Other nights you don't even get time to go to the bathroom. I like the busy nights because time flies. All of a sudden the next shift is coming in and you wonder why."

"Do you always study on the slow nights?"

"Yep. It's really the only time I have. When I get off, it's catch up on my sleep or drive Kerrie around, or on Saturdays go out to the bee farm and help old Grandpa Lane. He's a cool guy. Knows more about bees than anyone in the state.

"Kerrie can't go out to help her grandpa unless I tag along. She can't get behind the wheel of her little car anymore. We got a baby coming any day now. Seems like all I do lately is watch her incubate."

The phone rang. Pecos answered and started taking notes.

"Will do," he finally said and hung up. "Mind the store, Marcie. I have to give this to Rip."

She could barely hear them talking. Pecos said there was a wreck between Clifton Bend and Honey Creek, but still in the sheriff's county. Two state troopers were at the scene, but they needed a deputy to take care of a few drunks trying to direct traffic.

She thought she heard Rip cuss as his boots stomped toward the door.

When Rip reached for his coat, he turned and yelled, "If it's that one-winged Joey Hattly causing the trouble again, I swear I'm going to run over him on my way to the wreck."

Marcie fought down a giggle. If Joey was the town drunk in Clifton Bend, he was doing double duty.

She glanced at the huge wall clock. Three more hours and she could fall asleep. She couldn't remember how long it had been since she'd slept. She didn't care if her new bed was a rock, she planned to curl up and dream a while.

Half an hour later, Rip called in on the office line. The wreck was between two cars packed with teenagers. Four were not hurt, and one of the troopers was driving them to the sheriff's office so LeRoy could call their parents. Four were headed to the clinic with minor injuries, and two ran.

Pecos flipped the phone to speaker. Rip's voice came through loud and clear. "We've got our hands full with the ones in the back of our cars. When it settles down I'll circle back and pick up the runners. By then they'll be walking back to town freezing their tails off." He hesitated, then added, "Wake the sheriff. He'll want to call the parents."

"Will do," Pecos said.

About the time Rip hung up, two state troopers herded four yelling, cussing fifteen- or sixteen-year-olds into the office.

"Pick up the paperwork from the troopers and try to get them settled down before the sheriff gets here," Pecos said to her.

Marcie squared her shoulders and tried to act like she knew what she was doing. The paperwork was easy, but getting them to settle down was impossible. One was crying and kept saying her parents were going to kill her. Two boys were yelling at each other and one of the girls swore she had to have a smoke.

LeRoy's booming voice almost shattered the windows as he hit the door. "Quiet! I should be asleep but, no, I can hear you babies cussing from the parking lot. Thanks to you pups it'll be another hour or two before I can go back to sleep, so my patience is short. Shut up and sit down."

They all plopped down on the long bench and stared at the sheriff like he was mean as the devil.

LeRoy marched in front of them. "If you four don't remain silent, unless I ask you a question, I'll lock you up for the night. We only have the drunk tank available, and it hasn't been mopped. You'll be standing in ankle-deep vomit and piss till dawn." He pointed to the back door. "We haven't got anyone back there tonight, so no one has turned on the heat, but the rats never complain."

One of the two girls started crying. A boy who didn't look like he shaved yet threw up in the trash can.

The sheriff handed Marcie a clipboard. "Get their names, addresses, and parents' numbers. I'm about to ruin some folks' night." He looked at the four perched on a bench like crows on a line, but he spoke to the crying girl. "You four are the lucky ones. You're not at the clinic. It's a bloody mess over there."

Marcie remembered those wild high school days when she thought she was invincible.

As she moved down the line collecting information, she watched them lose their attitude as it sank into each one what had happened and what was about to happen when their parents arrived.

Only the last girl on the row remained silent. She looked angry.

"Your name?" Marcie asked.

"Star Summers."

"Address."

"I live behind the only bakery in town. At 101 Fourth Street."

"Parents' names?"

"They're dead. I live with my sister, Adalee Summers. She's going to be madder than hell, again. She screams and cries every time I do anything, but I know she doesn't want me around. She just got stuck with me."

Marcie knew how Star felt. She'd been that kid no one really wanted around.

Chapter 32

Colby

Colby stayed late at the office researching Brand Rodgers. Nothing. The man really was a ghost. He found a Honey Creek high school graduation picture. He'd been in ROTC in high school and joined the Marines after a year of college. He made about fifty thousand a year selling a special breed of quarter horses. That wasn't enough to keep a small ranch running, so Brand either had a trust fund or the guy had a business on the side. He had a few credit cards he never used except to buy books on the Internet.

Marcie, on the other hand, had lots on the Internet. In her early twenties she'd been in a band, even played at a few bars in Nashville. Her brother had been arrested a few times, but hadn't served any time. Her dad was dead and her mother's last address was in Denver. Not-so-dear-old mom had listed her occupation on an online dating site as bartender. Marcie's runaway mom had listed her age as forty-one, which would have made her ten or eleven when she had Marcie.

Brand and Marcie didn't go together. A loner with a military background and a singer whose last boyfriend was in jail.

Colby almost laughed. These two were even a worse match than he and the mayor were. The only thing the mayor and he had in common was work. They both loved their jobs.

Colby asked for a few hours off on Friday. Before he drove into Honey Creek he planned to drive out to Brand's ranch.

He leaned back in his chair. Piper had said, "Come home." Maybe it was time to stop pretending she didn't mean something to him. He didn't have to ask her to marry him, but he did need to tell her how much she meant to him.

She might get over being mad. If they still broke up, at least she'd know that she'd meant a great deal to him. More than any other woman he'd dated.

That is, if she believed him when he swore he'd never said *I love you* to another woman.

Chapter 33

Jesse

The evening was one of those perfect nights in Texas. Cold enough to wear a jacket but warm enough to sit out and watch the stars. Jesse rocked slowly as he studied them from the wide wraparound porch. There had been a time when he knew the names of a hundred stars and constellations. In a few more years he'd get his old telescope out and set it up for Zak. He'd teach his oldest, then Zak would teach Danny, and Danny would teach Sunny Lyn.

He loved his kids. He knew they'd always be a part of him, but someday he wouldn't be a part of them. They'd grow up and marry and be on their own. Sometimes he thought that the first two to marry would have to pick one of the grandmothers to take on their honeymoon. Either that or both old ladies would move in with him when the kids married.

Who knows, maybe he'd sell the farm and move to town. He knew deep down that he'd never travel or have grand adventures. He'd grow old loving his family, including the grandkids that would be coming someday. He'd go to church on Sunday and live his life by the seasons. His ways had always been simple.

Adalee had given him a great deal to think about lately. But as much as he liked the idea of getting to know one another better, bringing someone else into his life would be too much. He didn't have time, much less love, left over for anyone else. He took little bites of life, not big ones.

The baker was like a dream he kept all to himself. In his mind he felt like a parallel life was playing out. The real world and the might-have-been. How could a woman be all wrong for him and feel so right?

The phone rang and for a moment he thought it might be Adalee reading his thoughts. Knowing how much he wanted to hear her voice, even though deep down they'd soon be saying goodbye.

"Hello," he whispered, hoping the phone hadn't awoken one of the kids.

"Keaton?" a man's voice snapped.

"Yes."

"This is Dr. Donovan. You've had my daughter's bay out in your barn since the day before the storm."

"Yes, sir, I've got Princess. Let me know when you're coming to pick her up and I'll make sure I'm here to help."

"I won't be coming. Not right now." The doctor's words dripped with importance.

Jesse always smiled when doctors felt the need to identify themselves by title. He never announced himself as Farmer Keaton, and he bet his day was just as busy as the doctor's.

"What would you charge to board the horse for another few weeks? My daughter wants to go visit a cousin in Austin."

"Thirty a day." Jesse heard one of the guys at the co-op meeting mention that Donovan's daughter had been expelled. He hadn't paid enough attention to hear what the problem was. Something about a car wreck with half a dozen drunk teenagers inside.

"Don't I get a discount?" Donovan complained.

"Nope. The horse eats the same amount every day. Takes up the same stall. Gets exercise every day and has her stall cleaned." Jesse thought maybe times were hard on the dentist. "I know a few ranchers who'll keep Princess in a corral with the herd. That could cut the cost in half if you want to move her somewhere else."

"No, my daughter, Pamela, wouldn't like that. I'll pay. I just don't have time to tend to a horse right now."

From the looks of Princess when she arrived, no one had been taking care of her properly for a long time. Hooves needed tending, mane and tail matted, and the horse had an infected sore on her left knee joint that Jesse treated twice a day.

Jesse didn't bother to tell the doc about the horse's problems. He knew from experience that Donovan wouldn't care.

"I could cut a bit if Pamela wants to come out and exercise her horse every day."

"No, she's busy with soccer right now." The doc let out a long breath. "Sometimes I wish Princess was a toy horse that we could put in the attic. Pamela still loves the horse. Can't stand the thought of losing her beautiful Princess, but there's no time to ride anymore."

Jesse didn't ask any more questions. He had a barn full of horses and none of the owners seemed in any hurry to pick them up. "I'll take good care of the bay."

"Thanks." Donovan hung up.

Jesse thought about going back to the porch, but it was getting late. He'd go to bed and think of Adalee. He knew it wasn't practical for them to ever see each other on a regular basis, but she could fill his dreams. They'd been empty for a long time.

Wednesday

Chapter 34

Marcie

Marcie sat beside Pecos as he explained that Wednesday was a great day to cover, but Thursday was an iffy night. One time it would be dead at the station and next week you'd think some drunk must have sent out invitations to join him at the sheriff's office for a party.

"It depends on if there's a Thursday night game, I've decided. If so, we'll have bar fights. Sometimes couples start fighting before the weekend, like they're gearing up for the main event." Pecos answered a call from a Mrs. Davis. She was turned around again and couldn't find her house after leaving choir practice.

He gave directions and hung up. "I thought Mrs. Davis might be going into Alzheimer's. She's eighty-seven. Then I found out that her husband always drove. When he died last year, everyone noticed she had no sense of direction. I asked her if she knew north and south and she said, 'Of course, dear, they are sides of the Civil War.' After that I'd just tell her how to get home by landmarks. Last month she brought me cookies for helping her, then called me from the parking lot so I could direct her home."

Marcie wondered if big-city dispatchers had to put up with calls like Mrs. Davis.

Pecos folded his arms over his thin body and continued, "Now if it's a full moon, we get lots of calls. Don't know why. Folks go crazy. Babies pop out. Men are more likely to kill someone."

"What about women?"

"Nope, they always kill during their period. It's a known fact."

"Who told you?"

"The sheriff. He's had three wives, he should know."

Another call came in.

"You want to take this one, Marcie?" Pecos glanced at the caller and picked up the phone before she could answer. Suddenly he was all panic.

"Kerrie. What's the matter?"

Marcie knew they weren't allowed to take personal calls.

In the stillness of the room she heard Pecos's wife say, "I think my water just broke. We have to go."

"I'm on my way." Pecos's low, controlled tone was gone.

It took him three tries to hang up. "You'll have to take over. Call the sheriff if you need backup. Rip should be back soon to help." He stood up, then sat down to take off his headset. "I don't remember who else is on duty out there. I got to go."

Pecos looked like he was about to faint. "I'm about to have a baby! I got to get to the hospital."

Marcie stood and followed him out. "I can't take over yet. I haven't finished my forty hours of training."

"You've read the book. You'll be fine. Our water broke. We have to go. The baby could come out anytime now. We have to start breathing. I'll have to help Kerrie find her shoes. She can never find the right shoes she wants to wear. I have to go."

He was starting to sound like a windup toy with only one saying.

Marcie could see that to Pecos's way of thinking, this baby birthing was going to be a group project. She yelled, "Good luck," but he was already out the door.

In the silence of the office, Marcie suddenly felt totally alone. She sat in Pecos's chair. Read every report that had come in today. The huge clock seemed to be ticking louder and louder in the still room.

As she waited, the night wind began rattling the windows. It sounded like someone was trying to get in.

Panic crawled up her back like a hundred fire ants waiting to bite.

No calls came in.

About the time she was ready to call the sheriff and scream that she quit, Rip Carter came in. "What's happening, Pecos?" he yelled.

She stood and went to the open doorway. "Pecos isn't here. He's having a baby."

The deputy studied her. "You all right? You look like you've seen a ghost."

"I'm fine. I just don't like being alone."

Rip didn't look like he believed her. "First time on your own at the boards, right?"

"First time," she answered. "Maybe we should call in the sheriff? I'm not sure I can handle it. I was supposed to have forty hours of training before I had to take over."

"Lots of calls?"

Marcie shook her head. "No. It's too quiet in here."

"The sheriff will be madder than hell if he's called in for nothing. How about I move in there with you? I can do my paperwork on the empty desk as easy as here. If something happens, I'll call the sheriff, but it's too late now to worry. There's a good chance we'll make it through the night in silence." He moved into the dispatch room. "We're a team. I got your back. That's the way things work around here."

Marcie nodded. Rip was right. It was after two. "A team," she repeated as she sat down.

Rip got them coffee and they waited. He told her about Rip Ford, the hero of early Texas who he was named after, and she told him of her days in Nashville where the streets rang all night with music.

Slowly, she relaxed.

Pecos called in at six to tell Rip that he'd had a girl.

"That's great, kid. Any chance your wife was there?"

Marcie fought down a laugh and kept laughing while Pecos must have told Rip every detail. The young deputy looked like he'd just watched a horror film by the time Pecos finished describing the afterbirth.

When Rip finally hung up, he swore he'd never have children.

The sheriff showed up at seven and made a big deal about Pecos leaving his post, but Marcie had watched

LeRoy enough to know that the guy was full of hot air. The old sheriff thought of Pecos as a son.

When one of the day dispatchers came in, Marcie was ready to leave. As the old woman sat down, her knitting bag on the desk, Marcie walked out into the main office. She saw Brand standing by the sheriff's desk talking to Rip. All three men turned to face her. Marcie didn't need a lie detector. It was obvious they'd been talking about her.

She walked closer and just stared at them.

LeRoy broke first. "I was just saying you did a great job last night alone."

"Alone?" Rip snapped. "I was here with her."

Brand didn't comment. He just extended his hand and said, "Wanna go to breakfast?"

"You bet."

As they walked out, he whispered, "While we eat, how about we talk about what frightened you last night? Rip said you were pale when he came in from a call and found you alone."

"I can't," she answered.

Brand stopped and faced her. "Can't what? Go to breakfast or talk?"

Marcie jumped at the first life raft she could grab. She couldn't, wouldn't talk about how frightened she'd been alone. "I need to go see Pecos. He had a baby. You should have seen him. He looked like he might have a heart attack."

"That's interesting. Mind if I tag along? I've never seen a newborn human."

Ten minutes later they were standing in the short hallway where babies were born at the clinic. The four rooms were made up almost like bedrooms, only with a hospital bed, and a private bathroom. Each room had a couch for the husband to sleep on.

Mr. Winston was at the door of the Smiths' room as if he were the butler. When Marcie dragged Brand in, Pecos was holding a wrinkly newborn and Kerrie was asleep.

Brand took one look and let go of her hand as he backed away.

Marcie grabbed his arm and forced him forward. "Don't worry, Brand. She doesn't have her teeth yet. She can't bite you."

The nurse beside Kerrie whispered to Marcie, "Only stay a moment. This new little family all needs sleep."

With a look at Brand, she added, "That may be all the big guy can take anyway."

Marcie nodded as she fought down a laugh. Brand did look a bit pale.

Marcie said the baby was perfection. Brand set down the white teddy bear he'd bought at the pharmacy next to the clinic and then started pulling Marcie backward.

Pecos looked tired, but he was smiling down at his new daughter, barely aware that there was anyone else in the room. A tiny hand was wrapped around the tip of his little finger.

Marcie talked about the baby as they walked out, but Brand made no comment except that he never dreamed they come out so little.

"Wasn't she beautiful?" Marcie said.

"Looked a bit like a large tadpole to me." He scratched his head. "Horses come out looking like horses. Cows come out looking like cows, but I didn't know about humans. How long before she can stand and suck?"

Marcie jabbed him in the ribs with her elbow.

He winked at her to let her know he was kidding.

Marcie loved that the quiet man liked to make her laugh. "She is beautiful."

"If you say so," Brand added. "You know the parents should post a picture on the door so it's not so much of a shock when you walk in and see the kid."

Marcie stopped in the middle of the hallway and kissed him.

When Brand finally pulled away and asked her where she wanted to eat breakfast, she suggested they go back to Winston's house and she'd cook him something.

Even in the silent kitchen, the old house seemed to welcome them in the early morning light. Brand offered to help, but Marcie made him sit down and watch.

They ate eggs and toast in a tiny breakfast nook and made predictions of what the world would be like when the baby was twenty.

After they did the dishes, she showed him her room and leaned back on the bed. Brand sat down on the other side. "How about we talk now, Marcie? I'd really like to know why you were so afraid to be alone last night. I thought it might be about the scare you had a week ago, but it seems like something else. You know you can tell me anything. If I can, I'll try to make it better."

He laughed. "I think I've just said more words than I've said at one time in years." He leaned on his elbow, almost lying beside her as he brushed her hair with his fingers. "I guess I'm worried about you."

He leaned close and kissed her lightly. "Any objections?"

"Never," she answered as he kissed her again.

After a few minutes, he backed away. "I love kissing you."

"Me too." Her eyes drifted closed as he kissed her cheek.

She smiled as she circled her arms around his and fell asleep. The last thing she heard sounded like no more than a whisper in the wind.

"Marcie, are you asleep?" When she didn't answer, he added as he rolled closer. "Good night, my little koala bear. If you don't object, I think I'll stay right here until you wake up."

Thursday

Chapter 35

Jesse

After dropping his children off for breakfast at his mom's house, Jesse decided to stop by for one of Adalee's scones. He told himself he just wanted to see how her kid sister was doing, but the truth of it was, he just wanted to look at her. He'd spent so much time dreaming about her, he wasn't sure she was real.

He parked his old pickup, half full of feed, on the side street beside the bakery.

When he walked in, the woman who'd bewitched him smiled at him and pointed at a table closest to the counter. By the time Jesse took off his coat and got comfortable, she'd delivered his order. She hadn't even asked what he wanted. Proof she was a mind reader.

"Who is the new help?" he asked, thankful the old

woman he'd run into last time wasn't hanging out behind the counter.

"Her name is Wallis. New in town. Came to live with her grandmother."

Adalee poured herself a cup of coffee, but didn't sit down. She just stood at the end of the counter, ready if needed. "Because of the trouble with my sister, I decided I might need someone to take over from time to time. My help in the kitchen doesn't like the public. The feeling is mutual. I had a few regulars say they'd run for the hills if they saw her again."

Jesse grinned. "How is your sister doing?"

"Star got into more trouble. The sheriff found out she was drinking in a car full of underage kids. The drivers were racing and had a wreck."

Jesse saw tears in her beautiful eyes, which she was fighting not to let fall.

"I threatened to send her to my brother. He's a cop in Houston and swears she needs to go away to a camp where they straighten out out-of-control kids. I don't know what to do. I don't think I can send her away, so that means I'll have to work less."

The urge to touch Adalee's hand was so strong, he had to keep a death grip on his cup.

Her summer-day eyes let one tear fall. "Sorry I'm dumping my problems on you."

"You're not." He wrote his cell number on a napkin. "Call me anytime after nine if you need to talk. I may not be able to help, but I can listen."

She borrowed his pen. "And you do the same." When she passed him her number, their hands touched a moment longer than necessary.

One small smile and she was gone. The bakery was

busy. Jesse stood and nodded when he caught her gaze; she nodded back. No one noticed, but they made an agreement, a promise to be there for one another if only on the phone.

Somehow they'd find a way to stay in touch. He'd be home with his kids and she'd be watching over her sister, but they could talk now and then on quiet nights. It'd be nice. The bond between them might only be a thread, but it was there.

As he pulled into the barn twenty minutes later to unload, he smiled at another lucky turn of events.

He scanned the horse stalls. Three hundred and sixty dollars a day was dropping into his bank account, thanks to the horses people had brought over to board during the stormy weather. Yesterday, one came to pick up his horse, and two people who'd heard about the horse "hotel" brought in their *not so loved* pets.

Half of the horse owners had already asked to extend their arrangement because they were cleaning up from the flooding and didn't have time to mess with a horse. One even said he was moving and simply didn't want to worry about his wife's horse.

Subtracting the feed, and all the other things that go with taking care of animals, he figured he'd still clear over six thousand this month. All it would cost him was time, and since growing season was over, he could make the time.

Something rattled on the other side of the pickup, ending his mental calculations.

If an animal had somehow gotten into the barn, that could mean trouble. Jesse grabbed a rake and rushed behind the truck, hoping to shoo the animal out the open doors.

Just as Jesse raised the rake, a mop of red hair crawled out of the hay. For a moment dark green eyes flashed fear and then anger. "What are you going to do, kill me with a rake?" She looked around. "Where in the hell am I? Who are you?"

Jesse stared at the kid for a moment. Girl in boys' clothes. About fifteen. Red hair. Green eyes. She had to be Adalee's little sister. "What are you doing here?"

"What do you care, mister? Where am I? When I jumped in this smelly truck, I thought I was going to Arkansas."

"You're on my farm, about fifteen miles from Honey Creek."

"Great. My luck is nothing but a pile of shit."

Jesse put down the rake, trying to make sense of the kid. "Why'd you think you were going to Arkansas?"

"Your tags. Don't you even know what state you live in?"

He noticed the tags he'd forgotten to change when he'd bought the truck from his cousin six months ago. "Why are you going to Arkansas?"

"I'm not, thanks to you!"

He swallowed down his anger at her scornful tone. "What's your name?"

"Star, and that's all I'm telling you. I have places to be, and it isn't in this dumb barn. You know, it's illegal not to change your plates!"

Jesse didn't want to make this become his fault. "You're running away. You hid in my truck so you could get out of town. Right?"

She jerked her backpack out of the truck's bed. "I don't have to answer you. I'm bad news and not your problem. You don't want to mess with me. Just point me in the direction that heads away from Honey Creek and I'll thumb a ride."

"You're five miles down a muddy road with no traffic. Once you hit the pavement, you've got a ten-mile walk to Honey Creek or a thirty-mile walk to the next town if you turn the other way. Don't plan on anyone stopping to pick you up. You've got *runaway* written all over you. No one in their right mind would help you, so go back where you came from."

The girl glared at him. "I'm never going back to Honey Creek. Never, never, never. I'll die first." Then out came a string of cuss words that were starting to hurt his ears. "No one can tell me what to do! It's my life!"

The horses objected loudly and Star stopped cussing.

Jesse said calmly, "You're scaring the horses."

She turned to look at the stalls. "I'm sorry!" she yelled, not to him but to the horses.

"As skinny as you are, you'll probably starve before you walk the thirty miles, or maybe freeze, because it'll take you more than one day. That is, if the highway patrol doesn't pick you up. He'll take you straight to the sheriff, and my guess is LeRoy has probably seen enough of you."

Jesse saw that she was wrapping her arms around herself as if growing cold.

"Come to think of it, you won't freeze. This time of year the wolves are hunting at sundown."

"I didn't know there were wolves around here."

"Wolves, mountain lions, a few bears." Jesse lied. "You're lucky, it's too cold for the snakes."

She glared at him. "Then you'll have to drive me to another town. This is all your fault anyway for not changing your tags. That's illegal. You could go to jail."

"I can't take you anywhere. I have to take care of the horses first. They haven't had their breakfast, then I've got to brush them down and walk them."

"I haven't had breakfast either, but hell, I'm not complaining. Take me to the next town or I swear I'll scream my head off."

Jesse shrugged. "Much as I'd like to see that, I got work to do. You can help if you want, but I'm not leaving until the chores are done. I could call your kin or the sheriff to come get you."

"No. The sheriff and me aren't speaking and my sister is working." Star Summers glared at him as if adding him to her hate list. After a long moment, she said grudgingly, "Okay, I'll feed and water the horses, if you take me to the next town when I'm done. I'll be on a bus before anyone knows I'm gone. No one in Texas will ever find me."

Jesse headed for the first stall, deciding teenagers have Jell-O for brains. The knowledge that he'd have three in ten years gave him a shiver.

She dropped her backpack and removed her jacket as he brought out the first horse. "You know how to brush a horse down?"

"No, but how hard could it be?"

Thirty minutes later, she'd fallen twice and been stepped on once. To his surprise she seemed to enjoy the work.

"Horses are my spirit animals. You probably don't even know what that means."

"Nope," he answered. "Horses probably don't either. But that's a good thing, I guess." Jesse pointed toward the tack room. "See those mud boots over there? Put them on. They were my wife's. Those tennis shoes are wet."

"Won't she mind?"

"No." He turned the grooming over to Star. She'd gotten the hang of it, plus the pampered horses loved her talking to them.

Afterward, he saddled Princess and asked Star if she'd like to ride her around the corral, and the teenager actually smiled.

For the first time he saw the resemblance to Adalee. He wondered if big sister had been just as much of a hellcat at fifteen.

After exercising each horse, Star hugged their necks and talked to them as if they could understand every word she said.

Jesse didn't leave the barn. He watched her, making sure she didn't get hurt. Each ride was longer than the last. The kid really did love horses. He'd only seen that kind of devotion once. His Beth had loved horses. When they'd built the barn, he'd planned to use it for storage, but she'd insisted on at least two horses. The upkeep was worth it for the long rides they'd take.

He'd sold the horses after she died. Now, watching Star, he was thinking he might buy a few for the kids.

It was almost noon when Star put the last horse back in his stall.

"You want some lunch before we go?"

She nodded. "I'm so hungry I was thinking of trying the hay."

They walked back to the house as she asked questions. Jesse pulled a frozen pizza from the freezer and told her she could wash up in the kids' bathroom.

"Your clothes are really dirty. I've got a few things that should be your size. I'll toss them on the bed in Sunny Lyn's room."

"You said your daughter's four. I can't wear her clothes!"

"No. But you're about my wife's size."

"Your wife . . . Where is she then? Did you run her off with your work ethic?"

"Nope. She died when Sunny was born." He kept his tone level. Just tell the facts, nothing more, even if it did hurt inside. Sometimes talking about Beth hurt less than not talking about her.

To his surprise, Star didn't make any comment. She simply nodded, and headed toward the bathroom.

From down the hall she yelled, "I'm guessing the room decorated in unicorns is Sunny Lyn's."

"You found it."

Jesse pulled the pizza from the oven when Star walked in wearing a blue sweatshirt and jeans. The jeans were two inches too short and the shirt a bit too big, but they'd do. He handed her a pair of red boots.

She made a face. "I'm going to look like a damn cowgirl."

"It's that, or the mud boots, or your tennis shoes covered with your favorite word."

"What's that?"

"Shit."

She sat at the table and put on the warm socks, then pulled on the red boots. "They feel pretty good," she said more to herself than him.

"You can have the boots if you want them," he said as she studied them.

"I do. They fit like a glove." When he didn't comment, Star added, "I'm sorry about your wife, mister."

He handed her a bottle of Coke and changed the subject. "How'd you learn to ride, kid?"

"When I was in grade school my best friend's family had horses. We rode every day during the summer, but I never had to care for them. Would you show me how you clean the hooves? I'm going to own horses one day."

"Sure, that reminds me, I want to ask you about something." He passed her a plate with three pieces of pizza. She suddenly seemed much more interested in the food than talk.

Jesse picked his questions carefully. "If you leave after lunch, you won't get to the next town before most of the buses have gone. Might even be a chance you'd have to get a hotel."

Between bites she explained what a dumb idea that was. "I can't get a hotel. I only have money for a bus ride, and I don't know if it's enough to get me out of this state."

"So you'd sleep on the street?"

"No, I'd curl up in a doorway. I saw people do that all the time in New Orleans."

"Did you see any little girls sleeping on the street?"

"No. So what? I can take care of myself." Her words were determined, but he saw doubt in her eyes.

"I know you can, Star, but how about you stay around here for a few days, maybe a week, and help me out with the horses. I'd offer room and board and twenty dollars a day for helping me. By then you'll have a hundred dollars to get you down the road, and most of the horses will be gone. You could sleep in my daughter's room on the extra bed. Only, there's one rule, you got to let your sister know where you are."

"I knew there was a hitch. My sister will never let me stay here. She'll come get me one minute after I call."

"Think about it, kid."

"She'll never let me stay. She thinks she's in charge of me. She's not my mother. We're sisters, that's all."

Jesse took a big chance on Adalee. "How about I

promise if she doesn't let you work for me, I'll drive you to the nearest bus terminal before she has time to get here."

He knew she didn't have much choice. He'd bet she didn't have twenty dollars on her, but she bargained anyway. "You got any food besides pizza? That stuff's not even good pizza."

"I got a freezer full, but I can't cook much. Beth's mother comes over once a month and cooks ahead a few dishes."

"Then, if I stay, one rule. No, that's not right. This is my first rule. I have a feeling others will come along. Number one: I get to cook supper."

"You can cook, kid?"

"Duh, I grew up in a bakery."

Jesse smiled. "You got yourself a deal. How about we go feed the chickens after we eat?"

"You've got chickens? That means you've got eggs. Why are we eating bad pizza?"

He laughed. "I got guineas too, and goats, and bees a half mile down near my fields."

"Holy moley! This place rules. I love animals, but I never had one. Bakeries and pets don't go together. Please talk my sister into letting me work here."

"I'll work on it."

When he drove into town, he left Star playing with Zak's pet rabbit while she sat beside a pregnant goat.

He told Star not to leave the goat's side in case she went into labor.

"What'd I do if it does?"

"Watch," Jesse answered.

Chapter 36

Jesse

Adalee was closing the bakery early when Jesse walked up.

"Evening." He touched the hand she held on the half-closed door.

"Good evening." She didn't step away.

He smiled. "I thought I'd drop by and tell you a plan I've come up with, if you have a minute."

"I'm sorry, I can't. My little sister will be home any minute and I feel like I have to be there. Maybe another day." She looked truly sorry.

Even turning him down, she was beautiful. "It is about your sister," he said in a low voice. His fingers brushed hers as if comforting her.

She hesitated, then opened the door wider to let him

in. "I really can't stay but a few minutes. I want to be sitting in the kitchen when she walks in. That way she'll know I'm there for her."

He had no idea how to start without frightening her. "Your sister is safe. She ran away this morning. But she's safe. She's at my farm right now babysitting a pregnant goat."

"We'd better sit down." She sounded more interested than frightened. "Start from the first."

When her gaze met his, she shrugged. "This isn't her first teenage escape attempt. If she's safe, I'll continue breathing."

They took a seat in the shadows, where anyone passing by the bakery wouldn't notice them. Jesse held her hand and slowly told her the whole story, including the bargain he'd made with Star. "That kid loves horses. All animals, I'm guessing. Maybe a few days out there will do her good. It's got to be better than her being on her own at fifteen."

Adalee cried when he described how her little sister talked to the horses. Then she smiled when he told her how Star stopped cussing around the animals because he said it upset them. "I don't know if this will work, but her staying out at the farm has got to be safer for her than walking the streets of New Orleans."

"She wants to go back there because that was her first home. I was twenty-seven and she was twelve when our folks died. I sold their bakery and moved here, thinking we could start over."

"I told her you'd let her stay at my place for a few days, but if you don't want to, I'd understand. I'm not so sure she will."

"You already have your hands full, Jesse. I can't ask you to take on more."

He shook his head. "I think she'll be more help than work. She even offered to cook supper." He tightened his grip on her hand. "I wouldn't be doing it for just Star, I'd be helping you. I'd like that. You mean a great deal to me." He laced his fingers with hers and smiled. It felt so good just to touch her hand. "You've been walking through my dreams since that night you found me in the rain."

"How can I ever pay you back?" She looked at their hands. She could have pulled away, but she didn't.

"Free scones for life if it works." He grinned, realizing she'd already given him a great gift. A chunk of loneliness fell off his heart. They were friends now and maybe someday they'd be lovers.

She smiled. "You've got a deal." In the shadows of the closed bakery, she leaned over and kissed him. One sweet kiss. "Will you keep me up on how she's doing?"

"I will." He wanted to kiss her again, but somehow it didn't seem right. They were in the friends category now.

"Jesse, one more question. How can I mean so much to you? We barely know one another."

He could feel his face reddening. That hadn't happened in a long while. All he could think of was to be honest. "Don't you know you fill my dreams some nights and my daydreams when I'm working? The days are packed with work and parenting and worry, but when I have a free minute, you come to me. I can almost feel you by my side."

She straightened and stared at him as if trying to see inside him.

"I probably shouldn't have said that. Forget it. Too much information. Sorry."

He was rattling now. Time to go.

He stood. He wasn't a polished lover. Hell, he didn't even know how to date. Beth had asked him all those years ago. Right now he felt like an awkward teen standing in the corner at a dance, afraid to make the first step.

Before he could dart away, her hand on his chest stopped him. "Wait. I need to say something."

He closed his eyes, wishing he could close his ears as well. How he felt about her had nothing to do with him wanting to help her sister. Helping Star was simply the right thing to do. Adalee didn't owe him anything. He had no right to tell her that she was in his dreams. He wasn't a poet. He was a farmer. She probably thought he was a pervert.

She cleared her throat and said, so low he barely heard her words, "You fill my dreams some nights, too. Every morning when I make scones I think of the way you touched me."

"I do?" He opened one eye. He'd never filled any woman's dreams and he'd always figured he was pretty much forgettable.

Adalee moved closer, pushing her full breasts against him. "You're my kind of man, Jesse. Kind and stable and funny, and my definition of sexy. When you touch me I know you're seeing me, just as I see you."

"I am?"

Her big eyes stared at him. "I shouldn't have said that. Too much information. Sorry. I probably scared you off."

He moved a strand of her auburn hair that had escaped from her ponytail. "I don't scare easy, pretty lady. It's been a long time since I've been attracted to a woman. You mind if I kiss you again?"

"No, I don't mind at all."

One long kiss, with her moving against him as if they were dancing just like she had in his dreams. Only this was better. This was real. His hand moved down her back, pulling her so close he felt her shiver when he deepened the kiss.

They didn't have to talk about when or how they'd be alone again. They both knew it would be near impossible. But both held on tightly, as if memorizing the feel of the other. Listening to the other's heartbeat hammering. Collecting sensations to build a memory on.

He took a deep breath, trying to learn the smell of her. He never wanted to forget the way her lips felt when he kissed her. He could feel her smile turn to need. He loved the way her fingers threaded into the back of his hair and held on tight.

"I'll see you in my dreams," he said as he stepped away and put on his hat.

"I'll be there."

Jesse walked out of the bakery. He was definitely out of the "just friends" category.

Chapter 37

Colby

The clock on the office wall finally moved to eleven o'clock. One more hour and Colby could leave Austin and head for Honey Creek. He already had a change of clothes packed. It had been less than a week since he'd seen Piper, but he could barely wait to be with her.

First, he had to meet Brand Rodgers and let him know someone might be coming for him, then somehow he had to solve the problem of Leon Newton bothering Piper's friend Marcie. Maybe he could talk to the man, change his way of thinking. By seven o'clock tonight he wanted to have dinner with Piper and tell her all was settled.

This time he was keeping her updated about what time

he planned to be driving into Honey Creek. He'd even told her he'd text when he left Austin.

Colby had a feeling if Brand got to the thin, bald guy first, the man who'd made the threats against Marcie and him would be moving a few states away or be six feet under.

Then, tonight, when all was calm, Colby planned to hold Piper close to him and tell her how much she meant to him. She wasn't just a girlfriend or a sometimes lover. He wanted her to know that he'd be there for her. He liked the idea that he was the one she ran to when she was in trouble. She was someone very special and he liked being her friend, not just her lover.

She had to still care for him. He'd been the one she called, not her brothers or the sheriff. He wanted to tell her she could always run to him.

Colby looked at the clock again. Long before dark he'd be in Honey Creek. Tonight he planned to hold Piper in his arms all night. Even if he had to fight his way through a mob of white-haired widows to get to her bedroom.

Colby ignored the racket in the office as he thought about how the old ladies would probably help him. They wanted to see Piper happy, and his goal tonight was to make her just that.

"McBride!" Dave yelled from four feet away. "Grab your hat and get ready to ride. We got a huge drug bust out on Interstate 35."

Colby headed out with four other rangers. As he passed the clock, he thought that with luck this might only take an hour or two. He could still make it to Honey Creek in time for dinner.

Long after dark, with his body aching from wrestling half a dozen outlaws into patrol cars and tagging evidence, one of the prisoners got free and elbowed Colby in the eye. As he hit the concrete floor of the holding cell, he focused his one good eye on the jail clock. Midnight.

He wasn't going to make it to Piper tonight.

Chapter 38

Pecos

The walls of the hospital were closing in around Pecos. Everything had been fine with the birth. It was just as gross and beautiful as the books described it. But pictures, even in color, could not compare to seeing it firsthand. The head crowning. A tiny little hand stretching out to the world. A baby covered in sticky blood, fighting to breathe as the doctor cleaned her nose and mouth.

Pecos had held his breath until she cried. Then, just like that, he knew he'd love this little girl for the rest of his life.

Kerrie was great. Strong. Excited. Sometimes terrified. Watching her step into being a mother was almost as exciting as seeing the baby. When the nurse put the tiny infant in Kerrie's arms, she looked up at Pecos, and thanked him. "I'm not sure I would have made it without you, but it's all over now. She's ours."

"She's ours." He beamed. "We're her parents from now on."

Kerrie just smiled that sweet smile he'd never stop loving.

A few hours later they called her parents, who of course rushed to the clinic. Kerrie questioned them before she'd let them hold the baby. Did they have colds? Had they washed their hands? Were their clothes clean?

All the while Pecos sat in a chair beside her, looking like a homeless person. He'd been wearing the same clothes for two days. His spotty beard wasn't pretty and his hair had gone completely wild.

In contrast, Kerrie had on makeup and a clean gown. Even her hair was perfect. The beauty queen and the frog, he thought. He feared it would always be that way.

Kerrie turned toward him about then and winked. Pecos figured she had a blind spot when it came to him, and for that he'd always be thankful.

All morning she'd been smiling at him. Of course, he was holding the baby.

Her folks did the strangest thing. When they first came in, all they did was fuss over Kerrie, but after they both got a turn at holding the baby, they seemed to forget there was anyone else in the room. Any worry he'd had of them not accepting their first grandchild was forgotten.

Pecos moved over close to Kerrie as they watched her parents. At one point the Lanes were giggling while playing *this little piggy* with the baby's tiny toes. Mr. Lane swore she looked just like Kerrie did as a baby. Mrs. Lane agreed.

Kerrie kissed Pecos's cheek. "Thanks for being there

with me, husband. You held my hand through it all."

"I held your hand? I thought you were holding mine." When he studied her eyes and pale cheeks, it struck him that she looked tired, very tired.

He reached over and pushed the call button. "Are you all right?"

She nodded. "It's just hot in here."

The Lanes kept talking to the baby as the nurse ran Kerrie's vitals. One look from the nurse told Pecos that something was wrong.

The nurse turned to the grandparents, who were now trying out names that their grandchild would call them. "If you'll excuse me, I need to take baby Smith to the nursery. Time for a nap. If you'll wait in the waiting room, we also would like to examine your daughter."

"What's wrong?" Mr. Lane demanded.

"We're not sure anything is. That's why we are examining her. Please step out. The doctor is on his way."

Pecos moved to Kerrie's side and took her hand. He could hear Mr. Lane asking, "Why's he staying in the room? We're her parents."

For once Pecos turned all the world off as he squeezed Kerrie's hand, trying to push strength into her. She'd closed her eyes and he could see her blood pressure dropping on the monitor. "I love you," he whispered. "I always have and I always will. Remember that, wife. I might be just your best friend, but you are my life."

Two more nurses and the doctor circled through the room poking her, examining her while they whispered among themselves.

Kerrie must have drifted to sleep because she let go of his hand. The loss of her touch made him feel hollow. Without her, there wasn't much of him.

Finally, the doctor put his hand on Pecos's shoulder. "You need to step out for a few minutes. Go talk to that baby of yours. She's probably wondering where her daddy is. We'll be finished here soon and will come get you when Kerrie wakes up."

"Is Kerrie all right?"

"Yes. She'll be fine."

Pecos saw the uncertainty in his eyes.

As if sleepwalking, Pecos left the room. He turned his back on the waiting room and headed straight to the nursery. His baby was the only one there. An aide sat at a desk doing paperwork as she watched over baby Smith.

Pressing his hands against the glass, Pecos watched his baby move in her sleep. She was so perfect. She was his daughter, for sure. She had her fist up, ready to fight.

"Your mama is going to name you today," he whispered. "She said when you look at her, when your eyes meet hers, according to her, she'll know your name."

Pecos heard his words echoing off the entry hallway. "It doesn't matter what she names you, I'm going to call you Button. I have a feeling you're going to be beautiful, just like your mother."

The need to talk to someone was so great he felt like his emotions might explode. "Your mom's going to be fine. The doctor said so. Just a complication. Giving birth is hard." Pecos smiled. "I bet it wasn't easy on you either. There for a while I was wondering if you were ever going to come out to meet us."

Pecos pushed a tear off his face. "Don't think nothing about me crying, Button. My eyes just leak now and then. Sometimes just because I'm so happy."

He closed his hand into a fist against the frame of the viewing window. "Nothing is going to happen to her. I won't let it. If God tries to take her, I'll make Him take me instead. You need her a lot more than you do me."

He stared down at Button. "I don't see how I can love something so small so fast. I thought I'd never love anyone but Kerrie, then you popped out and all it took was one look."

A hand touched his shoulder, startling Pecos.

"Now you know why I hate you so much," Kerrie's father said. "Someday this little angel is going to grow up and want to marry some bum of a boy like you. He won't be good enough for her."

Pecos saw tears in Lane's eyes, as his grip grew tighter on Pecos's shoulder.

"I just pray he'll be half the man you are, son."

He watched Mr. Lane walk away, wiping his eyes as he headed back to the waiting room.

"You see that, Button? I think I'm growing on the old guy." Pecos thought he saw the baby smile at him. Probably just gas. "You'll have him wrapped around your little finger in no time."

A nurse stepped out of Kerrie's room and waved him in.

Pecos kissed his fingertips and pressed them against the glass. "See you soon, Button."

He ran down the hallway, but the nurse didn't let him in. "She's resting. Nothing to worry about. Just a minor thing that could have been a problem. The doctor said he'll explain the procedure when she wakes up." The nurse gave him a stern look. "Do not wake her up. We'll keep a close eye on her, but I've watched you two and I know she would want you close. So, I guess you can stay."

"Can you go tell her parents she's all right? I just want to be with Kerrie."

"I'll tell them and ask them to come back during visiting hours."

Pecos stepped back in Kerrie's room and sat in a chair beside her bed. "I'm here," he whispered. "I'm not going anywhere. We've got Button to raise."

After a few minutes of listening to the sounds of machines, he rested his head next to her pillow and fell asleep.

Friday

Chapter 39

Colby

Friday morning was warm for late fall, when Colby pulled off the main road and started up to Brand Rodgers's small ranch. It wasn't easy to find. No signs. Gravel road. Trees blocked the view along a rugged hillside. This land was far more compatible for raising horses than any kind of crop.

Colby had the coordinates, but thanks to all the overgrown vegetation along the road, he missed the entrance to Brandon's place twice. This guy didn't even have a mailbox. Of course, why would a ghost need a mailbox?

Once he pulled onto Rodgers's private property, Colby had a feeling he was being watched. The place looked too perfect to be a working ranch. No ruts in the drive, no piles of junk waiting to be hauled away. Not even any horse-shit piles. It was almost like someone had taken a picture of the perfect little place to hide away from everyone and created the Rodgers Ranch.

The house was small, but well kept. The barn looked freshly painted and seemed oversized. No chickens or dogs that might interfere with surveillance paraphernalia. No overhead cable lines. A man like Brand would have electricity, cable, the Internet. All underground, of course. That couldn't have been cheap.

Colby pulled up twenty feet from the porch and killed the engine on his Harley. The second it died, silence surrounded him. If Brand was within a mile, he'd probably heard the bike coming. This would be no surprise visit.

Colby pulled off his helmet and waited for Brand to appear. He'd thought of coming up dressed like a ranger. In truth, the Texas Rangers didn't have an official uniform, just like the first rangers didn't. But everyone knew today's rangers wore tan or gray slacks, a white shirt and boots. When Colby signed on, he'd even gotten an allotment for his hat, gun belt, and western boots.

But today he came in jeans and a dark brown leather jacket. He didn't want to make this visit official. He wanted to offer his help if Brand needed it, and he'd accept the man's help if the ghost offered.

After last night, Colby had enjoyed the morning drive, and this place seemed a million miles from Austin.

He'd needed to clear his mind of all the mess Thursday night. A car pileup on I-35. Three vans full of drugs involved. A dozen men pumped up on pills were traveling as guards.

When he got home at two a.m., adrenaline was still running in his blood and his eye hurt like hell. It had been too late to call Piper, but he'd texted so she'd wake up to know he was still coming. It would just be a day later than he'd planned.

He'd explain when he got to Honey Creek. She had two brothers who were rangers. She'd understand it wasn't an eight-to-five job.

He'd stick to his plan. He'd talk to Brand Rodgers first. Maybe stop by LeRoy's office and then let Piper know he had her problem in hand.

Colby almost laughed at his plan. Nothing in law enforcement was ever that simple.

A screen door banged against the frame just as he thought about how happy Piper would be to see him.

A tall man stepped onto the porch. Blue western-cut shirt, gray vest, jeans, and boots. He was big, but Colby would guess there was not an ounce of fat on the guy. If Colby hadn't seen Brand's face once, he still would have known the man by his stance. He moved easy, deceptively slow, like a lion in tall grass. Brand Rodgers stood still and waited. Colby had no doubt he was taking the measure of him as well.

Rodgers's stance was wide, ready for anything coming from any angle. His eyes narrowed as he studied Colby. His face gave nothing away.

Colby swung off the bike and pulled off his gloves, leaving them with the helmet.

"Mr. Rodgers, I assume."

"Right," Brand answered. The man didn't ask what he was doing on his land. He knew he'd find out soon enough.

Few men made Colby nervous, but he was staring at one who did.

He decided to be honest. "I need your help. I'm—"

"I know who you are." Brand's voice was low. "The

state trooper who saved lives almost six months ago during a fire in Honey Creek. You and the town's new fire chief not only got the two women out, you also caught the arsonist."

Colby relaxed a bit. He wasn't a complete stranger to the man. That was great news.

"You're Colby McBride, Texas Ranger now. Congratulations. You deserved it." Brand stepped out of the shadow of the porch. His gaze never left Colby and his next words came slow. "I met you once before, a few years back, on a back road behind a warehouse just outside of Austin."

"Good memory, sir." Colby walked a few steps and was glad Rodgers didn't react. "You ended a drug war that night. I heard they recovered a hundred guns from that warehouse and almost as many bodies. Must have been some fireworks inside that tin building."

"I wasn't there to shoot anyone. I was there to make sure one man didn't get killed." Brand relaxed a bit. "One undercover cop who would go on and make twenty bigtime arrests in the weeks that followed. He's the one who ended a big operation."

Colby smiled. The guy trusted him or he wouldn't have given any information away. They were on the same team.

"I've been following your career, McBride. Nothing professional, I just keep up with the little towns around here. Word is you're sweet on the mayor."

"The news gets around. You know her?"

"Everyone in this valley knows everyone, at least on sight, but to her I'm just a rancher and I'd like to keep it that way." Brand finally smiled. "No one here knows I have a *part-time* job."

"I'll keep it quiet. You have my word."

"Just so you know, Ranger, if you break that mayor's heart I won't bother coming after you. Those two brothers of hers will get to you first. They stop by now and then. We went to school together. We enjoy fishing now. Never catch more than a skillet full of trout, but they fill me in on what's going on in town and at the capital."

Colby knew he wouldn't get any answers if he asked, so he waited.

"You want a beer?" Brand asked.

"Sure."

Brand nodded toward two chairs on the porch and stepped inside. A minute later he brought out two longnecks. They talked about the weather and the storm last week. Colby drank his beer and Brand took one draw on his.

Finally Colby got down to what he came for. "I wanted to come out and warn you that some guy is bragging about coming after you. I don't think it has anything to do with your occupation."

Brand showed no surprise. "It doesn't. I stopped him and a few of his friends from raping a woman. They weren't too happy that I broke up their party." Brand shrugged. "They don't know it, but I went easy on them."

Colby told him what Piper had said. "The man who bragged about his plans is tall, thin, middle-aged, bald."

"I know the one. I had no trouble tagging him. Leon Newton. Lives just outside of Clifton Bend but does his drinking over in Someday Valley. Unemployed when he can't find anything to steal. If he comes after me, he won't come alone. I'll know he's coming when he turns off the main road. Don't worry about me."

"I'm not. Soon as I recognized you, I knew you'd have it covered." Colby thought that men like Brand were rare, smart, and more than a little lucky.

"Mind telling me where you were trained?"

"In the Marines and around."

Colby knew that was all the information he'd get.

"The sheriff in town just knows I'm retired army intelligence. Nothing more."

For some reason Brand trusted him. Colby would make sure that trust was never misplaced. He also wouldn't be surprised if Brand knew everything about him.

Brand's voice was calm, matter-of-fact. "My bet is it won't be long before Leon messes up and LeRoy will catch him for something. He's been in the county jail so often, they should put in a revolving door for him. As for him gunning for me, in no time he'll find someone else to hate. He's selling drugs, small time. LeRoy is watching him. Chances are I won't have to do a thing. Problem solved." Brand set his beer under the chair.

Colby made a mental note. The man didn't drink.

"I'm afraid it's not exactly solved on my part. Piper saw him threatening a friend, Marcie. The woman you rescued the other night." Colby didn't miss Brand's eyes widening slightly and knew he'd just told the ghost something he didn't know. "If Leon saw them talking and he knows Piper saw him, this Leon Newton could come after not only Marcie but the mayor as well."

Brand was silent for a while, then asked, "Do you know what he said to Marcie?"

"Yeah, most of it at least, but I promised I wouldn't tell anyone."

Brand nodded. "I understand, but if I knew what you know and it was Piper in danger, would you want the details?"

"I understand. Marcie means that much to you?"

"She does. She's my girl, but she doesn't know it yet."

Brand's smile was almost shy, as if this was the first time he'd realized it.

Colby told him that Newton said he was going to kill Brand slow and watch him bleed out. He tried to remember the exact words Piper used. "He planned to cut Marcie while he rapes her. Claims he'll smear her own blood all over her until she's red. But he wouldn't kill her in case he wanted to come back again. Even told her that it's easy to cut open scars, so this isn't his first time, I'm guessing."

Colby expected Brand to react, but he didn't. He just stared out over his land.

The calmness was another one of his strengths. He didn't react, he planned.

Finally, he turned to Colby and said, "You are right. He's done this kind of thing before. I'd bet on it. Probably several times and getting more violent each time. The night I saw the gang of drunks, Leon was the leader, pushing the pack along. But he wasn't drunk, and he backed away and let the others charge me.

"I think Leon had planned the attack on Marcie for a while. If he let the other men take a turn first, they'd never talk. Leon could have even killed her and the others wouldn't have turned him in."

Brand leaned forward in his chair. "Can you search the files for women cut while raped? He'll probably follow a pattern. Small towns. Maybe finding them in bars and following them home. His victims will live alone."

"Will do," Colby answered. "In the meantime, what can we do about Piper and Marcie being safe? Piper thinks she's protected in her own town."

"I'll watch over Marcie. Piper is safe in Honey Creek, but ask her to leave her office before dark. I'll put a tracker on Leon. If he gets within ten miles of Honey Creek, I'll be standing behind him."

The two men stood and shook hands. Brand followed him to the bike. "This conversation didn't happen, Ranger."

"This conversation didn't happen. If I see you again I won't recognize you, but if you ever need me, you know where to find me."

Brand nodded and pulled a plain white business card from his pocket. It had numbers in black ink, nothing more.

"My number." Brand stepped away.

Colby started the Harley and drove toward town. He was almost twenty-four hours late and couldn't tell Piper where he'd been this morning. He hoped she'd be in a forgiving mood; after all, she'd told him to come home and that had to mean she was over being mad at him.

On the way to Honey Creek he thought about how calm Brand had been. He'd expected him to swear and threaten to bash bald Leon's head in for frightening Marcie, but Brand slowly reasoned out the facts.

Brand hadn't even asked Colby about his black eye. He just said the law could go after Leon for selling drugs or theft. That would put him in jail for a few years. If they could charge him with being a serial rapist, they could put him away for life.

Brand hadn't made a single threat, but Colby had a feeling if Leon was found guilty but somehow got away, he'd just disappear.

Colby laughed, thinking of something an old ranger told him. *Some people just deserve a free ticket to hell.*

Chapter 40

Marcie

In Mr. Winston's quiet old house, Marcie slept the day away. Pecos and Kerrie were at the hospital and Mr. Winston, who'd become part of their family, was either with them or out spreading the news that Kerrie's baby was born.

Brand had disappeared without waking her hours ago, but he left a text on her phone. Would you be open for a date? Pick you up before sunset.

It was almost dark when she texted back that she had to play at Bandit's tonight. Wayne was expecting her.

In what seemed like a blink he texted back. I'll meet you there. I may be late, don't leave the bar until I get there.

Marcie smiled. Brand didn't even know about the guy

who was threatening her—he was just protecting her. He was a good man and he kissed great. She usually wasn't attracted to good men, but she'd make an exception with Brand. He didn't drink. He didn't cuss. He must be a health nut because he worked out like a madman.

Most of the men in her past had been passing through. They spoke of adventures and told her how hot she was. A few left without remembering her name when they said goodbye.

But Brand was different. He was stable, quiet. She could almost believe he was a virgin who knew little about the world. If it wasn't for the scars on his body, she could easily believe he'd never left the valley. She'd only seen the scars from a distance, but whatever hurt him had been bad, real bad. No wonder he didn't like to be around people. When they'd been at the bar in Honey Creek, she felt he was on guard. He didn't take a deep breath until they stepped outside.

As she played to an almost empty bar at Bandit's, she thought of him holding her as she'd slept. Any other guy she knew would have felt her up or tried to have sex, but not Brand. He seemed to really care about her.

But, she'd been fooled before. One rising star in country music had told her when she was eighteen that she was his soul mate and he'd love her for the rest of their lives. He even wrote a song about her. Two days later he left with her money and didn't bother to pay the week-long hotel bill they'd run up.

Tonight, in the dusty bar, her songs were sad as she thought back over her short-time lovers and almost friends.

Halfway through her last set and Brand still hadn't shown. Marcie decided she'd ask Wayne to walk her to her car, then she'd drive straight back to Honey Creek.

She wasn't upset that Brand didn't show up. Knowing her luck, she would have been surprised if he had. He'd probably forgotten about asking her for a date.

As she played, letting the music relax her, she noticed a group of men move from the pool area and head for the bar. They were laughing. None of them looked familiar except one tall, skinny bald guy bringing up the tail of the migration.

The music stopped. She couldn't move. She simply stared at the boots of the men passing. All wore steel-toed work boots like linemen or riggers wear. All but one. He wore an old pair of western boots. The heels were worn down and muddy. The leather uncared for.

She watched those boots walk closer. She knew who was coming.

The man who'd frightened her earlier walked closer and dropped a dollar in her tip jar, then whispered, "When I come back to you for a second round of fun, I'll cut you in the same places while I take you. A scar is easier to open when the first wound isn't completely healed. If you don't fight or scream too loud, I might only cut you in a few new places. You can't hide from me, Marcie. I'll find you. No one cares about trash like you. We can play our little cutting game all night. I'm in no hurry. So, move back to your trailer to make it easier on me, or I'll make it hard on you."

Marcie closed her eyes and heard him whisper, "Go back home tonight where you belong and leave the door unlocked, or you'll be real sorry."

When she opened her eyes again, he was gone. It was closing time. No one seemed to notice she'd stopped playing. She scanned the room, making sure he wasn't standing behind her or hiding in a corner.

She sat unmoving on her stool. Her eyes wide, her
hands shaking, staring into the smoky room. Wishing she
was anywhere else.

When the door opened she held her guitar so tight she
was surprised it didn't crack. The yellow ribbon she'd
tied to the neck wiggled as she shook.

Then Brand walked in. Big, strong, safe Brand.

She wanted to run to him, but she couldn't. Somehow
she had to stand on her own. This was her problem, and it
wasn't fair to bring him into it. She couldn't go to him
every time she was afraid. He could take care of himself
in a fair fight, but she knew the bald guy wouldn't fight
fair.

She packed her guitar and did her best to smile as
Brand walked toward her.

He took the case. "I missed all your playing tonight?"

"Yep." She linked her arm in his, ignoring the money
in the tip jar. "Now, if you want me to sing, you'll have to
feed me."

"I can do that. Name the place."

"The truck stop outside of Honey Creek is probably
the only place open this late. You want to follow me to
my place at what Pecos and I decided to call the Winston
House? Then I'll ride with you to pick up food and we
can eat it in my sitting room."

She wouldn't tell Brand the bald man had frightened
her, but she wouldn't go back to the trailer tonight, or
ever.

"You have a sitting room?" Brand asked as if he hadn't
seen it.

"Of course."

He walked Marcie to her car, then followed her back
to the Winston House. When she slid into his truck, she

moved over next to him and said, "Since this is a date, mind if I have my good night kiss first?"

He laughed and kissed her. Both of them forgot about eating for several minutes. His kiss was warm and inviting, but not hungry. This man seemed to think a kiss was the event, not the preshow. She loved that about him.

By the time they got back with day-old fried chicken that had been in the warmer oven so long it looked dehydrated, both laughed and tossed the meal in the trash. They split a bag of Oreos and a half gallon of milk that she insisted they drink from wine glasses.

Marcie had slowly calmed down. She wouldn't let the bald guy scare her. He was just playing with her mind. If she was careful there was no way he could get to her. She was safe here, and even safer at the sheriff's office. She got off after sunup and would make sure she got to work early.

When the Oreos were gone, they moved to the front of the house, far away from the other bedrooms. As she played, she decided not to tell Brand about the threats. It would only worry him.

Tonight she played low and slow; in case anyone was above and heard her, they'd listen and drift back to sleep. Unfortunately, the music worked on Brand as well.

For a few minutes she tried to figure out how to wake him up. He looked so comfortable in an overstuffed chair, probably bought in the '50s. Laying her guitar on the couch, she pulled off her boots and crawled up in his lap.

He sighed and circled her with his arms.

Marcie closed her eyes, feeling completely safe.

When she woke later, she knew Brand had carried her to bed and covered her with a quilt. As she rolled over to cuddle further under the covers, she thought he was a good man, too good to get mixed up with her.

She wanted to drift back to sleep so she could dream his arms were still holding her even though he'd left.

But dark dreams haunted her, as they did now and then. She'd been braiding her doll's hair when a man opened the door of their trailer. He'd asked where her dad was. When she'd said she didn't know, he'd stepped inside. For a long time he just watched her, and then said they might as well have some fun. It was time she learned a few things.

Marcie cried in her sleep as the dream continued. The man had called her names she didn't know the meaning of and he'd slapped her hard when she made any sound while he hurt her. When he'd left, she ran out into the trees. She curled up in the brown grass and dead leaves, wishing she could disappear. She cried until no more tears would come.

Marcie jerked awake and sat up. She was through crying, finished hiding, over feeling sorry for herself. She'd always be that hurt little girl if she didn't do something. She couldn't let one man frighten her now.

As the day dawned, she dressed and headed out. Her plan might not do any good, but she had to try.

Saturday

Chapter 41

Brand

Long after midnight, Brand left Marcie at Mr. Winston's place, and drove around. He'd broken half a dozen laws, so what would a few more matter? In the twelve hours since he'd talked to Colby, he'd secured Mr. Winston's place and checked on Widows Park's security to make sure it was working. He'd put trackers on all three of the junk cars in Leon's front yard.

Brand had watched the man enough to know he lived alone, but now and then a buddy would crash at his place. Through a cracked window he saw Leon watching a big-screen TV.

Brand waited. One hour. Two. Three.

He was standing fifty yards away when Leon pulled out of his yard half an hour before dawn. Maybe he

planned to make a drug deal, maybe he thought he could
steal something. Or, he might be planning a visit to Marcie.

If Leon thought she was still in her trailer, he might
figure she wouldn't be expecting him in the darkness before sunrise. No one would be up this early. No one
would see him. Over the years, Brand had learned to
think like his targets. They all followed patterns. Leon
had been on his radar since the night he knocked on Marcie's door. If he was lucky, Leon wouldn't cross Brand
before the sheriff had enough evidence to put him away.

Brand had left her sleeping in Honey Creek. He knew
Marcie wouldn't be at the trailer and Leon would never
find her.

Brand walked toward Leon's house. He thought he
would have to break in, but it turned out Leon had left the
back door unlocked. Brand stepped over several trash
bags and switched on a flashlight. Pig sties were cleaner
than this place. It looked like the trash truck had pulled
up to the door and dumped a load. Old paper, half-eaten
food, dirty clothes. The bathroom was worse. In a back
bedroom there was nothing on an old stained mattress but
a rag of a blanket.

Brand touched nothing, but was sure some of the stains
were blood. Could have been Leon's blood, of course.
Maybe he had frequent nosebleeds. Brand had a feeling,
though, that the spots wouldn't match Leon's blood type.

Brand backed out of the house and checked the tracker
in his truck. Leon was heading to Someday Valley, just as
he'd guessed the guy would.

Leon was making a wasted trip.

He thought of calling to check on Marcie, but she'd
said she had a few things she had to work out, and needed

time to learn the kitchen and where everything was in the huge house. Mr. Winston would need help getting everything ready for the baby.

Marcie was safe in Honey Creek. Brand relaxed.

Brand drove around for a while, fighting the urge to go check on her. He knew he was getting too close to Marcie too fast. There were a thousand rules in his occupation, and the first one was: Don't get too involved. Don't get close enough to people that they might notice you disappear from time to time.

He told himself he was simply helping Marcie out of a bad spot. A few kisses didn't mean commitment. Once everything settled down, they might see each other now and then. They'd probably drift into just being friends.

Man, he was going to miss those kisses though.

When he pulled up to his house just after dawn, he sensed something was wrong even before he saw the barn lights were on. He cut the engine and silently walked toward the open barn door.

The barn was silent except for the occasional shifting of the horses.

Brand moved along the left side, all his senses on full alert.

Then he saw Marcie, standing in the center of his workout space. She had on gloves and was punching at the bag. The bag didn't move. Her long ponytail was flying behind her as she battled without any progress.

"Morning." Brand jumped onto the mat. "You beating up my equipment?"

She lowered her head. "I'm afraid the bag is winning."

He walked over to her and unstrapped the gloves. "What are you doing here, Marcie?"

"I couldn't sleep after you left and I remembered seeing this equipment earlier. I want to learn to fight. I'm tired of being afraid. Will you teach me to defend myself?"

He saw the panic in her hazel eyes and decided her fear took precedence over his need to check his security system. She was a mouse who wanted to roar. "It's a great deal of work, honey. By the time you learn how to fight, every part of your body will hurt."

"I have to learn to survive. I have to be prepared to fight."

He understood. He'd seen her broken the night of the almost rape, and again when she'd been left alone at the station. He saw her afraid at the bar last night, but she hadn't told him why. He wanted to hold her and tell her he'd watch over her, but she needed to know how to feel safe when no one was around to protect her. He knew she was right. He couldn't promise to always be there.

He smiled at her. "First, you've got to learn to fall. How to roll and be back on your feet before anyone can kick you. That one skill might save your life if danger does come."

"Teach me."

They began. Working out on the machines to strengthen her core and improve her balance. Then he taught her to stand so she could put power into her hit and avoid being hit.

After an hour of hard work, she strapped on gloves and he showed her how to hit the bag. No, not hit just the bag, but swing like she was going through the bag.

The second time she hit, the bag moved.

The morning passed. No matter how many times she

fell, she got up and wanted more. When he tried to slow down, take it easy on her, she would have none of it.

When she was out of breath and barely able to stand, he stood in front of her and asked, "You want to tell me what this is all about?"

"No!" she yelled. "Can I come back tomorrow?"

"All right." He tossed her a towel and they walked outside to his truck.

He opened the passenger side and helped her in. "You mind if I drive you home?"

For a moment she held his hand tightly. "I don't want to be alone. Can I stay with you for a while?"

They didn't say another word as he drove her the fifty feet to his front door. Once they were in his house, she disappeared down the hall and he made cocoa. He stepped outside to cool off as she took a shower. Twenty minutes later he found her curled up in his bed.

He sat on the other side of the bed and leaned his head against the headboard. "Glad to see you've made yourself at home. I love these sleepovers we're getting into."

She didn't say a word, so he drank the cocoa and turned out the lights. He tugged off his boots and shirt and got under the covers.

After a few minutes she pulled his arm toward her and cuddled her body around it.

"You awake, koala bear?"

"I'm awake," she answered.

"Did you forget something?"

"No. I don't think so."

"Well, unless I've lost all sense of feeling in my arm, you forgot your red pajamas." He rolled slightly toward her and ran his free hand down her entire body. Her skin was so soft.

"I need you to hold me."

He swallowed hard. "I'm afraid I'd like to do much more than that."

She wiggled closer, making him groan. "I was thinking the same thing."

Brand didn't know what to do. His mind was telling him one thing. She was afraid. Maybe she just wanted to thank him? Maybe she was bored? Maybe she didn't want to be alone and any man would do right now?

Then there was his body that was all in for adventure, passion.

"Are you sure about this, Marcie?"

"I wouldn't be naked if I wasn't. I want to sleep in your arms with nothing between us. We can go back to be kissing friends later."

He still didn't move. "I . . . I . . ."

She rose on one elbow. "Is something wrong? Are you broken, maybe from the army? I saw the scars on your back. Do you have scars I haven't seen? Oh, Brand, I'm so sorry."

"I'm not broken." He could barely form words as he stared at her body.

She flopped on her back. "You don't want me. I thought from those kisses that you did. I'm fine if you just want to be friends. I'll get up and put my pajamas on."

"I want you, honey."

She rolled back on her elbow, her breast pushing into his side. "I give up. Why are we hesitating?"

Brand was glad the room was dark. He had a feeling he was blushing for the first time in years. "I . . . I . . ."

"You've already said that part," she reminded him.

"I don't do this kind of thing very often."

"Sex?"

Even in the dark he could feel her looking at him as if he was an alien. "Yeah, sex."

"When was the last time? I know you're a quiet man, but I figured you talked sometimes. With your body you wouldn't have to talk much to get a girl to go home with you."

"I don't want to talk about it now." He tried to pull away but her grip was still around his arm.

"Why? Were you hurt badly by a woman? Did she break your heart? Believe me, you'll heal."

He thought of a girl in high school. They'd kind of learned about sex together. He'd asked her to wait for him when he joined up, but she didn't. By the time he got home he hadn't cared. He was on another path by then.

"That was part of it, but I don't think my heart was involved at eighteen," Brand said honestly. "Once I healed from being shot, all I wanted to do was fight, and the career I chose kept me busy. In my job in the army and afterwards, I traveled. No time to date."

He brushed her hair back away from her face. "I'm not the kind of guy who does one-night stands. I want it to mean something. I want to care about the woman I make love to. The few times I didn't follow my rules, the sex was great but afterwards I felt hollow inside. Or, I walked away and probably hurt someone. I didn't like that."

Marcie sat up. A tiny sliver of sunshine from a slit in the curtains played off her beautiful breasts. "Are you saying you don't want to sleep with me?"

"No, I do. I just want you to know I may be a bit rusty."

She didn't move. "Are you saying you care about me?"

"Yes. I've loved you for a long time. I just didn't

know how to say it. If we do this I'm not just playing around. This is no one-night stand. This is the start of something that might last forever."

Marcie let go of his arm and jumped off the bed.

Brand watched her stomp around the room looking for her clothes. She was cussing the world and her bad luck. She was breathtaking.

Finally, she whirled at him. "I should have known better than to get involved with you, Brandon Rodgers. I knew from the start that you were too good for me. I should have seen the signs. You never felt me up or asked to borrow money. You never hinted about what we might do if you had me alone."

She glared at him. "You probably don't even know how to talk dirty. You even slept with me and just slept. I should have spotted the signs of crazy."

Brand turned on the lamp by the bed so he could see her better. "You're mad at me for caring about you?"

She pulled on her jeans, forgetting underwear, and found one boot. She thumped around looking for the other leather boot. "I've got along just fine for years without anyone caring for me. Every time a man says he loves me, the next thing I remember him saying is good-bye."

She picked up her other boot and threw it at him.

When she came close to pick it up, he grabbed her arm and pulled her back in bed. He rolled on top of her and braced her head with his hands. "Do you have any idea how beautiful you are right now? Cuss and scream at me all you want, but I won't stop loving you. You're worth the loving, and I'm not going anywhere. I've been saving love up most of my life, and I'm afraid you're the one who has to take it."

Tears bubbled out of her eyes. "Promise," she whispered.

"I promise. I've loved you since that first time I listened to you play. I don't care how many men you've slept with. I'm not too good for you. You're the only woman I want to sleep with and drink cocoa on the porch in every season with."

She wiggled her arms free and wrapped her arms around his neck. "I thought I'd never say this, but Brand, shut up and make love to me."

Brand whispered that he couldn't turn away from her if bombs were going off in the yard.

"Say it again," she whispered.

"About the bombs?" He laughed.

"No, about loving me and drinking cocoa on the porch."

He whispered that and much more as his hands learned her body.

She did sleep in his arms with nothing between them. Twice during the night he made love to her as if she were the most cherished woman in the world. When they settled back into sleep, he kissed her gently and she'd sigh and say, "Thank you," as if he'd given her a gift.

Chapter 42

Colby

The afternoon sun was already starting to dip before Colby pulled into town. Honey Creek always reminded him of a postcard paradise. He wondered if every traveler passing through thought of living here.

But all was not calm; the day had gone downhill since he'd talked to Brand, and he'd promised he wouldn't find Piper until he had news.

The agent had suggested Colby drive over to Someday Valley before he headed to Honey Creek.

He needed to get to know the lay of the land. Brand's suggestion made sense. Which told Colby that Brand thought, or maybe feared, it might figure into their investigation. If the thin man Piper had seen with Marcie was planning something, Colby needed to know how to move in his world.

Neither man mentioned what "just in case" might be. Colby simply took Brand's advice, knowing he'd be lucky to see Piper tonight.

As he pulled into Someday Valley, the first thing he saw was an old gas station junked up with broken car parts and used tires. A sign on the glass read, WE'RE OUT OF ICE. DON'T PET THE DOG. An OUT OF ORDER sign had been taken off one of the pumps but left on the ground.

An old man came out when Colby pulled up. He sat down in a metal lawn chair so old he'd worn off the paint.

Colby bought a few gallons of gas and looked around. The town had been built midway up a hill. Beautiful trees behind the place, and rolling grassland spread out all the way to the river below. A mix of houses spotted the landscape to the river. A few two-stories that could be beautiful if painted, and several small cabins that looked like a fisherman's retirement home.

From this angle the valley looked peaceful and calm.

Off to the side, behind the bar, was a cluster of shacks laid out in no particular order, like someone built the homes but forgot about putting in a road. Colby remembered seeing something like them before. His dad called it *Pigtown*, where wooden houses had been cleared to make room for a mall. They'd been set out on an acre of land and left to rot. Only the rats and druggies moved in.

Some of the houses in the valley below made the trailer park across the street look desirable by comparison.

Less than half of the mobile homes looked occupied. The rest looked like they'd been left to rot.

Colby looked at the old man. "You know who owns the trailer park?"

"I do," the old guy said. "You looking for a cheap place? I got a few empty trailers and one cabin near the water." He pointed one arthritic finger toward the park. "It used to be nice over there, before the drugs and the bums moved in."

Colby put the cap on his tank and handed over money for the gas. "I might go take a look, if you don't mind?"

"Nope."

Colby saw he could pass through the Bandit's Bar parking lot. From there, if he didn't turn in the main entrance but circled around, was a road that looked like it went above the trees that banked the back of the park. A back entrance to the trailer lot that few would notice.

"What about that spot beyond the park?" He saw a grassy area that looked perfect for a house. Beautiful view in every direction. The river in front and the hills in back. "Any chance you'd sell that land?"

"I own it, but it's not available."

"Why not? All it's got on it is an old picnic table. You could name your price on those acres."

"I told you it ain't open for discussion. Private property."

Colby kept picking on the old guy. "You saving it for yourself, old man?"

"No. I'm saving it for a little girl I once saw playing there. She planted wildflowers all around that old picnic table and they still bloom. You should see it in spring. I'm keeping it like it is now so she can come back whenever she wants to. Her special place will be there when she needs it. She don't know it but it will be hers when I'm gone."

"Sounds like a plan." Colby strapped on his helmet. "You got a soft heart, old man."

"Don't tell anyone or I'll tell the locals you're in the Hells Angels. The last one who came through here slept with half the wives in town. All the husbands will take it out on you."

Colby waved as he headed up the back road. He climbed up a road no car could have managed, then crossed through the trees and came out with a clear view of Someday Valley. The beauty of the place shocked him. Close up, the houses and trailers were old and in need of repair; but from far above, the town seemed peaceful, sleeping in nature's arms.

If Brand had been keeping an eye on Marcie, this would be the place to see all. From this point he could see the entire valley, and it was a straight devil's ride down to the last trailer in the park. Piper told him that was where Marcie had lived. Last trailer near the tree line.

He'd heard that Marcie moved to Honey Creek, but the last trailer in the park was where she grew up. When people are frightened, they run. He needed to know where she'd run to and make sure he got there before that creep, Leon, did.

Reason told him she'd never come back here, but people do strange things when they are afraid. He pulled out his binoculars and watched for a while.

When he walked back to his bike, Colby called Piper's office and her cell but she didn't answer. He left messages, then headed back to Honey Creek and drove around for a while looking for that ugly old van of hers.

This weekend was starting out to be a rerun of last
week. It seemed he came home to play hide-and-seek
with the mayor again.

After he'd left Brand's ranch he'd called Widows
Park, and Piper's grandmother had told him Piper was at
the church in a meeting. He'd guessed it would be over
by now, but maybe not. He drove over to the church and
parked in the back beside her van.

Half an hour later, she walked out the back door of the
church and waved, but she didn't smile. Several people
darted to their cars to avoid the wind, but Piper slowly
walked over to him and merely stared at him.

He'd forgotten how beautiful she was. He loved that
she always wore high heels, even if she did take them off
every chance she got. He also loved how her chestnut-
colored hair danced along her shoulders. His mother was
going to love her. A classic beauty, she'd say. They had a
long way to go before he took her home to meet the family, but he could see it in their future.

When he took her back home, Mom would make them
sleep in separate bedrooms and his dad would wink and
say Colby got lucky finding a girl like Piper. Of course
he'd have to explain that they were just dating. She'd
never mentioned anything more. Lover didn't seem to
mean mate and lately he wasn't sure he even fit in the
lover category.

As she neared, he silently swore that the next time he
came to Honey Creek, he'd drive his car so they'd have
some privacy when he kissed her hello. The need was so
strong he thought about ignoring the other people. He
wanted to start with light kisses tasting her skin, then
when he finally reached her mouth, he wanted one long,
deep kiss.

When he swung off the bike to kiss her cheek, she backed a foot away.

Like a daydreaming fool, he didn't notice she wasn't smiling until she was three feet away.

"Evening, darlin'." He grinned without taking his sunglasses off. He didn't want to talk about his black eye. In truth he didn't want to talk at all.

Piper put her fists on her hips. "I thought you were coming in Thursday."

Colby felt the urge to duck. For a moment he couldn't form words, which made him look like he was trying to think up a lie. "I had lots to do. A bad wreck Thursday night on I-35. After that, paperwork and interviews to try to make sense of it all." He couldn't tell her what or who he was interviewing out here with people so close, all acting like they weren't listening.

To his shock, she turned around and walked away.

Five minutes later, when she pulled into the Widows Park driveway, he was right behind her.

Now, Colby was plain mad. "What is going on, PJ?" He climbed off the bike and met her before she got out of her van. "First, you ask me to come home and now you don't talk to me."

"I wanted you to help Marcie, not me. I can take care of myself." Piper closed her eyes and lowered her voice. "Thank you for coming down to help. I understand you're probably worried about me, but the more I think about it, this 'me and you' thing won't work. You remind me of an old jack-in-the-box I had as a kid. I never know when you're going to pop up."

"You're breaking up with me?" He kept his voice low when he saw three white-haired ladies watching from the window ten feet away.

"Were we ever together?"

She stared at him a moment with those dark green eyes and added, "Maybe we were just two people caught up in passion. I'm independent. I don't need any man to take care of me. You were there for me six months ago when Boone Buchanan tried to kill me, but that was just part of your job. I'm all right now and I don't need a knight in shining armor following me around waiting to be the hero. You did a good job and you got your Texas Ranger badge and I went back to my job, being mayor. Our lives don't fit together."

Colby had never wanted to hold her so badly. His darling PJ had on her professional mask. She'd face any storm head-on, and right now he seemed to be the storm. When they'd talked before, she'd been frightened for her friend and she'd turned to him. But between then and now she seemed to have found her footing.

She had to know that he cared about her from the night they met, and that caring had nothing to do with the job.

Maybe he hadn't told her, but he'd shown her. He'd never cared about someone so deeply. She'd rocked his world when they'd made love, and now she turned away as if she barely remembered him.

Piper stepped into the big house where all the Mackenzie women lived. He couldn't help but think that she'd grow old there. She was married to her job. She'd make a great governor of Texas one day.

He wanted to yell and demand she come back out and talk to him. But he had the feeling if he yelled, one of the old ladies would rush out and bop him on the head with her cane.

As he walked back to his bike, he thought about what his mother would never have the opportunity to say. Piper was a classic beauty, but she'd never be his.

Strange, Colby thought. *At the moment I lost her, I finally realized that I love her.*

Chapter 43

Jesse

Fifteen-year-old Star Summers stumbled into Jesse's kitchen looking like she'd been on a three-day drunk. Strands of her hair created a stringy curtain over her sunburned face and the eye makeup she'd had on yesterday had drifted down her cheeks. For a moment Jesse thought she might be auditioning for a part in a horror film. You know, the unnamed teenager who runs the wrong way and bangs into the monster in the first scene.

"Morning," he said, fighting down a smile.

"What's good about it? Sunny Lyn woke me up jumping on my bed. When that didn't work, she tried talking me awake." She sneered at him. "Who taught that kid to talk?"

"Sorry about that. I forgot to tell you she's our alarm clock around here. You want orange juice or coffee?"

The teenager kept glaring at him. "Coffee, of course, I'm not a child."

He figured if she was old enough to run away, she was old enough to drink coffee.

When he slid the cup across the bar, Adalee's little sister almost smiled. She added milk and three spoons of sugar, as his kids gathered around her. Zak stared at her like he'd discovered a new life form. Danny seemed to think she was their new pet, and Sunny Lyn climbed up in her lap.

Star calmly accepted the kids as if they were extra appendages. They'd circled her all day yesterday, so it must feel normal by now.

Jesse passed out juices and set the makings for breakfast burritos in the center of the bar. The kids each made their own burrito. Zak added a touch of hot sauce to his meat and cheese. Danny liked extra cheese and lettuce on his eggs, and Sunny Lyn put blueberry jam in hers.

Star made a face when the four-year-old offered her a bite.

Jesse couldn't hold back a laugh as he went over what the plans were for the day. Care for the horses, of course. Three had been picked up yesterday, heading back home, and two new ones came in. The owner had bought them for his kids, but the mare needed some gentling first. He booked two weeks at the horse hotel for both horses.

With Star keeping an eye on Sunny Lyn, Zak, and Danny, Jesse could get a few stalls cleaned out and ready in case they were needed. He'd had several calls. Who knew horse hotels were in demand?

As he went down the list of chores to do, Star interrupted. "You make your kids work?"

"Everyone works on a farm."

"Why?"

Jesse smiled and repeated what his dad used to say. "We share the fun."

"Yeah," Danny said. "As soon as that kid pops out, I get to name it."

"What kid?" Star looked around as if she'd miscounted.

"The baby goat," Jesse explained, then shook his head. "City girl."

"Farmer," she shot back.

As days off from school often did, daylight passed with chores and fun. While Jesse cleaned out all the stalls, Star let each of his children ride Princess when she walked the horse around the corral. The royal guest was as gentle as a rocking horse. When Star lifted Sunny Lyn up to kiss the horse goodbye, Princess shook her mane so hard all the kids laughed.

All morning he heard laughter. When they sat down for a lunch of peanut butter and jelly sandwiches on the porch, one invisible chip seemed to have fallen off Star's shoulder. Once, Jesse looked up and saw all three of his kids following Star to an old windmill, like ducks in a row.

Jesse didn't ask her questions; they just drifted through the hours. She sometimes played with the kids and sometimes helped him. Again and again he saw how much she loved animals.

When she asked if she could ride one of the horses outside the corral, he said, "Sure, if you can saddle him."

"I can do that, farmer, if you show me. It's not a skill we learn in school."

"It's a pity," he said as he began the lesson. "You don't do this right, or don't double check, or do something stupid to scare the horse, he'll toss you off. When that happens, I don't want to hear any complaining."

"Agreed."

"Stay in sight of the house."

"Agreed."

Jesse thought of another ten things to tell her, but he figured she'd stopped listening. As he boosted her into the saddle, he said, "Get to know him. Remember, he wants to work with you."

As he'd expected, the wild teenager was gentle with the horse and the bay wasn't even sweating when she brought him back to the barn.

"Thanks," she whispered when she slid off the saddle.

"No problem. You can ride anytime you want."

She turned to face him. "Thanks for trusting me. Most people don't."

Jesse nodded once. "Their loss, kid."

She smiled. "Right. Their loss."

When Star disappeared about five, Zak told him she'd gone in to make supper. "You think she can cook?"

"Don't matter. We're going to eat it either way."

Zak grinned. "I guess if I can eat your cooking I can handle about anything."

An hour later she stepped on the porch and yelled that supper was ready. Jesse washed his hands as he eyed quiche and salad on the table. His children stared at him like they were not touching it until he ate some.

Jesse took a bite and declared it great.

Star smiled. "My mother taught me to cook when I was no bigger than Sunny Lyn."

"Will you teach me, Star? I only had a mother for one day."

"Sure. I'll teach you one thing a day. We can make supper together." Her smile didn't reach her eyes. "I was lucky. I had a mother for seven years."

After dinner they watched a movie Jesse had seen a dozen times. He stepped out on the porch as Danny sat next to Star and told her what was about to happen next.

It had been a good day, he thought. A peaceful time. In a way he felt closer to Adalee. Maybe he was helping her. Star might not be at home but Adalee knew she was safe.

When the movie ended, everyone was ready for bed, even Star. "I can't believe I'm going to bed with the chickens. Until today I had no idea what that phrase even meant."

Before long the house was silent. Jesse walked out to the barn and dialed Adalee. He told her every detail of the day he could remember.

"Thanks," she said when he was finished. "For everything."

"You're welcome. Oh, one other thing. Didn't hear a cuss word all day."

Adalee sounded like she was crying. "I don't believe it."

The conversation changed directions when Jesse said in a low voice, "Talk to me. I like hearing your voice."

She seemed to understand. She told him the details of her day. The people, the customers.

He sat down and listened. It felt so good to be talking to someone his age, and as he listened he could almost feel his hand touching her.

The conversation moved into how to handle Star as if

she were their child. After several ideas they agreed to let her stay a few more days at the farm, then suggest she go back to school. He could drop her off at the bakery when he took his kids to one of the grandmothers' houses. Adalee and Star could visit while they had breakfast. She promised to keep it light and not make a fuss if Star wanted to come back to the farm.

"We need to rebuild our relationship," Adalee admitted. "She's right, Jesse, I'm not her mother. I'm her sister. Maybe it's time I started acting like one."

"She's welcome to stay over here at night. In truth, she's good with the kids and the horses. If I bring her home, she won't have time to run around with her wild friends."

"I'm not sure Star isn't the wild one. Can I come out sometime?" Adalee asked.

"You're always welcome." He hesitated, then added, "I'd love to see you, and it has nothing to do with your sister. In another world, I'd love you to come out and sleep over, but that's not happening."

She laughed. "Someday?"

"In our dreams maybe," he echoed.

They were both silent for a while, then she whispered, "Think of me tonight."

Jesse closed his eyes. "I usually do."

Neither said goodbye. He didn't want to and he guessed she felt the same.

When he went back inside and turned off the lights, he glanced in each bedroom, checking one last time that all was well.

Star's face shone in the moonlight. As she slept, and with no dark makeup, he saw she was just a kid pretending to be grown. The thought crossed his mind that if she hadn't climbed in his pickup yesterday, there was no telling where she'd be tonight.

He lay in his bed doing what he said he would, thinking of Adalee. A peace settled over him. They might not get together often alone, but they could be friends. They could help one another raise the kids. They would talk. They could dream of someday.

That was enough right now. He'd gone from lonely to someday.

Chapter 44

Colby

Ranger Colby McBride climbed on his Harley and rode over to the fire station. He knew he could use Sam's computer to contact his friend David Hatcher back at headquarters. Colby had slept on one of the bunks upstairs last week, so he was considered one of the guys. Sam, the fire chief, even told Colby he'd have to go out if a call came in.

When the information he'd asked Dave for started coming in, Colby called headquarters, guessing that David would be the only one still in the office.

"What did you find?" Colby asked.

"Good evening to you too." Dave didn't waste any time. "I found plenty. Reports of rape where the woman was cut are coming in from several counties. I've eliminated those solved and those accounts where the woman knew her attacker. When I matched those locations up with places Leon Newton had worked in the past five years, several lit up. A few had the exact MO. Apparently when he moves, he only travels one or two counties over. Two years back, reports of incidents with bad knife cuts started coming in from emergency rooms. Most of the women were not willing to press charges. Too afraid. The cuts were getting deeper. At first he cut deep enough to bleed, but the last few victims required stitches.

"The description was the same. Balding man, tall, thin, with a knife. Not much for the police to go on. None of the cases have been solved lately. Several of the women had been drinking. None knew the name of the attacker or where he lived."

Dave was silent. "I've been reading the records. Only two crimes in the same county. Or at least only two recorded. When you think about the fact that less than half of the rapes are reported, no telling how many we're looking at.

"First cut is usually just below the collarbone and the second's on the breast. Several women commented that he liked to tell her what he was going to do." Dave took a long breath. "If I'm following the same man, he's cutting more and more. It's like the rape isn't important, it's the cuts he's going for."

"What about the women? Do they follow a pattern?"

"They live alone. He followed some home; others he caught getting in their car or walking. Most were women who hung out at bars. One was a secretary in the building across the street from a popular bar.

"Some disappeared after they gave their statement. They never followed up with the police, and the cops had nothing to tell them anyway."

"Thanks, Dave. If you find anything else, call me. I'm off tomorrow. I think I'll stay around Honey Creek."

"Yeah, I'm off too, thanks to our all-nighter." He laughed. "I think I'll spend the weekend here in the office. Unlike you, buddy, I don't have a life. Maybe one day I'll ride along with you to Honey Creek. I lost my wife for what looks like a month. She went to Galveston to plan her sister's wedding. I may never see her again. I might as well drop by Honey Creek and look for a date. The mayor have a sister?"

"No, but she's got a grandmother."

"Great. I like older women. After we marry and you marry Piper, I'll be your grandfather."

Colby didn't want to mention that he was no longer with Piper. It seemed every time he showed up late, they were off again. "Sounds like a great idea, Grandpa Dave. I'll get you nuts and socks every Christmas. See you Tuesday."

When Colby put the phone down, he felt a chill. Leon was close. He could feel it. Piper might think she was safe, but he planned to stay on guard.

Chapter 45

Leon

Leon Newton lay in the weeds across from Mr. Winston's house in Honey Creek. Marcie's car was not parked in the drive. Which meant she was running around somewhere. Probably out drinking and going wild, like tramps do.

He'd tried the trailer every night, thinking she'd come back like he told her to, but she hadn't. Then Joey told him she'd packed up and moved to Honey Creek.

But Leon looked in her windows. It looked like her stuff was still there. She'd be back. If he couldn't find her here in Honey Creek, he'd find her in Someday Valley. It would be a better place for their date anyway. So many people had moved out of the trailer park, it was almost a ghost town. Nobody would hear Marcie's screams.

Thinking about her screams made him smile. He could almost smell her blood, warm and dark as he smeared it over her hot skin.

He patted the knife in his pocket as thoughts of what he'd do flashed in his mind. He'd started cutting his women deeper, thinking it would leave a wider scar. The first cut would be on the inside of her thigh. A few weeks later, when he circled back for another date, he'd get a kick out of examining the scars forming before he cut again. Most of his dates disappeared, but now and then he found one still around. They never screamed as loud the second time.

Leon would bet Marcie would be a screamer every time. He'd take it slow with her. One, maybe two cuts a night after the first time. She had nowhere to run. No one would believe her or help her. They could play his little cutting game again and again.

Leon moved a few feet closer in the grass. The big old house she'd rented a room in was silent and dark.

Who knows how late she'd stay out tonight, but when she came in she'd probably be too drunk to fight much. If she parked across the street, he'd grab her and take her back to Someday Valley. If she went to the trailer, he'd find her before dawn. Either way he'd have a date with her tonight.

On a night this dark, she'd be no problem to catch. He'd simply push a knife into her side, deep enough to bleed, and make her drive him back to her old place. Or better still, they could go back to his place. He could keep her all weekend there. But then, no one would notice or care what was going on at the last trailer, and he wouldn't have to clean up the blood. He'd leave her tied up for a few days and just drop in whenever he wanted to play. If no one came by, it wasn't his fault if she died.

In his mind she was the cause of all his troubles. His fishing buddies weren't hanging out with him anymore because they blamed him for them being hurt.

Wayne, that nosy bartender, must have seen her shiver when he stopped to talk to her the last time she sang. The barkeep told him not to come back to Bandit's, which meant he had to drive all the way to Honey Creek to buy beer.

He'd applied for two jobs yesterday. One look at his bruised face from the fall over Joey, and he was turned away. That wouldn't have happened if Marcie had cooperated.

Leon took a gulp from the bottle of whiskey he'd stolen from the gas station. It was almost gone. He was shivering, and the tramp had stood him up. Tonight was supposed to be the night.

He stumbled to his feet and decided tomorrow night he'd go after that rancher who thought he could butt into his business. Joey and the other boys would go with him on that one. If he could come up with a plan, he could talk that gang into anything after a night of drinking. He'd tell them that he was going out to get even. Make them think he was just going to beat Brand up and maybe steal a few things lying around. Once they got to the ranch, Leon knew he wouldn't be leaving until the rancher was dead.

Then, he'd tell Marcie all about how Brand died. It'd give them something to talk about when he finally got her alone.

Sunday

Chapter 46

Piper

Piper wasn't surprised to see Colby eating at the Honey Creek Café the next morning. He looked tired. For a moment she thought of stepping through the kitchen and leaving without talking to him, but he had come because she'd asked for help, even if he was two days late. The least she could do was thank him and wish him a good life.

As she walked toward him, she remembered how they'd made love upstairs many times, and laughed that the spirits who haunted the place were watching. Loving him was so easy. He was funny and caring and easy to tease. They'd hidden out and playfully made love on her little office couch just before the fire six months ago.

When the smoke and the heat surrounded them, Colby never left her. He put her life above his own.

He'd stolen a piece of her heart that night, but they lived in two different worlds. Who knows, they might get together again sometime, but it would be as friends, not lovers.

He was a ranger. He lived the job. And she was a mayor with goals to make life better for the citizens of Honey Creek.

And now, in a crowded café with people watching, she had to say goodbye. Maybe for good.

When she reached his table, he stood.

"I wanted to thank you"—she used her very proper mayor voice—"for helping me with the legal matter. It was kind of you to come."

"I have news." He stopped her farewell speech. His worried glare said so much more. Both were being professional, but there was so much more than that in his eyes. A longing. A loss he feared was coming.

Colby pulled out a chair and she slid into the seat across from him. They were both behaving like strangers.

A lump filled her throat. How could they have slid from lovers to strangers so quickly? Even now the need to touch him was strong.

"I've had a friend checking files," Colby said calmly, in a low voice so no one around would hear. "This guy who is bothering your friend may be a serial rapist, and he's getting more violent. We don't have enough to arrest him yet, but my partner believes his next target may not wake up from the attack."

Piper felt the blood drain from her face.

Colby continued. "I can't give you all the details, but you need to let your friend know she's in great danger."

"I tried to call her last night. Her phone went to voice-mail."

"I'll go with you to look for her. I have an idea where she might be."

"No. I know where she is. I'll go over to Mr. Winston's house. It's on my way home. If she's not there, I'll check the sheriff's office." She tried to keep her words from sounding harsh. "I know you have to get back to Austin. I'll let you know when I find her."

Colby nodded. "Promise me you'll stay in town. I worry that this guy knows you're her friend. He might come after you just to hurt her."

"I can take care of myself. Don't worry about me, Ranger McBride."

This was it, she thought. They were no longer lovers, or even, apparently, friends. All ties were breaking. But he couldn't seem to walk away without saying something.

He stood and offered his hand. "I'll walk you out."

She took his arm, holding on a bit too tight. She had to be brave and let him go. If he yelled at her or blamed her for not holding on, then she'd say nothing and walk away.

But he said nothing as he walked beside her. In the parking lot, between her van and his bike, he finally turned and faced her.

"A part of you will always be in my heart, PJ." His words were barely a whisper between them. "You can always call if you need anything."

Piper couldn't find the right words for once in her life.

"I'm not sure what went wrong, but it was all my fault. I'm sorry if I hurt you." His words were so low she barely heard them.

She stood there, straight and proper. He'd apologized

for the third time. He turned away as if there was nothing else to say.

She watched him walk back into the café. Maybe he was hoping she'd come back in, but she couldn't.

Piper climbed into her van and headed toward Mr. Winston's house. All that she loved about the area—the fall leaves, the sunshine over her town, the way everyone waved at her as they drove by—was lost on her. Not even the distant movement of the river could call to her today. She was wrapped in worry and hurt. She could feel trouble coming and all she wanted to do was have Colby wrap his arms around her.

Piper concentrated on not allowing a single tear to fall. She was used to being on stage. She knew how to not let her feelings show. Until he'd turned away from her, she'd thought deep down that one day they'd patch up whatever broke between them, but somehow that magic moment had passed.

She knew it was over. More than the sorrow of losing him was one fact that broke her heart. He was hurting as much as she was. Part of her wanted to run back to the café and hold him close and say she was sorry, so sorry, that she wasn't sure what she'd done wrong, or what he'd done.

As she turned a bend where the trees shaded the road, a man yelled for help. "Mayor, can you give me a hand? I ran over a stray dog and I'm afraid he's dying."

Piper jumped from the van and pushed through the bushes, listening for the whine. This was a blind corner. A driver couldn't see ten feet in front of the car until he was almost to the turn.

The silence told her the dog was probably already dead.

"I don't see the dog," she said a second before something hit her hard in the back of her head.

She felt herself floating down. Her last thought was that her heel was stuck in the mud one step away from the sidewalk.

Then nothing. All went black as if someone turned off the sun.

Chapter 47

Leon

Leon lifted the mayor and threw her over his shoulder. In less than a minute, he was driving away with the mayor stowed in the trunk of his car. Not a car or a person on the road. He'd made a clean getaway.

He hadn't had much time to plan. It was pure luck that he saw the mayor walking into the café. All he had to do was wait and think up a hook to catch her with. He was good at thinking on his feet. That's why he never got caught.

In a few hours he'd have Marcie. She'd come to save her friend. She'd do anything he asked if he promised to let the mayor go. He'd have her just where he wanted and this time she'd have nowhere to run.

He was finally fishing with the right bait.

Chapter 48

Marcie

It was too late for breakfast, but Marcie was starving. She wanted to cook for Brand. They could eat it in bed, then make love again. They'd gotten up twice before dawn and ended up boomeranging back to bed. This time she'd dressed before she started cooking. When bacon, eggs, and biscuits were on the table, she went back to the bedroom.

Brand was standing beside his closet wearing only his Levi's, and they weren't buttoned all the way. When he turned, his smile made her warm all over. The thought occurred to her that this quiet man said a lot with his hands and his brown eyes.

Right now he looked like he wanted to push her back on the bed and make love again. She didn't mind one bit, but at the rate they were going they'd starve to death.

A slow smile made him irresistible. "You coming back to bed, honey? I'm ready. I'm half undressed."

"You are half dressed, and breakfast is on the table. We have to eat. I'm starving." She couldn't stop herself from brushing his bare chest.

"I'm not that hungry for food. Cold breakfast is fine with me."

She moved closer. "Brand, you don't have to make up for lost time all in one day. I'm right here and I don't plan on going anywhere. You look at me like I'm your Christmas present and you know I'm going to be broken or lost by the end of the day. I promise, I'm going to stay around."

"For how long?"

"For as long as you want me."

He stood staring at her. "Then it's settled. If I get to choose, it's forever."

He pulled her up into his bear hug and kissed her as he carried her to the kitchen. "We'll eat fast. I want to make love to you until we lose count and have to start all over again, and again, and again."

She smiled when the meal caught his attention. He was eating before he sat down.

"I didn't think it would be that easy," he said after a few bites. "I thought we'd have to talk about it for a while."

"Talk about what?"

"About you being mine. You said I get to choose. You're my girl. I'm keeping you."

She brushed his hair. "No, cowboy, you're my guy and I'm keeping you."

He took another bite and seemed to swallow without even chewing. "You need to understand something. I've been yours for a long time. I was just waiting for you to notice."

She stood and straddled his lap. "I'm noticing now, Brand."

He forgot about food as his hands slid beneath her shirt and found her breasts.

She was laughing when her phone rang.

When Marcie saw that it was Piper she pointed to the front door and mouthed, "Piper."

Brand nodded and went back to devouring everything on the table.

She closed the door, not wanting Brand to hear their conversation. Marcie didn't want him to know she'd been threatened.

"What's up, Piper?" Marcie smiled, thinking about Brand waiting for her.

There was no answer to her question.

"Piper, are you there?"

A low voice whispered, "Oh, she's here. The question is where are you, tramp? We're going to have a little race, and no matter what happens you're going to come out the loser. The only question is, do you save the mayor, or do you die with her screams in your ears?"

Marcie couldn't breathe. She knew the voice well, it haunted her. "What have you done with the mayor? If you hurt her I swear . . ."

"Don't threaten me. Your friend is fine for now. But you're the only one who can save her. And if you don't do exactly as I say, she'll be nothing but ashes when you see her again.

"Pure, proper, Piper Mackenzie is tied to one of your old bar chairs in your trailer. I broke up the other one for firewood that is stacked around her. If you're not here in ten minutes, I'm going to roast her on a fire like she is nothing more than a little piggy. Since the fire is in the middle of your trailer, it'll all burn around her."

Marcie couldn't breathe, couldn't move.

"I read in the paper that the mayor has been afraid of flames since she was caught in that fire at city hall. I'm betting she'll scream real loud as it climbs up to her. She'll breathe in the smoke first and hot air will make her sweat. Maybe she'll pass out, but as the fire catches her clothes, I'm betting she'll wake up. She'll scream and beg me to help her, poor dear. But I can't. That was your job. She'll cuss you for not following orders.

"If you tell anyone, or take time to make a call, she'll be dead before you get here. Come on home, tramp, where you belong. You've been enough trouble to me. The timer on your oven begins NOW." He yelled the last word as if starting the race.

Marcie heard a muffled scream.

She dropped her phone and ran to her car. She had to save Piper. She was the one who got her friend in this mess.

Memories of Piper being kind to her in grade school flashed in her mind. Piper always stopped to talk to her, even though Marcie was no one and Piper was the mayor.

As she backed away down the drive, she glanced at Brand standing on the porch in his bare feet.

There was no time to explain. He'd try to stop her, or worse, want to go. Leon might kill all three of them then.

Turning onto the road, she took the curves at full speed. All Marcie could think about was getting there in time. Somehow she'd stop the madman. She'd trade her life for Piper's, if it came to that.

Almost to the paved road she realized she should have yelled at Brand. What would he think? What would he do?

He'd wait for her to come back. He said he'd been waiting for her all his life.

And if she didn't come back? Tears ran unchecked. He'd said she was his one love. It hurt her more to think that Brand would be forever alone than about what was waiting for her at the trailer.

She'd never be there to sing to Brand. To make love to him. To let him know how much he meant to her.

If Leon cut her and left her alive, she could never come back to Brand. She'd finally be too broken.

There would be no good ending in ten minutes. The best she might do was make herself the only one shattered.

Chapter 49

Colby

Colby McBride sat back down to a meal he could no longer eat. He'd watched Piper drive away and knew there would be no getting back together. It wasn't fair that they both had to choose.

He took his time drinking his coffee as he tried to figure out if there was one thing he could have done differently. When the crowd waiting for a table began to grow at the front, Colby paid the bill and walked to his bike.

He just sat there for a while, not wanting to leave. Maybe if he tried to talk to her one more time? Would it help if he said "I love you"? She deserved that. She needed to know that it was love from the first. He was just too dumb to see it.

One more try. Give love one more chance. She was

worth it. If he walked away now, he'd regret it the rest of his life.

He took the alley to Winston's place, thinking she'd be with Marcie. But the old guy said they hadn't seen Piper or Marcie.

She'd had over thirty minutes to get there. Piper must have gone somewhere else.

Colby drove the few blocks to Widows Park, thinking she might have changed her mind about talking to Marcie first. If she was upset, she'd go to her grandmother.

Determined to tell Piper the truth of how he felt, Colby banged on the front door at Widows Park. The sweet little ladies invited him in, but all said they hadn't seen Piper.

Colby dialed her number. No answer. He tried her office. No answer. Piper's aunt even tried, thinking that she might be screening her calls.

He tried to remain calm and told the ladies that he must have just missed her. He'd backtrack to the café. Maybe she had a flat in that old van.

The old dears turned into a cheerleading squad. Patting on him. Encouraging him all the way to the porch.

As soon as the widows closed the door, he was running for his Harley. Something was wrong. He could feel it in his bones. *Maybe she's had a wreck*.

He drove back toward the café slowly, expecting to find her sitting on the curb waiting for the town's only tow truck.

The van came into view at the bend in the road. Parked sideways with the door left open and one tire up on the sidewalk.

At the curve he saw something red lying amid the carpet of rusty-brown leaves.

Piper's shoe.

Colby ran up on the sidewalk and reached for the shoe without climbing off his bike.

Before he could make sense of anything, his phone rang. He thought of not answering it. Nothing was more important to him right now than finding Piper.

Then he saw the number. The one he'd seen in black on a white card.

The ghost.

He had to answer.

Chapter 50

Brand

Brandon was running toward his truck when Colby finally picked up on the third ring. He didn't waste time. "Marcie got a call from Piper a few minutes ago. She stepped out on the porch to answer, and the next time I looked up she was running to her car. I couldn't catch her before she drove away."

"Piper left me about half an hour ago to go talk to Marcie. She must have caught her by phone." Colby's tone relaxed a bit as he seemed to be thinking out loud. "No idea why Piper would leave her van by the side of the road. Maybe Marcie picked her up and they were in a hurry?"

Brand climbed in his truck as Colby kept talking. "The way the van is parked, the open door. Something is wrong, Brand. Piper left one of her shoes in the mud by the van. She'd never do that. This is looking more like a crime scene."

The ranger's last words were loaded with worry.

Brand slammed the truck door and flipped on the tracker he'd planted in Leon's car. "You know where Piper is right now?"

"Negative. She was headed back to town but obviously didn't make it. Something's wrong. Real wrong. There are two sets of footprints in the mud by the road."

Brand was silent for a moment, then yelled at Colby over his roaring truck engine. "The tracker shows Leon's car at Marcie's trailer. Piper must be there also. He somehow got her to stop, then kidnapped her."

Colby said what Brand was thinking. "Leon's got Piper's phone. The call Marcie got was him calling, not Piper. I called her cell and it went straight to message."

"Anything else missing?"

"No. I can see her purse in the front seat. She didn't leave willingly."

"Leon has more than just her phone. He has Piper, and it seems Marcie is headed toward them," Brand answered as the noise of the truck driving over rough road almost blocked his words. "We've got to find them fast."

"But why would he take her to the trailer?" Colby didn't bother with a helmet. He yelled as he took off on his bike, "It's miles away."

"To pull Marcie back so he can finish what he started." Brand paused as he jumped a ditch with all four tires off the ground. "Marcie took off running to help Piper, just like Leon hoped she would. I saw her face as she backed out of the drive. It was total panic."

"I'm on my way to Someday Valley." Colby swore.

"Right." The roar of his truck made Brand also yell. "You go in on the back side. I'll get there first and go in the front. Leon has a plan he wants to act out. His own kind of party. But he won't be expecting us."

"He'll be armed and ready for you this time, Brand."

"I know, but he better be fully loaded because it will take more than one hit to stop me."

Neither man said another word. Every second counted. They had to get to the trailer before Leon hurt anyone.

Brand was ten minutes away at full speed, but Colby was twenty if he pushed ninety.

Chapter 51

Pecos

Pecos was standing by the dispatcher table, ready to leave. All he could think about was getting home to Kerrie and Button. She had to stay in bed most of the time, so Mr. Winston had set up a table for two in their room. Marcie had cleaned out the connecting room and made a small living area and a nursery. It was like they had a real apartment. Mr. Winston even found a rocking chair in the attic.

Pecos had thought of taking off a few days, but his mother-in-law convinced him a new mother's mother was supposed to be around the first few days. He talked her into making it nights so he could be with Kerrie all day.

Since the birth, every time his wife opened her eyes

she searched for him. Even with the baby in her arms, she wanted him holding her. Pecos had become her rock.

When he'd kissed her lightly as he left for work, she'd whispered, "More."

"More what?"

"More of you, husband. Or should I call you Daddy? I want you closer, every minute. Touching me, holding me, loving me."

Pecos studied her. What had happened to his Kerrie who always rationed out her touch and her kisses? "Are you saying, when you recover, of course, that you want me to truly be your husband?" He looked up to make sure no one was in the room."

Surprisingly, she nodded. "When I saw you shaking when the doctor told you to cut the cord, I realized you were the most handsome man in the world. You're Button's father and it's time you were my husband for real."

He'd kissed her again and almost ran from the room. If he'd stayed any longer he might never leave her.

Pecos had thought about what she'd said all during his long shift, and now he just wanted to go home and hold her.

A 9-1-1 call came in, shattering his daydream.

He looked around just as the day dispatcher sat down. She had her sewing basket, several snacks, two bottles of water, and a box of tissues.

"I'll take this call while you settle in," he said, seeing that the old dear was emptying her sewing bag.

Kerrie would have to wait a few minutes. It wouldn't matter. They had the rest of their lives.

"Nine-one-one. What is your emergency?"

"Pecos!"

Pecos turned up the volume to full blast as he tried to

make out words over the noise of a Harley running at full speed.

"Ranger McBride here. I need backup ASAP. Kidnapping in progress."

"Shoot me the location, Colby."

Ten seconds later Pecos was back in the chair, yelling facts. Every man in the office was loading up and heading out. When a Texas Ranger was in trouble, LeRoy figured they'd need an army for backup.

Pecos was sending every deputy on patrol to Colby's location. Someday Valley Trailer Park.

He heard rifles being pulled from the racks and the front door banging as everyone headed out with LeRoy shouting a stream of orders.

The 9-1-1 number sounded again. Marcie's phone number popped on the screen. Before Pecos could get out a hello, a man ordered loud and clear, "Patch me into the sheriff. Kidnapping. Mayor involved."

Pecos didn't know who the man on the call was, but he didn't waste time asking questions. "Will do," Pecos answered as his fingers were already flying over the keyboard. "He's on his way to his car now."

As they waited for the sheriff to pick up, Pecos asked, "Mayor's location?"

"Someday Valley. Marcie Latimer's home. Last trailer on the lot."

"Sending to all units now. Second nine-one-one request to that location." In the silence, Pecos asked, "Where's Marcie?"

The low voice answered, "She's headed into trouble. Big trouble. I don't know for sure, but I'm betting she's heading toward Piper."

Whoever the guy was, he seemed to know the situation.

The sheriff answered on the radio as he fumbled with his keys. Pecos patched him through to the stranger calling, and listened in, writing down details.

Kidnapping. Piper in trouble. Marcie headed that way. Two men within ten minutes of them.

When Pecos leaned back to look at the other dispatcher, who should be settled enough to take over, she wasn't ready. She was shaking with panic. "I can't handle this. Tell Rip to come back. This is too much."

"You handle all other calls. I'll stay on this one." There was no way Pecos was handing over his post.

He worked like a pro. Putting the fire department on call. Directing an ambulance to the scene and reminding them to stand clear until the area had been secured.

He could feel his heart trying to pound through his chest. In a few months he'd be a deputy ready to run toward trouble. Right now all he could do was do his job. Maybe, if he did everything right, he'd help.

Chapter 52

Piper

Piper fought to wake up from a terrible dream. She felt she'd fallen down a well. The world was dark and cold. Her entire body ached. She couldn't move as the smell of smoke filled the air.

The nightmare mixed with a memory from almost six months ago. Fire barreling down the hallway toward her office on the fourth floor. Colby covering her with his jacket. His only thought had been to get them to safety. "I'll get you out, PJ," he kept yelling. "I swore I'd protect you. I swore."

The feeling that she was going to die this time, without Colby, smothered all other thoughts. He should be by her side. They'd be fine together.

But she'd walked away from him. He'd turned his back after she'd said they were over.

She heard banging and tried to scream. Something smelly was shoved in her mouth and tape ran from cheek to cheek, holding the rag in place.

"Shut up," a man close to her ordered. "You are not the one I want to hear screaming. Shut up or I will hit you again."

She shook her head and tried to fight free. Smoke seemed to fill her lungs. She had no way of knowing if it was real or brought on by fear.

Then a fist hit her cheek so hard it slammed her head against her shoulder. The cover over her mouth wouldn't allow the scream out.

"Be still!" the low voice said, angry now. "If you don't just sit there, I'll hit you again."

Reality wedged its way into her thoughts and she opened her eyes. The scene before her was far more frightening than a nightmare. It was real. The cold, the foul taste in her mouth, ropes binding her to a tall chair. Her head reeling from the blow.

Her legs dangled off the high chair, not able to touch the floor. Both her shoes were gone.

The man she'd seen talking to Marcie was standing in front of her, saying something about how he shouldn't have hit a mayor. He stepped backward and took a long draw on a whiskey bottle.

"That wasn't my fault, Mayor. You made me do it."

Her mouth was taped. She couldn't scream or ask where she was. Ropes hurt as they crisscrossed over her body, tying her in place.

She tried to wiggle free, but the ropes wouldn't give.

The man kept staring at her as if he couldn't understand why she was trying to fight. Finally, he must have decided to talk to her. "You ain't going anywhere, girl, so you might as well stop fretting." He tightened the rope already cutting into her throat, then tested each rope as he pushed his fingers between the rope and her body. His hand pushing into her breasts, her rib cage, her stomach. "I ain't going to hurt you unless I have to. You're just bait for that tramp."

He touched her hair in a gentle stroke. "I don't bother women like you. It's the trash who hang out in bars that I punish. Women should be home with their children, not out picking up men. My goal in this life is to fix them so they won't be attractive to any man."

Piper saw the insanity in his eyes. His thin body was jerking with excitement.

He moved closer, as if he needed to explain himself. "Once they've got scars, they hide away and don't go looking for trouble. Sometimes I have to circle back and remind them to be good." He laughed. "They don't like that much. Their eyes tell me they know what's coming when they see me. But women like them have to be taught how to behave. I wash away the evil in them with their own blood."

Piper looked around, trying to figure out where she was. A trailer home. It was neat except for the floor around her chair. She could see dead branches, newspapers, wadded-up clothes built up like a bonfire.

The creep kept flipping a lighter on and off, as if he couldn't wait to light the place up. While she watched he pulled a strip of a rag off the pile and lit it. He waved it close to her hair, as if playing with a trapped mouse.

He jerked her dress down over her knees, then burned

a hole in the hem as if testing to see how fast the material would burn. "Marcie's on her way to save you. If she gets here in time, she doesn't know it yet, but she'll get to take your place atop the bonfire. I plan to teach her a few lessons first. By the time I finish she may not even feel her skin burning." He pointed with a jerk of his head to a pile of belts and ropes lined up along the couch. "You'll have to stay tied up until I finish with her. She's got a few things to be punished for before I put her in the chair and light up this place. You can watch if you want to."

He leaned closer and she smelled the whiskey on his breath. "If either of you gives me any trouble, I light the rags and dead weeds under you. You'll try to scream because it'll burn your feet first. She'll be tied up over there and she'll have to watch you burn."

"I got this all figured out if you turn out to be more trouble. Once you're burning, I'll carry the tramp outside. A few blows to the head and she won't even wiggle. I'll put a blanket over her and take her to my house. Then I can take my time raping her and every time I do, I'll cut her in a few more places that no one will see as long as she keeps her clothes on. As more and more blood comes out, she'll settle down. If she dies I'll bury her where no one will ever find the body. All they'll find of you is ashes, so you better be good, hear.

"If Marcie and you don't give me no trouble, I'll take you out and put you in the trunk of my car while I burn the tramp. Someone might find you, maybe if they think to look. If not, and you die, you're not my problem. I'll just dig another hole. You wouldn't be the first to die on me."

A car pulled up outside, with dirt and gravel flying against the outside of the trailer.

The bald man jumped with excitement. "'Bout time she got here." He waited, a knife in one hand and ropes in the other. He pointed the blade at Piper's throat, pushing just enough to draw blood.

Footsteps ran up the steps, and Marcie barreled through the door.

The moment she saw Piper, horror registered in her hazel eyes. Then she saw the man who'd been pestering her, and the knife in his hand. Shock and anger flared but she couldn't seem to move.

In the silence the timer on the stove went off. Three dings to say the time was up.

Piper stared as Marcie took a step toward them. "I made it on time, Leon. Let the mayor go. This fight is between you and me. Leave her out of this."

"I'll let her go, but first I got to tie you up on that couch. I don't want you bothering me. No one knows where you girls are, so we can take our time."

Piper slowly shook her head, trying to tell Marcie he was lying. She felt the blade at her throat press further into her neck, but she had to warn Marcie. She wanted to scream for her friend to run while she still could, but no words escaped the gag.

"Hold your hands out in front of you, tramp, or I'll poke a hole in the mayor's neck right now."

Marcie lifted her arms high, but when she turned to face Leon, Piper saw no fear in Marcie's eyes, only determination.

Leon didn't notice. "Now you mind just like that, tramp, and we won't have no trouble." He lowered the knife and lifted the noose-shaped rope. "I'll bind your hands first, then I'll tie this noose around your neck. That way I can lead you around, and if you try to run I'll cut off your air."

He was so excited he made a mistake. He switched the knife to his left hand.

When he was within reaching distance of her hands, Marcie raised them higher.

He moved closer, so excited that his hand shook as he reached to loop the rope over her hands.

Piper tried to scream. She rocked in the chair, making a sudden thud against the floor.

Leon glanced back.

In that second, Marcie shifted her left shoulder forward as her body turned slightly and her right hand dropped behind her like a pitcher throwing a fast ball. Her fingers curled tightly when the momentum powered her swing.

Before Leon could react, her fist slammed into his gut. She was not aiming for him, but for the wall behind him. Just like Brand taught her.

When he leaned forward in pain, her knee hit him between his legs with enough force to lift the thin man off the ground for a moment. He crumbled in pain. Her elbow connected with his nose as he fell, and the crack of bone seemed to echo in the tiny space.

Marcie grabbed the knife while Leon curled up in pain on the floor. She cut Piper free.

As soon as Piper's hands were free, she jerked the gag off and shouted, "You were great. How did you know to do that?"

"I had to act." Marcie's hands were shaking. "I could take no more."

Piper stepped away from the pile ready to burn. "What do we do with him? Help him or tie him up?" Piper knew she sounded insane, but adrenaline and fear were running at lightning speed through her.

Leon started cussing. "I swear I'm going to kill you both." His hand reached for Piper's ankle. "I'll break every bone in your body. I don't care if you are the mayor!"

Piper grabbed a broken chair leg from the pile of trash and hit his hand so hard he screamed. "Stop cussing!" she yelled, knowing she was rattling. "You don't cuss in public. It's not polite." Fearing he didn't get the message, she hit his hand again.

His fingers pointed in strange, unnatural directions.

He cried out as he dragged his bloody, broken hand away.

Piper dropped the chair leg. "So what do we do, Marcie?"

Marcie's voice had calmed. "I say we tie him up before one of us accidentally kills the rat."

If Piper hadn't been so afraid, she would have laughed. Her friend sounded like a 1920s gangster.

Marcie put the noose over his head and looped it over her one ceiling beam. It was a fake, and if it didn't hold him, it would hit him on the head when it fell. If it held, Leon wouldn't be able to move without choking.

They worked together to tie his hands behind him. Piper taped his mouth. Around and around his head she went until she ran out of tape.

Leon had to blow blood out of his nose before he could get air in. When he tried to kick them, Marcie stomped on his instep so hard that the heel of her boot pierced leather. He stopped trying to scream and started crying as blood bubbled over his boot.

"I can't stand to look at him," Piper said as she turned a wicker trash can over his head. "He was going to kill us."

Her words sobered them. Tears came as they hugged once more.

"We're alive," Marcie whispered. "We'll be all right."

Both held the other tightly, letting their hearts slow.

"We need a phone to call this in. I don't have one," Marcie said.

"I don't know what happened to mine," Piper answered.

A low voice joined the conversation. "I have one. I've already made the call. Every lawman in the valley is on his way here."

They whirled around and saw Brand standing in the doorway, his arms folded and a smile on his face.

A minute later they heard the roar of a Harley, and Colby came flying in.

"What happened? I heard screaming all the way up the hill."

"Not me," Marcie said.

"Not me." Piper smiled.

Colby looked at the six-foot, blood-dripping, ugliest piñata he'd ever seen. "What is that?"

"Leon," all three answered.

Colby lifted the trash can, took one look at the guy with his nose on sideways, and put the can back down. He studied the man up and down. The only other wound showing, besides a broken nose, was blood dripping out of the hole in the instep of his boot.

"How did that happen?"

Piper said softly, as if testifying, "Marcie accidentally stomped on his foot while he was trying to kick her for knocking his balls into his tonsils. Her heels are high, but I think the poor quality of the leather may be at fault."

Marcie confirmed the account by nodding, and Brand just smiled and added, "That's my girl." Brand opened his arms and Marcie ran to him.

Colby slowly closed the distance between him and Piper, and gently held her as she cried.

In gulps she confessed, "I broke his fingers. That's probably illegal."

"Probably is," Colby answered as he tied his handkerchief around her throat.

By the time the sheriff arrived, both men present seemed more upset than the ladies. They'd looked around and had no problem telling the sheriff what Leon had planned to do to the women. LeRoy turned to Piper and she nodded. Marcie filled in every detail.

The sheriff ordered them all outside. They watched him look inside, then slowly step in and begin to collect evidence and take pictures.

Finally LeRoy lifted the trash can, then put it back on Leon's head. He kicked at the pile of trash built with a chair in its center. Finally, he stormed out to the steps. "Damn it, which one of you men beat up my criminal?"

"I didn't touch him," Brand answered with his head down.

"Then you, Colby. Hell, you're a lawman, you know we don't go around beating people up when we arrest them. You got him hanging like he's nothing but a punching bag."

"Not me," Colby answered. "He was having to tiptoe to keep from hanging himself when I got here. He could have yelled for help if he had a problem, but I didn't hear him say a word."

Leroy stormed back and forth. "He couldn't yell 'cause you two gagged him."

Both men shook their heads.

"Damn it to the moon and back, he didn't do that to himself. So who did it?" the sheriff demanded.

Both Marcie and Piper raised their hands, as if to answer a question in school.

The sheriff looked from one to the other, then back at Brand and Colby. "Are you trying to tell me that my new dispatcher and the mayor did that to this man?"

The men didn't even blink as they nodded.

LeRoy turned to his deputy and yelled loud enough for the whole valley to hear. "Well, Rip, what do you think happened to him?"

Rip, who'd been standing by the door, took one more look at Leon and answered, "Looks like an accident to me."

LeRoy waved the ambulance in and ordered them to keep him tied up until he was cuffed to a hospital bed. "As soon as he's patched up, I'm booking him for every crime I can spell."

He turned to Colby. "Ranger, I know I don't have the power to boss you around, but take my squad car and get Piper to the hospital. I'm guessing she doesn't want to ride with Leon. I see blood dripping out of the back of her head. Her neck is also bleeding. Have the doctor check her right leg, she's limping."

Colby moved close to her and tenderly lifted Piper. "I warned you about those high heels. I knew one day you'd twist your ankle." He'd already tied his handkerchief around her neck, but he hadn't seen the back of her hair.

She put her head on his shoulder. "I knew you'd come."

As he carried her away, Piper heard the sheriff tell Marcie to get a few hours' sleep and if she felt like it, come in tonight to relieve Pecos at the station. "When the kid heard you two were in danger, he wouldn't let anyone take over. He's already making enough overtime to send that kid to college."

As everyone began to move away, LeRoy raised his voice. "I want to see you all in my office tomorrow to make statements."

Marcie wrapped her arms around Brand's arm. "I remembered everything you told me. You said if I have to fight, fight like my life depends on it. And I did. I saved us, because of you." They walked toward his truck as if the dozen people standing around were invisible.

"Now, my little koala bear, you'll have to come home and save me."

"What's wrong with you?"

"I'm dying to hold you. When I saw you make that last hit, I saw a warrior born. I saw my mate, strong and beautiful. Without you, my life will always seem dark and silent."

"I can save you, Brand." She put her hand on his chest and smiled up at him. "You know, when you said you loved me?"

"I remember."

He opened his pickup door and lifted her in. "We'll come back for your car later. I need you in my sight for a while."

She didn't argue. "I've been thinking about what you said, and I think I should let you in on something too. I think I love you. You know, with that forever kind of love."

"When will you be sure?"

"Probably as soon as our clothes hit the floor."

He smiled his slow smile that lit up her world. "It's going to be ten miles before we get back home. Why don't you start undressing now, and I'll drive and watch."

She laughed and followed his suggestion. "You want to know why I fought so hard?"

"I do."

"I had to get back to you."

Chapter 53

Colby

Colby sat beside Piper in the ER. A hundred questions kept running through his mind. He wanted to hear every detail she remembered from the moment she left him at the café, but Piper needed to rest. She'd had four stitches in her throat. She had a bruise on her left cheek that seemed to be turning darker by the minute. When the creep had hit her to knock her out and kidnap her, he'd left an open wound. She needed stitches in the back of her head. The area had been cleaned and bandaged, but the doctor wanted her to rest a bit before they started again.

He was glad she couldn't see the wound.

Colby thought the strangest thing of all was when he asked her how she was doing, Piper teared up and said that Leon burned a hole in her dress. The mayor was definitely delirious. She almost died and she was worried about how she looked.

Now and then he could hear Leon in the other emergency room at the clinic. He kept yelling, then he started crying when the doctor examined him.

One of the nurses said Leon planned to sue pretty much everybody. He was innocent and Marcie beat him up for no reason. He claimed it was his word against hers.

When the nurse reminded him that the mayor had been there, Leon said that Piper Mackenzie was a liar. He claimed she was just mad at him for hitting her in the head. He claimed he'd explained to the mayor that he was just using her as bait. He said he was taking it easy on her until she broke three of his fingers for no reason at all.

"I swore the cut on her neck wasn't my fault or the gash on the back of her head," Leon protested loudly. "How else was I going to get her in the trunk if I didn't knock her out?"

When the nurse talked to Colby a few minutes later, she just smiled and said, "I told Leon I'd write everything he said down, word for word, and would be happy to testify in his trial." She grinned. "I said he'd probably get out of jail."

"What happened then?" Colby asked the nurse.

"Leon hit himself in the head so hard he started crying again and cussing Piper. I reminded him that there were two Texas Rangers standing in the hallway named Mackenzie. Then he passed out."

Colby frowned.

Piper smiled. "My brothers are here?"

The nurse nodded. "I told them I'd ask if you wanted them to come in. They flew in on a private plane."

Colby swore. "Great. If I know your brothers, they'll blame me for this."

But Piper was all smiles as she hugged her two big brothers.

Colby moved to the window and stared out. He wanted to escape, but the brothers were between him and the door. Those two were great rangers, but they were about as cuddly as six-foot alligators.

Twenty minutes later, Piper had fallen asleep and no nurses were in the room. Colby braced for the battle.

Max left his sister's bedside and walked over to stare at Colby. If looks could kill, somebody should order a coffin.

For a moment Colby thought the big guy might not say a word. He might just explode with anger. But now, that would be too little.

Max's words came low and fast. "How in the hell did you let this happen to my sister? She could have been killed. That nut could have burned her to death. Where were you when this was going on? Don't tell me. My cousin Jennifer said you were eating breakfast while Piper was being kidnapped."

Max stepped back, apparently too upset to continue.

James took his place with pretty much the same song, but he included new names for Colby. Coward. Idiot. Fool. And a dozen more.

Colby made no effort to defend himself. He pretty much agreed with the two Mackenzies. He should have followed her back to town. He should have told her he loved her. Maybe she would have stayed with him.

The stitches in her head. The cut on her throat. Even the twisted ankle was all his fault.

Max pushed his brother out of the way. He must be ready for round two. "We sent you out here to watch over her. Some job you did. How are we going to explain to our grandmother that you didn't do your job? Our grand-father, if he was still alive, would shoot you on sight."

James leaned over Max's shoulder and added a few more names for Colby.

Colby had seen them interrogate suspected murderers with less malice. Finally, he broke.

He stood so fast, Max almost tripped as he stepped back.

"I didn't go with your sister because she'd just broken up with me. She walked out on me at the café."

Colby turned to James. "I was in town to date her, not be her round-the-clock bodyguard."

"Why'd you break up with her?" Max pushed his brother out of the way again. "What's wrong with you? She's perfect. Sweet. Kind."

"I didn't break up with her. I agree she's perfect. She broke up with me."

Piper's brothers looked at each other and nodded. Evidently agreeing that she might break it off. He obviously wasn't good enough for her.

Max glared at Colby and asked, "What did you do wrong? She told me she loved you. Three months ago she was happy. You must have screwed up bad."

James looked like he was about to jump in with suggestions, so Colby shouted, "I didn't tell her I loved her! She's my world. I don't want to come home every three months for a date, I want so much more."

He'd already spilled his heart out, he might as well add, "I want Piper, boys, but I don't want to marry her brothers. You two need to butt out of our lives."

James looked a bit insulted. Max still looked mad.

"Colby." Piper's voice came from the other side of the room.

Colby pushed his way past the brothers and rushed to her side. "What's wrong, honey?"

"Take me home. It's too noisy here."

"I can't. The doc says you have to stay overnight. But I'll stay right with you." He turned back to her brothers. "Go away. I'll call you if anything changes."

Max frowned. "Oh, so you think you can order us around. Didn't you two break up?"

Piper turned to James. "I want him back." She glared at them. "Undamaged."

James smiled at her. "I figured you'd like him, little sister. That's why Max and me sent him here six months ago. He's dumb as a rock but he was the best we could find."

"Don't tell her that," Max interrupted. "Now she won't like him if she thinks we picked him out."

"Leave," Colby ordered. To his surprise they both grabbed their hats and left.

He turned back to Piper. "So, Mayor, you want to keep me?"

"Only if you love me."

"I do." He leaned over and gently kissed her on the side of her face not bruised. "We'll work it out, PJ. We'll find a way. I love you too much to ever walk away."

"Even if my brothers are part of the deal?"

He smiled. "I'm thinking if we get them married off, they won't have time to bother us."

"It won't be easy."

"Nothing about marrying you is going to come easy, except one thing."

"What's that?"

"Loving you."

DINNER ON PRIMROSE HILL

New York Times bestselling author Jodi Thomas
welcomes readers back to the picturesque Texas
valley that cradles the town of Honey Creek—a place
where friendship and warm welcomes can be relied
on, and love always finds a way . . .

Benjamin Monroe is pretty sure how his life will play
out. He'll continue teaching chemistry in his small
college, and spend his free time biking through the
|valley. Eventually, he'll retire to putter around in his
garden and greenhouse.

His colleague, Virginia Clark, is not one for routines.
She's chatty, spontaneous, and bubbly, and before
Benjamin realizes what happened, she's talked him into
collaborating on a research project—studying the mating
habits of college students. Virginia knows her desire to
work with Benjamin is motivated by more than the
potential prize money . . . and hopes he might not be
quite as indifferent as he seems to be.

Ketch Kincaid, one of Benjamin's star students, returned
to college after serving in the army. He needs something
to get his mind off his recent breakup and collecting
research data might do it. And there's another distraction
on the horizon—a woman who looks like she, too,
knows about heartache.

Soon enough, their project, "The Chemistry of Mating," is gaining notoriety. Friends, neighbors . . . the whole town has become involved. But no matter what the data determines, one conclusion seems inescapable: love follows its own rules . . .

Available from Kensington Publishing Corp. wherever books are sold

**Read on for a special preview of the latest Honey
Creek novel from Jodi Thomas . . .**

SUNDAY AT THE
SUNFLOWER INN

*Available from Kensington Publishing Corp. in
May 2022 wherever books are sold*

Houston, Texas

Chapter 1

The Lost McCoy

McCoy Mason leaned his crutches next to his duffle bag and sat down on the bench just outside Houston Methodist Hospital's main exit.

If a cab came by, he might get in.

If he had any idea where he was going.

If he had enough money to get there.

Three 'ifs' seemed a long shot. He decided to sit on the bench until a few of his brain cells thawed. After three weeks in the hospital, his mind had slipped to frog IQ.

On the bright side, the sun was shining and the wind was low. Except for the fact he was headed nowhere, life wasn't all bad. Maybe he was just confused, maybe mixed up, maybe disoriented. Definitely handicapped. Broken. Homeless. Alone.

McCoy decided to stop thinking. He was running out of adjectives.

"I'm not lost, just nowhere to go," he said aloud. "Not brain dead, just wounded."

He almost smiled remembering what his crazy dad used to say when his mom suggested a vacation. "It don't cost nothin' to go nowhere."

Maybe he should stay here and save what little money he had left.

McCoy shrugged. Nowhere seemed as good as anywhere to go.

Mom must not have agreed with his dad, because one night she left with all their savings and never came back from vacation. Dad got up the next morning and went to work and never mentioned her again.

McCoy looked down at his new Wranglers. The nurse had to cut them to get one leg over the cast. He'd thought of yelling to cut off the plaster instead, but he doubted she'd do that. He could hop around on one leg, but he only owned one pair of jeans.

Right now, the break just below his knee was the least of his troubles. One broken bone seemed no big deal, considering his other problems. First, he'd had a head injury everyone thought would kill him after he'd totaled his Mustang on Interstate 45. He lived, but the car died.

Breanna Bell, his fiancée, stopped coming around after three days. She'd said staring at his bruised, broken body was too much to bear.

She should have seen it from his side of the fence.

Two days later, his new boss called and told McCoy he'd lost the job that he had moved to Houston for, and a week later his landlord texted that the apartment he'd signed a lease on was no longer available.

Last, Breanna left town, taking everything but one duffle bag with his work clothes stuffed in the bottom and the one outfit he'd bought the day of the accident. Jeans, a western shirt, and a Stetson hat.

Breanna had talked him into getting hundred-dollar tickets to a rodeo the night of his crash and of course, clothes to go with the date, but he'd never made it home to change. Now he felt like an imposter dressed up as a cowboy.

The one time he'd been awake enough to talk to Breanna on the hospital phone, she'd let him know how mad she was about him standing her up for their rodeo date. She also mentioned the moving van with all their junk would be on its way back to Georgia and she planned to ride along.

If he wanted any of his stuff, he could collect it the next time he was there. Since she'd picked out most of the household essentials, she considered everything more hers than his. Just before she'd hung up, his fiancée said she'd stuffed her engagement ring in the chest pocket of his work overalls.

He must have decided to go back in a coma about then because days later when he opened his eyes, he couldn't remember much else of what she'd said.

If the hospital hadn't saved his wallet and phone when they cut off his bloody clothes, she probably would have taken them as well. The cell was dead, but a few hundred dollars were still in his wallet.

He was in too much pain to think, so he gave up on time and dates completely. Hell, he didn't even care what year it was.

Now and then, one of the nurses would wake him up and ask him what his name was. If he got that right, they'd move on to, "Do you know the date?" like it was some kind of trick question.

How could he explain that he didn't know or care? The last construction site he'd worked on had relocated inside his brain, and the noise was blocking everything out.

As the sun started to set behind the buildings of downtown Houston, McCoy frowned, trying to recall Breanna part by part. Her hair was soft. Her breasts were rounded. Her mouth was always moving.

He grinned, remembering another one of his dad's sayings. He'd lecture, "Son, the right girl for you is the one who says 'yes'. Don't build up your hopes on more."

Night was moving across the huge parking lot, and McCoy didn't bother to care. He didn't have enough money in his pocket to start over, and no one was picking him up. He'd inherited being a loner from his dad. No sense making friends you'll just leave behind.

McCoy considered sitting on this bench until he starved to death. If he took the painkillers in his pocket, he probably wouldn't notice hunger or cold. Three weeks ago, he had a hot girlfriend, a new direction, and a great car. The job he'd moved halfway across the country for was promising to lead him toward the future he'd always wanted. He would have been the boss of this building site. Not bad considering he wasn't yet thirty.

Somehow one wreck had washed away all of his chalkboard dreams.

The janitor, who had cleaned his hospital room, walked by. "Evening Mr. Mason." The short man grinned as if they were old friends. "You finally getting out of this place or did one of them nurses just leave you out here by accident?"

McCoy smiled. "Evening, Roberto. I'm going to miss your great jokes. Most days you were the only one who talked to me other than the nurses asking questions."

Roberto set a lunchbox on the bench as he zipped a gray jacket that matched his uniform. As always, he seemed to have time to talk. "That pretty, long-legged blonde picking you up? I wouldn't mind hanging around to see her."

"No, she's gone. Moved back to Georgia. She left me with a bag of old clothes and what I'm wearing."

"You got family around?" Roberto might be short and forty pounds overweight, but he was one of the heroes in this life. He cared. "Friends picking you up?"

"Nope. My dad's in Alaska. He told me I've got a grandfather in some little town called Honey Creek. I couldn't even find the place on a map when I looked years ago."

"I know where that is." Roberto smiled. "My *primo* lives there. Runs a garage." He pushed his chest out. "I've got cousins in half the towns in Texas."

"Must be nice," McCoy lied.

Roberto asked a few more questions and then seemed to take over McCoy's life. "If you don't know where to go, you should head up to meet your *abuelo*. He'd probably be glad to see you. He's kin. He can't turn you away."

"I doubt that's a rule for my relatives. My family tree is more a fence post."

"My *primo* says the folks in Honey Creek are friendly. While you're not doing anything, you should look him up."

"I don't know about that."

"What else you got to do? There's a bus that heads that

way around midnight. I could drop you off at the station. It's not far."

To McCoy's surprise, Roberto picked up the duffel bag. "Wait here, I'll get my truck and take you. You'll be in Honey Creek by dawn. You got forty-three bucks for the ride?"

McCoy hesitated.

Roberto stared at McCoy. "You got any better place to be?"

"Nope." His head hurt too bad to argue. He could starve there as fast as he could here. "Maybe the bus will be warm and I can sleep. The fare is probably cheaper than a hotel."

A few minutes later, when Roberto helped him into an old Chevy pickup truck, the little man told McCoy that his cousin would meet the bus and help him find his kin when McCoy got to Honey Creek.

It crossed McCoy's mind that this could be the plot of a kidnapping movie. But what else could they do to him? Sell him into the sex trade? There couldn't be much demand for a scraped-up fool with one working leg and no memory of what day it was. Plus, he considered he might not be that great in bed if Breanna only took three days to forget him.

On the bright side, his always absent grandpa might let him sleep on the couch for a few nights.

After dark McCoy climbed onto the bus heading north. He stretched out on the back seat and tried not to breathe in too much of the air that smelled of whiskey and piss. He guessed the couple falling in love on the seat in front of him were the origin of the smells. They were deep into slapping tongues. The sight made him want to forget even thinking about sex or eating.

He had no future, no love life, no job, and no relatives except a grandpa who his dad had mentioned a few times in passing. Dad had said he didn't remember ever having a mother, and when he was seventeen, he told his father he was leaving, and Sadler Mason simply said, "So long."

McCoy's head kept pounding, keeping time to the throbbing in his leg. It didn't matter where in the hell he was heading. Forget the pills in his pocket. He'd take the pain. It was the only thing letting him know he was alive.

He told himself he wasn't a quitter; he was simply tired.

If Sadler didn't let him stay, he'd find a place to lie down and sleep off this nightmare.

Chapter 2

Midnight

Jessica Ann Mackenzie, 'Jam' for short, sat near the bend in the Brazos River where hundred-year-old cottonwoods lined the shore. Her thin frame blended with the trees' shadows making her invisible to anyone on the water or at the café looming behind her.

Not that it mattered, no one would be either place after midnight.

She'd worked late. Every couple wanted their Valentine's dinner at her place, even if a few looked like the love had been strangled long ago.

She'd heard one couple arguing over money and another complaining about each other's parents. The love songs playing in the background hadn't seemed to reach the couple talking low about divorce.

Sometimes Jam swore romance had disappeared with knights in armor. Loving was meant for movies and books, too flighty to survive real life.

As she'd cleaned up after all the couples left, the love songs still playing had simply made her sad.

By the time she'd prepped for the breakfast run at dawn, it was too late to bother driving home. She'd decided to stay upstairs above her cafe in one of the rooms she'd planned to turn into a bed and breakfast someday.

Only there was no time for 'someday.' She was too busy with today.

The farm, where her clothes and books lived, was becoming more of a get-away place, and the sea captain's old house, turned restaurant, had become her life.

Somehow, being alone upstairs always made her uneasy, but exhaustion let her sleep. Stories of ghosts haunting the place never seemed to die. They were as much a part of the building as the studs and tile.

The house by the water had been built over a hundred years ago by a Captain Barron. He'd had three wives who gave him four homely daughters. It was said all the wives died in childbirth. Then the captain gave up on marriage and hired a housekeeper who ran the place until the girls were grown. As the story goes, she left one morning without even saying goodbye.

The few men brave enough to come courting the captain's daughters were turned away. As the years passed, sorrow seemed to frequent the family. Two daughters died of a fever while still in their teens, the oldest daughter drowned in the river, and the last daughter just disappeared one night. Rumor has it, she took her life, but a few believe she ran off. The captain put up her marker beside her mother's grave and lived his remaining years alone in his huge house by the Brazos River.

Tonight, no more than thirty feet from her café, Jam felt like she was the last human alive in the world. Not even the wind moved across the land still sleeping in winter. She'd bought the house when she was in her twenties and spent years turning it into the best café around. Only now, after eight years, she felt like she might be like the captain. She'd grow old and die here, alone.

When moving amid all the couples having candlelight dinners tonight, she tried to remember how long it had been since she'd even been kissed. Really kissed. First date kisses didn't count and neither did drunk kisses.

She felt lonely all the way to her bones.

No one would kiss her goodnight on this Valentine's Day. No one would call her "sweetheart."

At thirty-two she'd achieved her dream of owning the best restaurant for miles around. The Honey Creek Café was successful. Her finances were solid. The whole town seemed to be her friend.

But she'd dreamed too small. Somewhere between making bread every dawn and polishing off the accounts after dark, she'd lost herself.

Lowering her head to her knees, tears fell unchecked. No one would hear her. Over the years of building a business, she'd lost all her other goals. She'd learned to work, but she'd forgotten to live.

The river splashed against the shore as if demanding attention.

Jam often sat out near the water to think, to plan, to rest, but never to cry. Tonight, she felt like she'd lost a lover she'd never taken the time to meet. She'd given up everything for one dream. The huge old house held a fine café that would never love her back.

Another splash came, louder, closer.

Jam raised her head listening in the night, trying to see across the river, but it was impossible. All she saw was the black flow of the water a few feet away.

Another splash and a shadow seemed to plop onto the bank. It landed a few feet from her with a hard thump, as bits of water sprinkled along her side.

Jam didn't move. Her first thought was Old Henry, the catfish locals claimed was as big as a man, must have jumped onto the bank.

No, not possible.

An alligator was her next thought. She'd never heard of one this far north. "Not likely," she mumbled as she made out two long powerful legs.

Then she heard cussing.

No fish. Definitely a man rose from the mud.

As he stood, she noticed he was fully dressed down to his boots. Army style, not cowboy boots.

Jam knew she should be afraid, but this was too strange. This has to be more of a joke than an invasion.

The impossible sight made her smile. "You know, mister, most folks swim in trunks or even skinny dip. You're a bit overdressed in that uniform."

He didn't look at her, so she reasoned he was just a figment of her imagination. She must have had too much wine. No one crawls out of the river dressed like a soldier. The nearest fort was hundreds of miles away.

Jam decided to keep talking to the vision. "The water flows too fast around this bend to be safe, but it calms a few miles down. You must be from out of town if you think you can swim here."

He slung his head, splashing water over her.

She couldn't make out his face as he began to strip off his clothes. The lines of his body were sketched against the moonlight. She decided he looked as good as she could have possibly conjured up. Wide shoulders. Slim hips. Muscles pretty much everywhere. "You real, mister?"

As he poured water out of his boot, he turned toward her, "Are you? I'm guessing not many people sleep in cottonwoods."

"Nope," she answered without hesitation. "I haven't been real for a long time." When she'd been in her early twenties, she'd always fallen in love with men who walked away like she was no more important than the half of sandwich they'd left on their plate. If she wasn't real then, she doubted she'd be now.

The mud man just stared at her. It had to be fifty degrees, but he didn't even look like he was cold as he stood there, his clothes were knotted in one hand and his boots in the other.

When she didn't say anything, he finally added, "I was fishing and flipped my boat when a water moccasin crawled in with me. I grew up in this valley, but I've been gone a dozen years, and apparently I've forgotten all I ever knew about fishing."

He sounded angry, not at her but maybe at the world. Jam wished she'd brought out a flashlight so she could see him better and, if needed, to use as a weapon. "What's your name?"

"What do you care?"

"I own this land you flopped up on."

His words were no more friendly than hers. "You want me to jump back in? It seems I'm in hostile territory."

He reminded her of a wild animal. Powerful. Primeval. Ready for battle. She had no doubt he'd dive back in the water if she ordered him off her land.

"No. You can stay. I've got towels in the kitchen. You can borrow a few. I might get arrested for letting you walk back to town naked." Bless her heart, Jam couldn't resist looking, just to make sure he was totally naked.

He didn't seem to notice or care. "Thanks. I'm Tucson Smith by the way. My younger brother is getting sworn in as sheriff tomorrow. If you want to file charges on me for trespassing, call him."

"I know your brother. I'm Jessica Ann Mackenzie. Everyone calls me Jam." She didn't say more. They knew one another's families. That was enough of an introduction.

Jam headed to the house. He followed.

As they reached the porch light's glow, she looked back. Mud man had Pecos Smith's coloring, brown eyes and hair, but this older brother was twice the deputy's weight and looked solid as a tree trunk.

"Where are you staying, Mr. Smith?"

"Nowhere. Pecos said I could borrow the mayor's boat if I wanted to fish, but to tell the truth, I didn't even bother to buy a pole. I just wanted to drift on the water for a while. I figured I'd just sleep out here, but I'm guessing my gear and the mayor's boat are both at the bottom of the river."

She opened the back door, reached in, and handed him a towel that barely went halfway around his waist. "Drop your things in the washer under the stairs. You can shower upstairs while you wait for the uniform. I can offer at least that to our new sheriff's brother. Your little brother may be young, but most folks in this county look up to him."

"Good to hear," Tucson said as he walked into the shadows of the stairs.

It crossed her mind that he could have gone to the farm where he grew up, but Pecos never mentioned their parents. Maybe they'd moved years ago or didn't speak to their sons.

She heard Tucson follow orders. He dropped his clothes in one of the café's washers. "It won't take long."

The only answer was the sound of the washer lid dropping.

Jam forced herself not to look as she turned on the prep table's light in the big kitchen. "You hungry? I could scramble you up eggs and make toast."

Halfway up the stairs, he turned. "I don't want to be a bother. I'll be on my way as soon as my clothes are ready. I got a rental car up the road a few miles. I can sleep in there. Come morning I'll buy something to wear to the ceremony."

She nodded and added, "Shower is the second door on the left. I'll watch your clothes. How many?"

He was on the landing. "How many what?"

"Eggs. I'll have them ready by the time you clean up."

"A dozen if you've got them." Then wearing only a towel, he disappeared.

"I've got them," she whispered. It occurred to her that the Valentine wish she always made might have finally come true. A lover for a night with no strings attached came wrapped in a towel.

Only the soldier seemed about as cuddly as a cactus, and he looked like he never bothered to smile.

She made him ranch eggs with sausage and peppers, then heated several pieces of homemade bread with butter and cinnamon-sugar on top. By the time he came down, wearing a bigger towel, she'd switched his clothes to the dryer.

Jam handed him the biggest T-shirt she had with the café's logo on it. It stretched over his chest like a second skin.

They sat on stools pulled up to the prep table. When she passed him a heaping plate, he grinned. "Thanks, I'm starving."

"I hope it's good."

He grabbed another fork from the rack and handed it to her. "Join me."

When he took his first bite, he closed his eyes and smiled. "Perfect."

She reached over and stabbed a bite, then agreed. She nibbled while he ate a meal big enough to feed a family of four.

Not covered in mud and almost smiling, Tucson Smith was an attractive man, and Jam had to fight her instinct to touch him. Somehow, he still didn't seem real. But, since she'd found him, she decided he was hers.

"I was told never to trust a slender cook, but you are a master." He winked at her. "And I am not saying that because I've been living on army food for a dozen years."

He ate and she watched him enjoy the meal. They didn't know one another well enough to make conversation. She refilled his milk twice, and he thanked her both times.

As he finished the plate, the buzzer went off on the dryer. He stood and moved to the shadows under the stairs.

With no hesitation, he dropped the towel, pulled out his wrinkled uniform, and began to dress.

Without hesitation, she watched.

"How can I repay you, lovely cook?" His back was to her as he buttoned his wrinkled trousers.

Jam stepped closer, almost near enough to touch the muscles on his back.

When he turned, she saw the surprise in his eyes, then a silent question, and then definite interest.

For one long moment their gazes locked. Two people truly seeing one another. His words came so low it seemed a thought passing between them. "Name it, Jam. What's on your mind? Name how I can repay you."

Lowering her eyes, she whispered, "If I could ask for one favor it, would be for you to give me a Valentine's kiss. But not a friend kiss or a thank you kiss. I think I'd like a real kiss. My café was full of lovers tonight, and I can't even remember the last real kiss I've had."

He frowned as if he didn't believe her. "You're sure?" He seemed to breathe the question in as he halved the space between them.

"I'm sure."

Slowly, like a man approaching a mirage, he moved his hand to the side of her face. She felt the warmth of his palm and closed her eyes, pretending he was real. Pretending he wanted her.

His arm circled her waist and pulled her against him gently, but his lips brushed her ear, not her mouth.

"If we're going to do this, Jessica Ann Mackenzie, I want to take my time. You may not believe this, but no one's ever asked me for this favor, and I want to do it right."

"Please." She brushed her cheek against his jaw. "One perfect kiss."

"You'll never have to ask me again."

Light kisses glided across her face. She couldn't open her eyes. If this wasn't real, she didn't want to know.

She'd expected a hard kiss, but the soldier was gentle and in no hurry. Slowly he pulled her closer until she felt him press along the length of her body. As his kiss deepened, she seemed to melt into his warmth.

One perfect lover's kiss from a stranger.

His hand moved down over her hip lightly as his free fingers laced into her short curls. While her heart pushed against his, the world slipped away, and passion rotated in the night, in his arms, in his kiss.

When she moaned, he lifted her and walked to the stairs. While kissing her throat, he slowly carried her up to the second room on the left.

Jam took a deep breath as dreams and fantasies blended with feelings she'd never let show. For just a few moments she wanted to believe in love. No, more than that. She wanted to believe someone could love her.

Without a word he laid her on the bed and covered her with the bedspread. Leaning down, he kissed her one more time and whispered, "I want to watch you sleep."

His hand moved along her body as he held her.

She was independent, strong, but tonight somehow, he sensed her need to be held. He feathered kisses over her cheek then leaned back beside her so close his breath tickled her hair. Just two lonely people needing companionship if only for a moment, she thought as she relaxed.

Jam drifted to sleep still floating on a dream that almost seemed real. A deep sleep welcomed her tired body and mind. She was safe from ghosts tonight. She was in the arms of a dream lover.

He'd watch over her this evening. The wind rustled the leaves on the old cottonwoods and the river whispered as it moved along, but she simply slept.

In the morning she stretched and decided she'd just had the best dream ever. It filled her thoughts as she showered and changed into a clean white chef coat and black cargo pants. A few brushes of her hair and she was ready to start the breads.

The dream of being kissed drifted in her mind as she rushed down the stairs smiling. "Almost real," she whispered. "Perfection."

She was still half-dreaming when she reached the prep table and saw the two stools pulled up and one dirty plate with two forks.

Jam froze. It couldn't be true. She'd been exhausted. She'd had too much to drink. The man from the river was only a dream.

Her employees wandered in. Most had worked the night before and still looked tired. Jam tried to be cheery. She met them with muffins and juice. "We've got a lunch for twenty from the sheriff's office. Other than that, the afternoon-run should be light. Folks don't usually turn out the morning after a big night out."

Her people yawned and shrugged. A light crowd would mean light tips but an early day.

"I've got eight mini red velvet cakes left over, so each of you can take one home. We should be out of here by two." On weeknights she was always the last one to leave. Being open early on weekdays for breakfast and lunch was enough. Then on weekends it was brunch only.

Her employees might work five days on and two off, but Jam was always there when the door was open. Now and then, she took a Sunday off.

If she could remember last night's kiss for a while, maybe she could smile and enjoy the day. She'd had a perfect night in the arms of a man who'd treated her as if he held a treasure.

Chapter 3

February 15
Honey Creek

The old gentleman put on his least tattered tie and looked in the antique mirror hanging on a wall that hadn't been painted in fifty years. Like the house, Charles H. Winston III stood solid against aging.

At sixty-seven he liked the man he saw in his reflection. He lived by the principles he set out when he arrived in New York almost fifty years ago. He was honest. Never talked about himself. He was kind and thoughtful. He lived his life by the clock and valued order.

Winston glanced at the tiny note taped to his mirror and whispered the words aloud. "A man is measured by how he lives today, not yesterday."

He grinned realizing later today his world might just change a bit. He was shifting his routine. At half past noon he had a lunch date with three ladies at the Honey Creek Café and he planned to pick up the bill. Charles considered himself a man much blessed and he would spend a bit of the wealth.

As he brushed his coat, he decided he might purchase a new tie if time permitted. After all, if his plan worked, he'd be proposing marriage soon. It would be an important thing, being engaged. Something he thought would never come in this lifetime.

Only the problem was, Mr. Winston wasn't sure which one of the ladies he was having brunch with to ask to marry. He'd loved all three for years. Maybe it was about time he told at least one of them.

Visit us online at
KensingtonBooks.com
to read more from your favorite authors,
see books by series, view reading
group guides, and more!

BOOK **CLUB**
BETWEEN THE CHAPTERS

Visit us online for sneak peeks, exclusive
giveaways, special discounts, author content,
and engaging discussions with your fellow readers.

Betweenthechapters.net

Sign up for our newsletters and be the first
to get exciting news and announcements about
your favorite authors!
Kensingtonbooks.com/newsletter